'. . . The Soviet Nuclear Arsenal. The Human Rights issue. Afghanistan. They were our weapons. We used them as rods to publicly chastise and castigate the Russian Bear. They were the pointers we used to demonstrate to our reluctant allies the insidious, unchanging nature of the Evil Empire in order to win acquiescence to our policy of nuclear escalation.

'. . . But now we have lost those weapons. The Russian Premier has disarmed us. His diplomatic initiatives in Afghanistan have given us the spectre of a peaceful solution and the withdrawal of all Soviet forces. . . . Furthermore, gentlemen, the Premier has seized the question of nuclear disarmament by the throat and paraded it all over the world, a gesture which has convinced the world that he is determined to see an end to nuclear weapons . . .'

'. . . It is not the President's fault. He is one of us, a cold warrior. But his hand has been forced: he had to negotiate the accord. . . . The Kennedy solution to our predicament, the predicament of our continued survival, cannot be applied to the President. Gentlemen, we cannot survive without a return to the Cold War. Which leaves us with one option only, one that involves collaboration with our sworn enemies, but one that will ensure that we can go on as before. That option, gentlemen, we are calling ASH . . .'

Also by James Murphy and available in Sphere:

JUNIPER
CEDAR

ASH

JAMES MURPHY

SPHERE BOOKS LIMITED

To Sue and Ben, for their great kindnesses

A *SPHERE* Book

First published in Great Britain by Sphere Books Ltd 1990

Typeset by Selectmove Ltd, London
Reproduced, printed and bound in Great Britain by
BPCC Hazell Books Ltd
Member of BPCC Ltd
Aylesbury, Bucks, England

ISBN 7474 0569 7

Sphere Books Ltd
A Division of
Macdonald & Co (Publishers) Ltd
Orbit House
1 New Fetter Lane
London EC4A 1AR
A member of Maxwell Macmillan Pergamon Publishing Corporation

'There are governmental services, and not a few individuals in Washington, who appear to assume that some sort of an ultimate military showdown between ourselves and the Russians is inevitable and that the priority ought to be given to the effort to prepare for it, rather than to the effort to avert it.'

George F Kennan, former US Ambassador to Russia, speaking in Newsweek, July 1987

'Where they make a desert they call it peace.'

Tacitus, Roman Historian, 55–120 B.C.

ENGLAND

T he sun was hot, and the air smelt of horses and hay. The ribbed, paving-brick path led past a wide expanse of lawn, across which a pair of frilly peacocks pecked their way in clockwork unison. Perched atop the weathervane on the Dutch barn, a watchful magpie, loitering with intent, scanned the environs with an eye to the main chance.

MacKenzie's purpose made him oblivious to his surroundings as he marched down the path, his bony frame set as stiffly as his upper lip. He felt sticky and uncomfortable, and his underwear clung to him like a damp hospital compress. That morning he had dressed in a dark, heavy wool suit and thick cotton shirt as the day had broken cold and overcast. But on the drive down from London, the weather had quickly cleared, and he was now suffering in the heat for his misguided sartorial selections.

He followed the path down to the whitewashed rails which enclosed a neatly cropped paddock where a man in a flat cap and jodhpurs was supervising the preparation of a nervous bay mare.

'Don't bother with the hobbles, Willy,' ordered the

1

stud manager. 'Just the twitch.' He took off his cap and mopped his brow with a red handkerchief. 'He'll be down shortly, Sir Robert,' he said without looking round. 'This is what he's come to see.' MacKenzie sniffed. The manager replaced his cap. 'Nice day for it, too.'

Willy finished bandaging the mare's tail, and picked up a short wooden stick, one end of which ran into a small loop of rope. He approached the animal from the near side, and, while his assistant held the mare by the snaffle bridle, he fitted the rope to the fleshy part of the bay's upper lip, and gave the stick a couple of quick turns. The mare tried to shy away but the two men held her easily.

A sleek black limousine drove up to the rail and parked. MacKenzie turned expectantly. But nobody got out. The smoke glass windows remained closed, reflecting the glare of the dazzling sun. MacKenzie stared balefully at the windscreen for a few seconds before rigidly resuming his observations.

'Shoes, Jimmy,' shouted the stud manager. 'In case she kicks out,' he added as an aside to MacKenzie. Jimmy gave an exaggerated nod of his head as if to say that he knew the routine without the prompts. While Willy held the mare steady on the twitch, Jimmy quickly fitted a pair of padded felt shoes to the animal's hind feet.

On the other side of the paddock, the head groom led in a chestnut stallion on a bridoon. The horse was superbly proportioned and its coat glistened and shone with health. It scented the air and curled its lips at the prospect in sight, and within seconds the stallion was fully drawn. Jimmy walked across to the horse carrying a bucket and he doused the animal's engorged sheath with disinfectant, damping off the excess with a dry, antiseptic cloth.

'Bring him on, Charlie,' said the manager. The head groom led up the stallion on the near side as Willy pulled lightly on the twitch and Jimmy lifted the mare's near foreleg. The mare adopted the Flehman's posture, throwing up her head, her eyes wide and protruding, showing the whites, and she shuddered in anticipation. The stallion, recognising the welcoming sign, skipped forward on its toes. At the last moment, Jimmy released the mare's leg and pulled her tail aside, as Charlie dropped the leading rein, allowing the eager stallion to jump the mare. With a little assistance from Charlie's expert hands, the beast rammed its member home. MacKenzie sniffed loudly and cleared his throat.

It was all over in two minutes. The panting stallion was led away back to its box. Willy removed the twitch and walked the mare round the paddock. Jimmy gathered together the tools of the trade. The stud manager wandered off in the direction of his office, drying his brow. MacKenzie leaned against the rail, waiting for the summons.

The passenger window of the limousine whirred open smoothly. MacKenzie approached, his arms clamped behind his back. 'Good morning, sir,' he said formally to the elderly, silver-haired man in the window.

'Good morning, Robert,' came the reply. 'Lovely day. Beautiful.' The old man's blue eyes twinkled with amusement. MacKenzie did not reply, nor did he meet the man's penetrating gaze, preferring to show his displeasure by taking a sudden interest in the polished coachwork. 'An English Derby winner and a French Oaks winner,' continued the man. 'Both have Native Dancer in their lines.' He smiled at MacKenzie.

'How very nice,' said MacKenzie.

The smile grew wider. 'Tut, tut, Robert. Is that all you can say. You know that it's always pleasure before business with me.'

'I didn't know you made a distinction,' replied MacKenzie sharply.

'Now, Robert. Don't try and spoil my mood.' He flicked a thin hand at MacKenzie. Only the thumb and forefinger remained. 'What a dour Scotsman you are, Robert. Nature in all its glory, the very act of creation before your eyes, a moment you should savour, and all you want to do is rush in to business.'

'I have travelled a long way at your invitation to discuss . . .'

Suddenly the bantering tone disappeared. 'Am I on the list, Robert?' demanded the man.

MacKenzie shook his head quickly, startled by the rapid change in mood. 'No,' he replied.

'Are you sure? Positive?' He narrowed his eyes at MacKenzie.

'The Home Secretary gave me the full list of names and all the case histories. I personally checked them myself. Thoroughly. There was no mention of you whatsoever. No reference at all.'

'That is good news, Robert. Very good indeed.' The man sat back in his seat. 'And you will make sure it stays that way.'

'Yes,' replied MacKenzie.

'As you well know, I am, er, shall we say, preoccupied with a very delicate proposition at the moment. I cannot afford to be disturbed or diverted by the Juden. There is too much at stake. Do you understand, Robert?'

'I understand, sir. I'll keep you informed of any untoward developments.'

'See that you do, Robert.' The window began to close and the car purred to life. It reversed along the brick pathway and turned the corner at the Dutch barn. Sir Robert MacKenzie, Director General of D15, followed in its wake as the magpie swooped down on the lawn to disturb the fussy peacocks.

BELGIUM

I

Garner rubbed dry his hair on the thick, white hotel towel and walked back into the steam-filled bathroom. He wiped the condensation from the mirror, making a circle on the oblong frame, and his blurred face stared back at him, unsmiling, somewhat grim, the brown hair tousled. He had the impression of a quickly taken photograph which had caught the subject unawares on a rainswept day.

The wall light was reflected in his hazel eyes and he looked deeply into them, something which he had only recently been able to do without feeling guilty and ashamed. He picked up his comb from the shelf and slowly combed his hair, using his left hand to press down and smooth the parting while his attention was fixed on the watery image before him.

His face had once been described as well-lived in. He had almost turned it into a slum. Gone was the gaunt, pasty, haunted appearance which had characterised the last two years in the *wilderness* to be replaced by an alert, interested expression and a ruddy, healthy complexion. The sagging, bloodhound bags beneath the eyes had receded and the dark smudges had all but disappeared, though the heavy flecture lines at the corners of his mouth were now a permanent feature, a constant reminder.

He plugged in his razor and began to shave, pulling the skin along the square jawline to attack the awkward thickets of bristles that grew there. 'The wilderness,' he mumbled to himself, and grimaced at his reflection. Veronica had called it the wilderness. Her parting note had mentioned it. Over and over again, as she had done during their bitter arguments which had preceded her moving out. And she had been correct, as he'd always known deep down inside his soul. Only he hadn't, wouldn't, recognise the fact. That is, until a year ago. But by then it was too late. She had already gone.

A year ago at night. Drunk as usual. But then when hadn't he been drunk while tamely existing in the *wilderness*. Falling down, puking, choking drunk, he had cursed and railed, heaving and spewing as he had crawled on hands and knees across the bedroom floor, dribbling a trail of stringy saliva and vomit, a human snail encased and protected by his own superiority, his acid wit, his tormenting pen.

There had been tears in his eyes as he had pulled himself upright in front of the bathroom mirror and tried to sponge the gobs of spew from his jacket. He had held on to the sink, swaying, the running tap splashing cold water over his sleeves. And then a foggy picture had emerged in the mirror; his own beetroot face had faded in the mists, and a clearer, sharper image emerged which transfixed him and made him stand upright unaided.

What he had seen was an ancient peasant woman in a shanty village high in the Andes, passing through the grey shadows of the arriving dawn, doling out a meal of sloppy maize gruel to a man in muddy battle fatigues, a man who sat alone, long-haired, bearded, silent. He was watched over by a cordon of jittery soldiers whose hushed whispers stalled on the cold air, and betrayed their nervousness. The man did not eat. And at first light came the rasping, staccato American voice to quell the gentle Spanish tones and startle the soldiers into action. The bearded man was stripped and made to stand to one side, an outcast in a village of outcasts, his trousers humiliatingly bunched around his ankles. Then the American gave the command. The soldiers shot the man to death.

Garner switched off his razor but continued to stare at his reflection in the mirror. 'Ché', he mouthed at himself. 'Ernesto Guevara Lynch de la Serna. Murdered by the CIA in the village of La Higuera in October 1967.' That had been the image his sodden mind has grasped a year ago in it's drunken stupor. 'It was six in the morning. It was exactly six in the morning,' he intoned to his mirror image. 'An old peasant woman brought a white shroud. At six in the morning.' He smiled sadly as he realised that he had unconsciously paraphrased Lorca's *Llanto*. Lorca and Ché, poet and pistolero. Both victims of the fascists.

A year ago he had embraced their spirits again.

He went through into the bedroom and sat down on the bed, putting on his shirt. How could he have forgotten? How could he have lived in the *wilderness* without a thought for the victims? He had forgotten what a powerful symbol Ché's death had been, forgotten the barricades, the mass marches in the capitals of the western world, the cries for change, for an end to war, for peace. He had been a part of it all in London. He had seen the hope in the faces of his fellow protestors. But he had forgotten. Until last year and the image in the mirror.

He pulled on his shorts and his trousers and slipped into his socks and shoes. He needed a breath of fresh air.

II

He stood on the steps of the hotel undecided which way to go. Not having stayed in Ostend before he did not want to stray too far as de Roos would be calling him in an hour or so. The prevailing drift of the strollers was away from the harbour, and as he observed the tranquil *paseo* in the balmy heat of the evening, his earlier tumultuous thoughts were accentuated. Unwilling to disturb the peace by his brooding presence, he took off his jacket, loosened his tie, and sat down on the top step.

He had recently been commissioned to write a short article on Sartre and he had later used it as the basis for a story in the small community newspaper he owned and edited in London. His research had brought back many memories of the sixties and his idealistic youth. Sartre had called Guevara the most complete human being he had ever met, and there was a great deal of truth in that statement, mused Garner. What had made Ché give up a comfortable middle-class life to fight for those who were denied the basics of life? Even Ché's enemies, those who did not share his vision, those who overtly opposed his militant communism, nevertheless respected him for his idealism and commitment to the eradication of poverty and oppression.

The angry students who took to the streets and barricades in Paris, London and Washington, had adopted Ché's message with a missionary zeal, and had attacked the **Establishment** for its abject failure to assist the poor and dispossessed of the world. He had been part of it himself in London. He had protested and marched, he had written, he had published, and he had developed a following. And the **Establishment** had been frightened; its windows were rattled and its walls were shaken, just as Dylan had prophesied.

Then nothing. The protests, and the dreams that had inspired them, had faded and evaporated. The streets were cleared and the barricades dismantled. What had happened? What had stilled all the angry voices? What had quelled the shaking fists? Nothing had come of it all. The **Establishment** was just as firmly entrenched as ever, if not more so, and war, poverty and famine stalked the earth with a renewed vigour. The demonstrators had all gone home to take on the middle-class life they had once despised, leaving behind a hard core that had to carry on the struggle.

He had stayed behind and used his pen in whatever journal or newspaper would publish his articles to try and renew the fight, but gradually the ink had run dry, his companions had grown fewer, and among those that remained the discussions turned to arguments on how best to carry the struggle to the **Establishment**. Until the day arrived when he found his criticisms were aimed more and more at his friends and allies than at the true enemy.

And from then on, the path into the *wilderness* had been laid out before him. As the internecine strife among the Left grew more heated and acrimonious, his writing took on a second breath, and he began to question the whole basis of the movement which had held his sympathy for so long. This was paralleled by a wider acceptance of his works, and his writing and critiques began to appear in the national press. Not only had he espoused the middle-class life which he had rejected, he had become its champion, and his scorn was reserved for those who now took up the struggle he had once led. Until the ghost of Guevara had returned a year ago to haunt him, to accuse him of betrayal, and to make him question the values he had upheld and promoted during his years in the *wilderness*. There was no point in asking where were the protesting youth of today: his scything pen had blotted out all hope of that.

Suddenly, the evening light disappeared. A hand grabbed his shoulder and arrested his thoughts. He looked up quickly, finding his feet, and was confronted by a giant of a man who towered above him, even though he stood two steps lower down.

'Little boy lost,' said de Roos.

'Christian,' exclaimed Garner. He jumped to his feet and wiped the seat of his pants before shaking hands with de Roos. 'You're early, aren't you?'

'Change of plans, Peter.' He guided Garner back up to the hotel entrance.

'Isn't Nihat with you?' He had been looking forward to seeing his friend again and he was disappointed by his absence.

'He'll meet us later in Diksmuide. Just get your toothbrush and a change of socks and meet me outside in five minutes. Red Volvo.' He gave Garner a friendly shove.

Garner did not argue: the tall Dutchman had that effect upon people. 'Okay,' he replied, and went in to the hotel to do as he had been told, informing the desk on the way out that he would be back the following day.

De Roos was waiting for him at the kerb, blocking the traffic, unperturbed by the blaring horns. Garner squeezed in and fastened the seat belt. 'Let's go,' he said and playfully nudged de Roos's intruding elbow.

There was not a great deal of room in the front of the car; de Roos's legs and knees dwarfed the dash, his right shoulder encroached upon Garner's seat, and his head, pushed forward on its long neck to avoid the roof, swayed from side to side as he pulled out into the traffic. The Dutchman was seven feet tall with the physique of a wrestler, which was not surprising as for many years he had been Holland's leading participant in the art of Judo, having attained the rank of fifth Dan before the age of thirty. Now approaching fifty, de Roos still retained the air of a man of action, and he looked no older than Garner. 'We should be there before dark,' de Roos said, as he swung the car round an island.

'In Diksmuide?' asked Garner. De Roos nodded quickly. 'So why the change of plans?' He should have known better than to ask: de Roos was a man who operated by instinct; plans and arrangements were always fluid.

De Roos bit his lip pensively before replying. 'The meeting in Bruges fell through unexpectedly. My contact failed to show.' He glanced across at Garner. 'And then there's the trouble in Diksmuide which I thought might interest you.'

'What kind of trouble?' said Garner. He didn't like the mention of the word trouble.

'Just what you need for your newspaper. The English groups have been fighting. Among themselves.' De Roos smiled broadly. 'The stewards couldn't contain it so the police had to step in. A few broken heads and a couple of arrests.'

12

'I thought you said the Vlaamse Militante Order always had it under control.'

'They usually do, but they've lost some of their more careful and capable men in the recent crackdown, so they didn't have the manpower nor the will to control the fighting when it began. They just threw in the towel and let the English get on with it.' De Roos's head swung violently from side to side as he brought the Volvo on to the Torhoutsteenwig.

Garner turned his right shoulder against the door to put some space between himself and his friend. 'I've got a good idea why the Brits were fighting. There's a split in the British neo-Nazi movement,' he said. 'Some of them are in favour of pulling the troops out of Northern Ireland, while the remainder back the Ulster Unionists and are all for annihilating the IRA and its sympathisers.'

'And they start fighting among themselves as soon as they are outside Britain,' said de Roos. 'And that's fine by me. Let them kill each other off. But you won't see any mention of this split in the British Press or even that a neo-Nazi movement exists at all. And even when these same Nazi thugs are orchestrating and directing soccer violence in England and Europe, the British press report it all as youthful high jinks with no mention of the political extremists behind it all, who use such activities as a training ground for future terrorists and murderers. The press and the British Government are all contrite and apologetic and make noises about controlling the thugs, but no one is prepared to identify the neo-Nazi leaders.'

'That's why I'm here, Christian,' replied Garner, hoping that de Roos would confirm that his task was going to be that simple.

De Roos negotiated the climb over the Ostend–Nieuwport canal. 'And I thank you for coming, Peter. But it's a long, uphill struggle. The top Nazis are known to the authorities in Britain, to the police, and to the Secret Intelligence Service, DI6. It's almost as if they refuse to recognise in their dealing with me that these outbreaks of violence are organised by the neo-Nazi movement.'

Garner smiled to himself. De Roos had called him earlier in the month asking him to join de Roos as an observer at the rally, to pinpoint the British contingents, and Garner had agreed. He had been working and reporting on various aspects of the fascist movement in operation throughout London, and the chance not only to see and work with de Roos again but also to witness some of the neo-Nazis' thugs in action had been hard to resist. But knowing de Roos of old he knew that there would be more to the simple job of observer, that de Roos had more to ask of him. 'But DI6 will have a team observing in Diksmuide, won't they?' he asked.

'Of course they will. DI6 like to keep an eye on their friends,' said de Roos archly.

Garner eyed the big Dutchman and saw the smile playing on his lips. Their exchange had been conducted very matter-of-factly, without any heat despite de Roos's reservations about the British which he always played up when he was with Garner. But that was de Roos's way, never hurried, never elaborate in word or deed, a master of the understatement, who had used his physical size and native cunning to attract the less fortunate to his side for help. The aura of the gentle giant, which Garner knew to be natural rather than cultivated, had led many an opponent to underestimate his intelligence;

and many a witness in the Dutch courts had been steered in to indiscretion, had been shown to be liars, under the genial but relentless probing of Advocat de Roos. It was as champion of the rights of the Moluccan Islanders that their paths had first crossed and they had been good friends ever since. De Roos's success in that particular endeavour had brought him several government appointments, and for the past five years he had been working for the Ministerie van Buitenlandse Zaken, the Dutch Foreign Office, where he held a special brief to investigate the burgeoning neo-Nazi movement.

'Is that how you think DI6 look upon the Nazis, as friends?' asked Garner sceptically.

'As I said, DI6 are of no help to us at all. They refuse to see any connection between the flag-waving racist thugs who typify the English neo-Nazis, and the neo-Nazis' terrorist organisations in Europe and America.'

'And there is a connection, is there?'

They turned off the Torhoutsteenwig and took the road to Sint-Pieters Kapeelle, passing through a region of drab, flat marshland, the Moere, which still bore the scars of the Great War. 'Tomorrow night in Bruges, at the den Anker cafe, the top neo-Nazis will sit down to discuss their future plans. They will come from all over Europe, from all over the world. And there's something in the air, something going on. I can sense it. John Heritage from the Miller Foundation is going to be there. And that says something.'

'I've heard rumours of him. And the Foundation,' said Garner.

'It's like a co-ordinating body for all the right-wing loonies in America and the main liaison between Europe and America. It raises funds for the fascist cause all over the world and then hands out money to organisations such as Freedom for Industry, the Freedom Federation and other similar rightist pressure groups. Aims for Commerce and Industry in London receives what they call a grant from the Foundation's bagman and Mister Fixit, John Heritage. Right now he's working with the British Freedom Movement based in Leicestershire.'

Garner nodded his head slowly. 'I've heard of that lot before. They've just opened an office in Lambeth.' He paused and stroked his chin, finding a tuft of bristles that had escaped the razor. 'So you think there's something happening and that it will all be discussed in Bruges tomorrow, after the rally.'

'I'm almost certain. The Yanks have always taken a big interest in the European neo-Nazis. More so of late. They think the climate of opinion favours them, particularly when books claiming that the Holocaust never happened, that it was all Jewish propaganda, are flooding the bookshops.' De Roos slowed down and drove in to a lay-by where he parked the car. 'With Heritage putting in an appearance in Bruges, and all the recent toing and froing all over the world, there's definitely something going on. There will also be three of the top English fascists at the Bruges meeting. That's my information.'

'And you want me to pick them out?'

'Hill, Parker and McWilliam. You'll see them at the rally in Diksmuide. Hopefully we'll get some good pictures of them for you to use in your newspaper.' De Roos sighed. 'But the important thing is that I told DI6 about the den Anker meeting and that Heritage would be there. And they told me they weren't interested. See what I mean? No cooperation from them at all.'

III

When he reached the Hotel du Sablon, Heritage crossed the Noordzanstraat and entered the narrow street directly opposite the hotel. Over his shoulder he carried a black camera case and a tourist map of Bruges protruded from his jacket pocket.

He ambled down the cobbled street, past houses and boutiques, until he came to a shop whose window was crammed with hand-made lace shawls and blouses. He stopped and scanned the window for a moment or two, just another tourist in search of a locally crafted gift to take back home, and then went inside. As he pushed open the door, a bell rang, and a grey-haired lady rose from her chair in front of the counter, leaving the magazine she had been reading in her place.

The shop was small and dull, painted in two shades of brown and the walls were covered in shelving upon which the stock of lacework was precariously stacked, wrapped in tissue paper. Heritage deposited the camera on the counter. The woman gave no sign of recognition. She took a key from beneath her floral apron and unsteadily climbed the wooden steps to the door on her right and opened it. Heritage followed her and passed through on to a tiny landing which gave access to a staircase. He waited until he heard the door locked behind him before descending into the gloom of the basement.

At the foot of the stairs he passed under an arch into a musty, vaulted chamber whose rough-cast walls glistened with damp under the glare of a single, powerful neon light.

In the centre of the room, Alex Hamilton and Willy Kohler sat at a stout Formica table.

'I thought you were staying away, Alex,' said Heritage.

'So did I,' said Hamilton. 'Emergency. That's why Willy called you over.'

'What is it?' said Heritage. He pulled out a chair and sat down.

Hamilton threw him a black disc the size of a penny piece. 'There were four of them altogether.'

Heritage weighed the bug in his hand, clenched it in his fist, then tossed it back to Hamilton. 'Who?'

'One of Willy's men,' said Hamilton, looking straight ahead.

The German scowled and his face reddened, except for the strip of white scar tissue that ran from the tip of his nose to the left ear lobe. He rubbed his hands on his denim shirt. 'Dieter,' he spat. 'The fucking bastard. I caught him myself.'

Heritage arched his eyebrows and looked to Hamilton for confirmation. 'Dieter?'

'Heard a rumour in London that there was a possible leak,' said Hamilton. 'And as Willy's men were setting up the den Anker rendezvous, I asked him to check. He caught Dieter placing the bugs. So I hotfooted it over here.'

'I recruited the bastard myself,' swore Willy. 'Treated him like a son . . .'

'Where is he now?'

'Next door with Stefano,' replied Hamilton. 'He's been working on him for most of the morning.'

'Let's take a look,' suggested Heritage. He walked round the table to the far wall, pushed it at waist height, and a narrow section swung inwards noiselessly. His entrance into the padded cell was greeted with a piercing shriek. Hamilton waited for Kohler to enter before pulling the door closed.

Stefano Pagliai did not look up from his work. He moved the dial again and the naked German in the chair arched his back and screamed. Pagliai let the current flow for a few seconds before turning it off again. Dieter slumped forward unconscious, drooling a thick mix of blood and saliva from his battered mouth, the leather leg and arm restraints preventing him from tumbling to the stone floor.

Heritage examined the collapsed figure of Dieter Klaus. Bright red weals discoloured the flesh on either side of the straps. The tips of his fingers were pulped and bloody, and he noted the pair of pliers on the table next to Pagliai's control box. The man's genitals and both nipples were blackened and blistered where the electrical clips made contact, and his face was badly bruised and swollen. Heritage snorted at the acrid smell of singed flesh and urine. He coughed and swallowed hard, then took a pace back. 'What's he told you, Stefano?'

The swarthy Italian put his bloody hands into the pockets of his blood-streaked white coat and grinned. 'Everything we wanted to know, of course.'

'Who gave him the bugs?' asked Hamilton.

'De Roos,' said Pagliai

'That bastard again,' cursed Hamilton.

'He's getting to be one pain in the ass is our Dutch friend,' said Heritage.

Hamilton shook his head in dismay. 'What was de Roos after?'

Pagliai shrugged his shoulders. 'He just wanted to listen in with the Belgians. We were all going to be sitting down tomorrow night talking and de Roos wanted to hear. That's all.'

'Dieter didn't say whether de Roos was after anything specific, anything in particular?' asked Heritage. He glanced at Hamilton who nodded an unspoken reply.

Pagliai shook his head. 'No. Nothing at all. He paid Dieter five grand to place four bugs. That was all.'

Hamilton turned to Heritage. 'What do you think, John?'

'Could be,' said Heritage slowly. 'But can we afford to take any chances?'

'Definitely not.'

Heritage pointed at Dieter but looked at Pagliai. 'Sure you got everything out of him, Stefano? He can't tell us any more?'

'He's empty,' said Pagliai grimly. 'I even know what size bras his mother and sisters took.' He laughed loudly. Kohler tried to smile but it didn't quite come off. 'I've just been having a bit of fun with him,' continued Pagliai. 'Waiting for you to tell me what to do with him.'

'Put him away, then,' ordered Hamilton.

Pagliai looked disappointed. 'Okay.' He reached for the control knob. Hamilton stayed his hand. 'No?' queried Pagliai.

'No,' said Hamilton. 'Too long, too noisy.'

Pagliai picked up a plastic jug and doused Dieter with water. Dieter came awake with a groaning splutter. Pagliai grabbed a handful of his hair and wrenched his head back over the chair, then slapped his face twice to ensure that he was fully conscious. A thin-bladed stiletto appeared in Pagliai's hand. He held it up in front of Dieter's face. Briefly it caught the light. Dieter's eyes widened with horror. Pagliai drove the blade up to the hilt through Dieter's right eye.

20

IV

'How much longer?' asked Garner. They had been parked in the lay-by for an hour.

'Another ten minutes,' said de Roos as he checked his watch. 'Ten minutes.'

'I take it this is the fall back location for your contact after the miss in Bruges?'

De Roos nodded. 'Recognise the procedure, do you, Peter?'

Garner could not see de Roos's face and was unsure about how to take his question. 'Yes,' he replied.

'I suppose in your time you've had one or two similar meetings on deserted country roads, eh?'

'One or two,' said Garner quickly, and he felt a hot flush of embarrassment grip him around the collar and the back of his ears.

'The CIA, so I've been told, have about four hundred tame journalists in Europe who promote the American way of thinking with disinformation, leaks, black propaganda, that sort of thing,' said de Roos. 'Am I right?'

Garner leant forward in his seat and caught sight of de Roos's face in the moonlight. His casual manner was misleading and Garner did not know whether he was probing or simply passing the time on a subject they both were well aware of. 'Probably more,' said Garner. 'And those same journalists do a similar job more or less for DI6 or France's SDECE. I worked with many of them. But it's not something I am proud of.'

'Did you have much contact with the CIA?'

'Quite a lot. But not as much as I had with DI6 or DI5. But I haven't had any contact with any of them for a year,' replied Garner forcefully.

'Didn't think for a moment you had,' said de Roos.

Garner decided to go on the offensive. 'But you're using me in exactly the same way aren't you, to push and promote the notion of a growing neo-Nazi threat to the world?'

'There's a big difference, Peter. I'm not asking you to bend the truth, or to report anything other than the facts, or to plant propaganda, or to sell to the West the notion that Russia and her satellites are the only bogeymen in this world.' De Roos switched on the engine but did not put the car in gear. 'All I want you to do is simply to heighten the British public's awareness of the neo-Nazi threat so that pressure will be brought to bear on the government, on DI6, so that some improved cooperation between the British, the Dutch, the Germans, the Italians and the Belgians results. And the reason for that is simple: the neo-Nazis pose a very real threat, a very great threat, to democracy and liberty.'

'So you're saying the British government institutions are aware of the threat?'

'Well, I get no cooperation from them, particularly DI6. And being a man who thrives on conspiracies, I am beginning to believe that inside DI6, there are a core of operatives who are covertly sympathetic towards the neo-Nazi, and who do nothing to hinder their growth. Or rather, they do a lot to obstruct any attempts to stop the growth. That's why I get no cooperation from them.'

'I'm still not fully convinced of that, Christian,' said Garner.

'Spend a few months with me, Peter, and I'll soon have you convinced.'

'Can't afford the time, Christian. Besides I have to pay all my own expenses.'

'Yes, yes, I understand,' said de Roos. He stared in to the rear view mirror but the road behind was merging with the night shadows. 'We'll give him a few more minutes,' he added quietly.

'You must think a lot of this contact, Christian,' said Garner.

'It's only the second time I've used him. But he knows what I want and he's the man who can provide it. Look, talking about convincing, remember what I was saying before about the Italian neo-Nazis being the most dangerous?'

'About them being out and out terrorists? With such men as delle Chiaie in their ranks.'

'Yes. You see delle Chiaie has been on the go since 1946. He's had membership of more Nazi groups than I would care to count. He's virtually led the Nazi revival on his own and he forms the link between the old SS Nazis and the new generation of neo-Nazis. In Europe. In South America. He's been involved with Klaus Barbie, the Butcher of Lyons, with Otto Skorzeny who rescued Mussolini from the partisans during the last war. He's helped to train death squads in San Salvador, Chile, Argentina and Bolivia. And before that, he worked for Franco in Spain and Salazar in Portugal. Delle Chiaie is an expert in terror. Nazi terror.'

'Wasn't he involved in the Bologna Railway Terminus bombing which killed eighty or more people?'

'Right. And he was also responsible for an earlier series of bombings and deaths in Rome and Milan. But the important thing to note is that all these outrages were blamed on left-wing groups. In fact several prominent members of the Left are currently under lock and key because of delle Chiaie. That's his strategy.'

Garner considered this for a moment. 'He must be a very clever man. I mean to say . . .'

'Oh, he is. Don't underestimate him. And he still wields enormous power from his prison cell in Bolivia. Anti-terrorist squads all over Europe are only now beginning to realise how delle Chiaie has led them astray for over twenty years.' De Roos slipped the car into gear and pulled out onto the road which would eventually take them to Diksmuide. 'All over the world, left-wing groups are being blamed for terrrorist atrocities while the neo-Nazis pass unnoticed. Sure the lefties are involved in terrorism. I'm not saying they aren't. But they carry the can for a lot of what delle Chiaie and his allies do. Do you remember the murder of the Italian Prime Minister, Aldo Moro, back in 1978?'

Garner nodded. 'Yes. He was kidnapped and murdered by the Red Brigades and his body was found in the back of a car.' When de Roos did not continue, Garner looked at him and saw that he was slowly nodding to himself. 'You don't mean . . .?' said Garner, as realisation dawned. 'Moro? Delle Chiaie?'

'Precisely. The evidence is just emerging that the Red Brigades were framed for Moro's murder by delle Chiaie.'

'But why? What was gained from it?'

'Remember the scandal of the Italian Masonic Lodge, P2, which emerged a few years ago?' Garner nodded. 'Well delle Chiaie was a member. And also among the membership was every right-winger in Italy. Moro's death forestalled a leftist government in Italy which was about to come to power with Moro's backing. And that government would have exposed a very nasty can of worms.

'I see,' said Garner. 'And instead, a rightist government followed Moro's death, and everything was kept under wraps.'

'Oh, the neo-Nazis do get away with murder, particularly when they have the right connections, as it were, and a sympathetic press which plays up left-wing terrorist activities. That's why it is so important to me to get the British to realise the connection between their own fascist thugs and the European neo-Nazis. They are all one and the same. And if they are allowed to go unchecked, there will be war.'

'You mean fighting in the streets?'

De Roos coughed and cleared his throat. 'I mean war, Peter.' He turned left on to the main Diksmuide road. 'Two years ago a nightclub in West Berlin was firebombed by terrorists and an American serviceman was killed and several others injured. The world was led to believe that Libya was behind the attack. Some days later, American warplanes, flying from bases inside England, bombed the Libyan capital in an attempt to kill Colonel Gaddafi. Thirty-seven civilians were killed.'

'I know,' said Garner sadly. He was embarrassed by de Roos's reminder of those awful days, for he, Peter Garner, had been one of the journalists who had been responsible for creating the climate in which such a murderous attack was justified. 'I remember. The Russians were warned off, threatened in fact, to keep out of it. The American attack could have been the spark which led to World War Three.'

'It could well have been,' confirmed de Roos. 'The Americans orchestrated such a hate campaign against the

Libyans that the retaliatory strike was welcomed by most people in the West. But the Americans were quite wrong to blame Gaddafi for the nightclub bombing.' De Roos's head began to shake violently on its long neck. 'That's right, Peter,' he said as he saw the look of astonishment on his face. 'It wasn't Gaddafi at all. It was delle Chiaie who bombed the nightclub. It was delle Chiaie who almost caused World War Three.'

V

From the attic window of the farmhouse Garner could see all of the town and the road up to the military cemetery. The march had been in progress for nearly an hour and the tail end still had a hundred metres to travel before reaching the gates. But the exhortations and speeches in honour of the dead of the Schutzstaffe were already in progress, and he focussed his glasses on the central monument around which the leaders of the various groups and organisations were jostling for the most prominent positions.

'I've got Willy Kohler again,' announced Nihat Sargin.

'Me too,' said Garner.

'Let me have a look,' said de Roos. He crossed the room and took Nihat's binoculars.

'Third from the left of the tall cross,' said Garner. 'Surrounded by the British contingent.'

'I see him,' said de Roos. He held his glasses steady for a few moments and then began to sweep the crowded cemetery. 'Hmm. Still no sign of Dieter Klaus.'

Garner put down his glasses. 'He seems to be a

big favourite of yours today, Christian. Any particular reason?'

'He should be there.' De Roos continued his search. 'Since Hoffman was forced to go underground Kohler and Klaus have jointly run the Wehrportegruppe Hoffman Truppe. They don't trust one another and where one goes the other is sure to follow.'

'So they've fallen out,' suggested Sargin.

'Maybe,' said de Roos. 'Kohler is the man of action; Klaus the diplomat. If Kohler has come out on top, then that means trouble.'

'Do you want me to carry on filming?' interrupted the Special Branch technician from the other window. He had the video camera trained on the graveyard. 'All the Fuhrers are in position.'

'A few minutes more, thanks Jan,' said de Roos. 'And make sure you get plenty of footage of the British groups for Mr Garner.'

Garner yawned and went over to the table and sat down on a cane chair. Nihat joined him, leaving de Roos and the Belgian technician to watch over the serried ranks of the Nazi world.

'Things won't pick up for a while, Peter,' said Nihat. 'Not until they get back to the Pacific Hotel. Then the drink will flow and the fighting will begin.' He laughed and lit up a cigarette.

Nihat Sargin was of average height and slim build. He had an unruly mop of jet black hair, a thick, drooping moustache and very narrow piercing black eyes. He had always reminded Garner of the stereotyped Mexican bandit, and from time to time, de Roos referred to him affectionately as Pancho Villa whenever he was out of earshot.

'How many times have you been to the Diksmuide rally?' He yawned again behind his hand. 'Pardon me.'

Nihat exhaled smoke through his nose and mouth. 'Let me see. I missed last year. Unavoidably detained by the security police.' He held up his hands to show Garner his twisted, nailless thumbs. 'But before that I was here three years in succession.'

'It's not an event I would like to make a habit of coming to see. All those flags and black uniforms give me the creeps,' said Garner.

'Oh, I've found my visits useful,' said Nihat. A blank look came over his face. 'The man who broke my thumbs was a member of the Grey Wolves, a fanatical Turkish fascist group. I recognised him from the rally the year before last. I asked de Roos to trace him for me.' His voice began to fade. 'The man's wife and children miss him very much.'

Garner shivered despite the warmth of the room. Nihat stared down at the glowing red tip of his cigarette, his lips pulled tightly across his teeth in a sardonic grin. 'Was it very bad?' asked Garner gently, and he reached out to touch Nihat's shoulder. The two friends had not seen each other for several years, and upon Garner's arrival in Dikmuide, they had sat up until the early hours of that morning drinking beer and reminiscing over politicians and pressmen, over boozy nights and hung-over days. But they had both avoided any mention of Nihat's troubles with the Turkish authorities and the many arbitary arrests and detentions Nihat had suffered as a member of the Socialist Party and editor of its weekly journal. Garner had refrained from asking such questions because he felt guilty for his years in the wilderness when he had turned his back on his friends and actively worked against them;

he suspected Nihat had done so because of the traumas he had undergone and a wish not to embarrass him by recounting them. But if they were ever to re-establish their friendship, there had to be an open and frank accounting.

There was a deep sadness in Nihat's eyes as he spoke. 'For me? No.' He shook his head slowly. 'For my wife, for my friends, for the Turkish people? Yes.' He ground out his cigarette under his heel.

'What are you two happy souls talking about?' asked de Roos. He pulled up a chair and sat down. 'Where's Adolphe?' he said looking round.

'Here,' came the reply. Inspector Adolphe Max of the Belgian Special Branch kicked open the door and entered carrying a tray of cups and a coffee pot.

'Good man,' said de Roos and stood up.

'Not for you, Christian,' said Max, swerving round de Roos's bulk and placing the tray on the table. 'You're wanted down at Police headquarters. Your Embassy want to speak to you. Urgently I'm told.'

'Ah,' said de Roos. He collected his jacket from the back of the chair.

'I'll walk down with you,' said Garner yawning. 'I could do with a lie down.'

The two men made their way down the creaking stairs to the first floor. 'Do you still want to walk round the town this afternoon?' asked de Roos. 'It could be dangerous.'

'We'll give it a try,' said Garner, knowing that his reply was what de Roos wanted to hear. De Roos wanted him to be involved.

'Okay, I shouldn't be too long.'

De Roos walked off along the corridor. Garner went to his room. The bed had been made up and his jacket was hanging on the back of the door. He went to the window, threw it open and breathed deeply, taking in the cool summer air. He was about to turn away when he saw de Roos below, crossing the cobbled courtyard towards his car. 'Bring back something decent for lunch,' he shouted. De Roos gave his the thumbs-up sign and unlocked the Volvo.

Garner yawned, rubbed his eyes and flopped down on the bed. He heard the Volvo starting up and he bent forward to take off his shoes. First the bed and then the room began to shake. The ceiling rained flakes of dusty plaster and the window pane jumped out of its frame.

Through the open window a bright orange flame leapt skywards, pulling with it a cloud of black smoke. Garner was deafened and thrown from the bed by the booming percussion of the exploding Volvo.

RUSSIA

I

The change had been slow and relentless, like a reluctant spring throwing off of the icy mantle of winter. Faces he had known for years, faces which had merged into the background of familiar features of his daily life, were gradually being replaced by other, unfamiliar, watchful, blank faces, all of the same school, but no longer there to protect him. There, instead, to dog his tracks, to spy upon him.

He could not be sure how long the metamorphosis had been in progress, but he was certain that it was almost complete. His phone was tapped as were those of his closest friends and associates; his mail was intercepted and read; his movements outside Moscow were carefully and obtrusively monitored; and his wife and children were finding themselves no longer welcome at the homes of their friends. It was not very subtle, simply classic KGB tactics. They wanted him to know that they had him boxed in; wanted him to feel the cold shudder down his spine, the hollow sensation in his stomach, every time he spotted a new face; wanted him to tremble at every unexpected knock at his door. The KGB were softening him up for the final blow. Gorbachev was ready to strike. But he was ready for Gorbachev and his allies; he had been for some time now.

Yuri Churbanov had lost his position as deputy Interior Minister when his father-in-law, Leonid Brezhnev, had died. But he had survived under the interregnums of Andropov and Chernenko: he had not forfeited any of the prestige, or the privileges, or the protection, usually afforded to the *vlasti*, the elite of Soviet society. That is, until Gorbachev ascended to power. Doors were still open to him, but the rooms now held an arctic chill.

His immediate superior, Minister of the Interior General Nikolai Shcholokov, had survived at his post until Chernenko had him arrested and imprisoned for a short period in Lefortovo jail. Upon his release, and while under constant supervision and surveillance, the General had managed to obtain a gun, and had blown out his brains while sitting on the lavatory at home. Irina, his wife, had soldiered on for another year, before she succumbed to the pressure and took her own life.

Churbanov stopped outside a small jewellery shop, attracted by the bright blues and greens of the displayed stones. He had just come back from Irina's funeral and had felt the need to walk in order to shrug off the stifling melancholia that pervaded his being. Above his head, two scruffy workmen in a cradle were busy repointing the brickwork. He glanced up and then about, surprised at the level of activity in Stary Arbat. The street had recently been converted to a pedestrian precinct and now many of the buildings were undergoing facelifts. Change, everywhere change, he thought. Glasnost. Perestroika. All change. Gorbachev in, Churbanov out.

He walked on slowly, grimly, shaking his head, angry at the transformations this old quarter of Moscow was suffering. He passed several bookshops, a street poet proclaiming his art, a spread of artists, two of whom were rapidly sketching the buiding opposite that had, as yet, not fallen under the wand of the renovators.

The shoppers, mainly young men and women, reminded him of shoppers in the centres of the capitalistic West; well-dressed, choosy and demanding. He smiled to himself as he remembered the days of the long queues and empty shelves, of the thriving black market and secret warehouses bulging with contraband which always had a ready line of customers. The queues and contraband were money in the bank to him and his friends. But those days were gone. At least for the time being. But they would be back, in the not too distant future, providing he kept his head. And his nerve.

He crossed the paved street to a *blini* stand and exchanged a few words with the old stallkeeper who reluctantly threw away her cigarette before spreading a lump of coarse grey caviare on to a paper-thin pancake. She squirted lemon juice on to the caviare and followed that with a spoonful of sour cream and a ladle of melted butter. Then she rolled up the pancake, presented it to Churbanov, and licked the excess butter from her fingers before lighting another cigarette.

Churbanov demolished the *blini* in two mouthfuls and ordered another. As he ate the second, he casually checked the positions of the three men who had been behind him since he had left the cemetery. He wiped his hands on the greasy cloth tied to the stand, paid up, and continued his stroll up Stary Arbat. At the junction with Kalinin Prospekt, he paused behind a group of men who were listening to a blond-haired young man who was warning them about the dangers of the Jewish conspiracy. The blond's companion was handing out leaflets. Churbanov refused the one on offer to him as he had seen it before. He smiled to himself as he watched the two men perform. They were dressed identically: black shirts, black breeches and shiny black, knee-length boots. Perestroika, mused Churbanov, worked both ways: the Pamyat, the Russian Nazis, were emerging once again under Gorbachev's liberating influence. Churbanov smiled. His old allies could now work out in the open where once they had struggled underground. When Gorbachev fell, the Pamyat, with its many tried and trusted friends in the West, would restore him again to prominence.

He wandered off and made his way along the Prospekt. It was too late for Gorbachev and his cronies inside the KGB. Even if Gorbachev had him arrested today and imprisoned him inside Lefortovo, he would spend no more than five or six weeks in custody before the Pamyat would release him. And the KGB would get nothing out of him, no matter what they tried because they would not know what they were looking for. Their main interest would be his black market activities, and he could spin out that saga for months, if not years. In the meantime, the plan would be nearing fruition, and nobody, not even the KGB, not even Gorbachev, would be any the wiser.

He had visited Geneva undetected some weeks before and had met up with the Englishman and the American. Now it was up to them. They would not fail. Their political and financial masters had too much to lose and so failure was out of the question. They would see it through even if he, Yuri Churbanov, was in the hands of the KGB. He would not fail them. They knew that too. What was it the Englishman, Hamilton, had called it? ASH? Yes, that was it. ASH. OPERATION ASH.

There was a spring in his step as he continued on his way, a spring that went undetected by his three shadows.

II

It was two o'clock in the morning when the black Zil with the Brest registration slowed to a crawl at the border crossing. The driver wound down his window as he edged the car towards the barrier and draped his arm through the opening. In his hand he held a piece of paper emblazoned with three red stars, and as he neared the Polish captain, who stood to the left of the red and white barrier bathed in a splash of yellow light from one of the arc lamps, he waved the paper impatiently and whistled at the Pole.

The captain watched the vehicle draw level, recognising it as the one which had passed through in the opposite direction some hours earlier, and he noted that a passenger was now installed in the rear. He clamped his arms firmly behind his back and rocked back and forth on the balls of his feet in what he hoped was a patient and authoritative stance, disdaining the summons of the boorish driver, and seeking to impress his own men who were gathered outside the administrative hut. Out of the corner of his eye he tried to gauge whether there had been any reaction from the Russian quarters fifty metres away on the other side of the demarcation line. As far as he could see there was no response to the car's arrival, so he decided to risk prolonging his performance despite the driver's angry grunts and scowls.

He glared at the driver who had been so insultingly dismissive of the major when crossing earlier in the night, and then he beckoned his sergeant. He instructed the man to collect the document from the driver, to ask for the passenger's passport and his final destination, and to do so in his own native Szczecin dialect. The sergeant grinned broadly as he listened to his orders, came to attention, snapped a sharp salute which just fell short of self-decapitation, turned and marched over to the stationary vehicle.

The captain despised all Russians and he particularly loathed the petty, officious types exemplified by the driver who looked down on the Poles as dross and cannon fodder. Whereas Major Sikorski bowed and scraped to anyone and anything that even hinted of Soviet officialdom, he, Captain Wladyslaw Zawodny, would rather die than raise a finger to the forelock. His father's two elder brothers had been captured by the Russians in 1939 and had disappeared into the snows of Katyn Wood where they had been murdered on the orders of Stalin together with fourteen thousand brother officers and enlisted men of the Polish Home Army. The captain would never forgive nor forget, and as far as he was concerned, all Russians were bloody savages. Though he personally could do very little to throw off the Russian yoke, his position as border guard gave ample opportunities in which to loosen it a fraction of an inch.

In the rear seat of the Zil, Nikolai Volsky gritted his teeth and checked his watch once more. It had been many years since he had encountered the stifling bureaucracy of the communist world, especially the Polish variety, and during the past week in Siedlce he had forced himself to smile bravely into the faceless masks of the incompetents who administered it, rather than make a fuss. But now, as he listened to the sergeant spouting off to the driver in some incomprehensible dialect, the tightness of his schedule would not allow him the luxury of a smile. He realised he could do nothing to prevent himself from falling victim again to the deliberate delaying tactics of the Poles.

He felt a momentary panic and then a burning rage as he heard the driver thump the side of the car in frustration and anger. The sergeant was striding back to his leader with the pass and he handed it over with the air of a man delivering the spoils of victory. Volsky contained himself, tried to relax, and decided that he had no option but to let the Poles play out their silly game. He was trapped.

Silently, Volsky cursed Stanislav, his control, who had ordered the meeting at such short notice. That it was an emergency of the highest priority was obvious from the fact that all procedures and protocols had been overridden, as had any fears for his safety and possible exposure as a KGB illegal living and working in the West. Nevertheless, Stanislav had made a very grave error. Volsky's only means of identification were his French passport in his cover name and the letter of authorisation from the Polish Ministry of Justice, in the same name, which granted him and his team certain privileges and facilities in Siedlce. But the red-starred pass, now in the hands of the Polish captain, identified him as Volsky, KGB colonel.

Should the captain demand to see his passport, the mistake would come to light immediately and he would be held at the border until it was sorted out. The Poles would know his true identity and his role as an illegal, which, in itself, would not be catastrophic. But the delay would mean he would not be back in Siedlce by eight o'clock that morning to meet his colleagues at the railway station and that would arouse a great deal of suspicion. Questions would be asked, explanations demanded, and the trust he had built up so carefully over the years would begin to evaporate: he would have broken the cardinal rule of not going off alone when working inside a communist country. His colleagues on the team, to whom suspicion and doubt were second nature, would label him as untrustworthy. He would probably lose his position which gave him direct access to the inner workings of the many Western governments. If that happened, Moscow Centre would have no option but to recall him, and that would break him.

The minutes ticked slowly by. Volsky clenched and unclenched his fists; the driver feigned sleep; the Polish captain doggedly perused the pass over and over again, occasionally casting furtive glances across to the Russian side; the sergeant stood with his men, grinning inanely, as he explained what was happening.

Suddenly there was a burst of activity from the Russian sector. A man came running down the no-man's land between the two border posts, his arms waving wildly above his head. He wore the green and grey uniform of the Polish Border Guard. He ducked under the barrier, dislodging his cap as he did so, straightening up, and began bawling orders at the captain and the troop.

As the barrier was being hurriedly raised, Major Sikorski marched unsteadily over to the car. Volsky lowered the window. Sikorsky returned the pass and began an obsequious apology for the behaviour of the captain. Volsky recoiled from the heavy smell of vodka

38

on the man's breath and he ordered the driver to proceed across the frontier before the major could finish. The driver grunted his approval.

III

Brest is a small city in the Belorussian Republic, one thousand kilometres south west of Moscow and a fifteen minutes' drive from the Polish border. It is an important rail and road junction and a centre for agricultural produce, timber and textiles. It owes its place in history to the collective decision of the delegates to the Petrograd Soviet who voted to accept the German peace terms as the only way of saving the nascent Revolution. The treaty was signed in the city, which at that time was known as Brest-Litovsk, in March 1918, and ratified two weeks later under the forceful promptings of Lenin and Stalin at the Seventh Party Congress. The only dissenting voice was that of Nikolai Bukharin who was, twenty years later, to pay with his life for his independence of mind when he became a victim of the Ezhovschchina, the second and most savage purge of the Old Guard Bolsheviks instigated by Stalin in the name of socialist solidarity.

The only solidarity Stalin recognised, mused Volsky, was that exhibited by corpses six feet under the frozen earth. He smiled to himself at his own black humour, then dismissed the thought from his mind. On his mother's side he was related to the Bukharin family; he had been named after the great man; and he had heard the dark tales, both the official and unofficial versions, of the repressions and murders which had terrorised Russia for almost thirty years, and which would not be erased from the collective memory until a much longer period of time had elapsed. That was the Soviet people's burden; and when coupled with the Nazi atrocities of the Great Patriotic War, then added to the viscious propaganda and Cold War posturing of the West, it really was a wonder, he thought, how Mother Russia continued to endure. She did so because her citizens were strong and steadfast and she would outlive and outlast the nations of the West because of that. For where as war was a matter of survival for the Russians, for the West it was a matter of profit. And as his dear old mother used to say, there were no pockets in a shroud.

'Almost there,' interrupted the driver.

Volsky saw that they were cruising through the darkened outskirts of the city, running parallel to a rail track, and above the noise of the car, he could hear the wheezing of a shunting engine further down the line. They turned left and began to slow: the driver flashed his lights, once, then twice as he pulled in to the pavement and braked to a halt outside a rectangular wooden building with a rusted corrugated iron roof.

'Here?' asked Volsky.

'Yes, sir,' said the driver. He took off his cap, cradled his head in his arms and rested them on the steering wheel. He was asleep before Volsky climbed out of the car.

As he closed the door behind him, Volsky saw a door open in the side of the building and a figure emerge. 'Stanislav?' he called warily as he approached.

'Come on, Nik. Hurry up.' Stanislav held on to the door as if trying to hold back the spill of light into the poorly lit street. 'Where the hell have you been?'

'I could throttle you, Stanislav,' said Volsky as they shook hands. 'Do you know . . .?'

Stanislav ushered him inside. 'Sorry, but you've no time for that. Inside. Don't keep him waiting any longer.'

They were in a narrow corridor which led to the main body of the building. 'Who?' asked Volsky.

'Straight ahead, Nik. I'm not coming in with you. This is for your ears only.' He shrugged and patted Volsky on the back. 'Off you go.'

Frowning, Volsky walked on into a workshop. Several lathes stood against one wall facing a pair of circular saws on the opposite wall, while the space in between was taken up with three lines of wooden work benches. There was a smell of pine resin and freshly sawn wood, and the floor was littered with sawdust and shavings.

'You'd think they'd clean up after themselves, wouldn't you?' said General Viktor Chebrikov. He was seated at an oblong table to Volsky's left, close to the first of the lathes.

Volsky's eyes widened in amazement, 'Comrade General,' he mumbled. He had not met the Chairman of the KGB before but he had seen his photograph, and he immediately recognised the pale thin features, the cropped white hair brushed back from the domed forehead, the blank, piercing gaze. Volsky came to attention and raised his right arm in salute.

'That will do, Nikolai Sergeyevich Volsky. We will dispense with the formalities.' Like Volsky, the Chairman wore a well-cut suit, white shirt and tie. 'Sit down,' he ordered.

Volsky sat on the short, three-legged stool in front of the Chairman. He cleared his throat and crossed his legs and clasped his hands round his knees. He resisted the temptation to avert his eyes under pressure from his superior's searching look.

'Your work has always been of the highest calibre, Nikolai Sergevevich,' began the Chairman. 'And your loyalty is beyond question. That is why I have called upon you today.'

'Thank you, comrade General.'

The Chairman blinked. 'Despite the Premier's attempts to destroy the myth of Soviet aggression, the Motherland is still under sustained attack from the West. In addition, fifth columnists and traitors from within are seeking to prevent the changes necessary to return the Motherland to the true path of Lenin's socialist democracy. The Premier's enemies are very clever and deeply entrenched and have had some success in thwarting the twin thrusts of glasnost and perestroika. But they are losing ground and so they are becoming more and more desperate in their attempts to stifle and halt the Premier's programme.' The Chairman dropped his hands below the table and produced a leather briefcase. He dialled the combination and opened it, then pushed it to one side after selecting a black and white print which he passed across to Volsky. 'You know this man?'

Volsky looked at the grainy print. 'Yuri Churbanov,' he said.

The Chairman nodded. 'The spider at the centre of the web. Arch conservative and black market racketeer.' He handed over a second print. 'Churbanov again, despite the blurring.'

Volsky compared the two prints. 'Undoubtedly, comrade General. But . . .'

'But why bother with poor prints when the archives are full of good, clear shots of the same man?'

'Yes, comrade General.'

'A lucky shot, Nikolai Sergeyevich. He was caught in the background. Our photographer was after someone else. Those pictures were taken four weeks ago outside an office block in the Bel Air district of Geneva. On the day they were taken, we had Yuri Churbanov under surveillance in his *dacha* at Sochi. Or at least we thought we had.'

'I see,' said Volsky with some surprise.

The Chairman selected another print from the pile and held it out to Volsky. 'This is the man we were after. Alex Hamilton. Among his many interests is an air transport company which has an office in that same office block in Bel Air.'

Volsky thought for a moment. He arched his eyebrows and slowly shook his head. 'Comrade General, you are saying that Hamilton flew him out of Russia and into Switzerland?'

'Why look so surprised,' replied the Chairman. 'He probably flew him back again, too. If a young West German student can fly a single-engine Cessna through our northern defences and land in Red Square, think of what a man of Hamilton's experience could do.'

'I do not know this man Hamilton,' said Volsky.

'Twenty years in the British armed forces, two of which were spent with the SAS. He also helped to train the American Delta Forces Commandos at McDill Air Force Base in Florida.

'Perhaps,' said Volsky reluctantly.

General Chebrikov dismissed the issue with a wave of his hands. 'How Churbanov managed to get in and out of Switzerland when he was supposed to be taking the sulphur waters at Sochi is not important. The point is he was there, in Geneva, with Hamilton. And Hamilton's interests extend far beyond flying illicit cargoes.' He delved into the case once more and brought out a large print. 'John Heritage.'

The picture showed Hamilton getting into a car accompanied by a second man wearing a cap. 'John Heritage,' said Volsky. 'I know him. Arms dealer. Former CIA resident in London and Madrid. He now works for the Miller Foundation.'

'An American fascist organisation. Very rich, very powerful, with many connections to the American military. And the White House.' Chebrikov ran his fingers through his hair. 'Heritage was also in Geneva with Hamilton and Churbanov. In fact Hamilton and Heritage seem to be spending a lot of their time together of late.'

'Very interesting, Comrade General,' said Volsky as he studied the print. 'What is Churbanov doing . . .?'

'We will not digress with questions, Nikolai Sergeyevich,' interrupted Chebrikov. 'Wait until you have heard the complete story.'

'Yes, Comrade General.' Volsky was tired: his head ached and the Chairman's droning voice was making matters worse. He wanted to get the interview over as fast as possible, but he now realised that the Chairman was going to pursue it his own way. He sneaked a look at his watch.

'Do not worry about time, either. Your colleagues in Siedlce will never know you left Poland. The Polish authorities will ensure you will meet your train.'

'Thank you, Comrade General.' After his experience at the border crossing, he had his doubts. But he kept them to himself.

Chebrikov clasped his hands together. 'A week after the Geneva meeting, Hamilton and Heritage turn up in Israel.'

'An arms buy?' suggested Volsky, then regretted his interruption as he saw the scowl on Chebrikov's face.

'Not an unreasonable assumption,' sighed the Chairman. 'Israel has become a centre for the illicit arms trade, and the two men have made several trips there for such a purpose. But on this occasion, they did not stay in Tel Aviv as usual, but travelled north to Nazareth.' As Chebrikov talked his fingers were sorting the photographs on the table. 'South west of Nazareth, across the Plain of Esdraelon, are the mountains of central Palestine. High in those mountains is a place known to the Hebrews as Har-Megiddo, the Hill of Megiddo, but better known to the Christians as Armageddon. The Old Testament of the Bible, Revelation Sixteen, names Armageddon as the place where the rulers of the world will fight the last great battle between good and evil.'

Volsky raised his eyebrows. He was about to speak when the Chairman got to his feet and walked over to the lathe, and with his back to Volsky, continued his monologue.

'It is no coincidence that shortly after taking office, the American President referred to Mother Russia as the Evil Empire. By implication, America is the Good Empire. At the Hill of Megiddo, Hamilton and Heritage met with the Reverend Jimmy Lee Lewis one week after their meeting in Geneva with Churbanov.'

'But Comrade General,' protested Volsky. 'The Reverend Lewis is a joke. Not only in America but also in Europe. Why the . . .'

'The Reverend Lewis and his fellow tele-evangelists.' He paused for a moment. 'I believe that is the correct phrase?' Volsky nodded. 'They hold sway over the minds of sixteen million Americans. Their churches generate vast amounts of money. The Reverend Lewis is on the board of the Miller Foundation. He is also the founder of ACME, Americans for a Christian Moral Environment. ACME has been endorsed by the American President. And some of the President's recent pronouncements show that he has become infected by the particular brand of Christian fundamentalism preached by Lewis and his colleagues.'

Volsky shook his head in disbelief. If he had heard this from anyone but his Chairman he would have laughed. As it was it took him a great deal of effort not to smile. Again, as he was about to speak, the Chairman interrupted.

'Yes, Nikolai Sergeyevich. This is 1988, the era of instantaneous mass communication, the age of scientific rationality and technological innovation. But it is an age in which, as many men believe, that man has lost his soul. Do we ignore the rantings of the mullahs in Iran? The Mujahedeen in Afghanistan? The rumblings of religious revival in our own Muslim Republics?' He stared at Volsky before resuming his seat. 'I know you may find it difficult to understand, but understand it you must. Many Christians in the West fail to understand the message preached by the Reverend Lewis. But the message he preaches is loud and clear: America is the Good Empire, Russia the Evil Empire. Confrontation between the two is inevitable, and because it is inevitable, it is incumbent upon men such as Lewis to work towards the advent of Armageddon.' Chebrikov's face had turned a shade of red, and he stabbed the space between himself and Volsky with his index finger. 'The end of the world is just around the corner. Only the chosen few will survive. Needless to say those chosen few are the Americans who contribute to the upkeep of the Reverend Lewis's religious empire.' He dipped into the briefcase and threw a snapshot across the table to Volsky.

'Hamilton, Heritage and Lewis,' said Volsky. 'But comrade General, this does not mean there is any connection with Churbanov and the Geneva meeting.'

Chebrikov took a deep breath. 'The Reverend Lewis is a firebrand preacher, or so I am told, revivalist, a fundamentalist, happily married, and, most importantly, totally beyond reproach. No scandal has touched him.'

'That is correct,' said Volsky. 'Recently a rival of Lewis's was removed from his church because of a sexual scandal, and Lewis, having pointed the finger, took over his rival's empire.'

'And now I find that Lewis, too, is involved in a sex scandal. Though it has yet to hit the headlines.' Chebrikov smirked. 'Lewis is involved with a young woman. In Baton Rouge. Unfortunately we have no photographs yet of Lewis and his mistress enjoying their particular sexual fancies, but we do have some excellent sound tapes of their antics.'

'Do you intend to expose him to the American media?' asked Volsky.

'That is our intention. In the future. But let us return to your earlier point about a connection between Churbanov and Lewis through Hamilton and Heritage.' Chebrikov began to gather in the photographs. 'The Reverend Lewis always begins and ends his sexual diversions with a prayer. To date, we have not been able to ascertain whether he does this on his knees.' Chebrikov smiled. Volsky followed suit. 'The latest tape, which I received yesterday, had Lewis insisting that his mistress join him in the opening prayer, something he has never done before. And then instead of the usual gropings, Lewis talked to her for two hours, trying to convert her to the Lord's path, as he put it. He told her Armageddon was at hand, that the final conflict between good and evil, between America and Russia, was about to take place. He pleaded with her to accept Jesus Christ or else she would have to suffer an eternity of hellfire.'

'A crisis of conscience?' suggested Volsky. 'Did she accept conversion?' He succeeded in keeping a straight face.

'She certainly gave it some thought which was why they spent all their time together talking.' The Chairman closed and locked his case. 'She asked him how he knew for certain that the end of the world was at hand. Lewis beat about the bush for some time, quoting biblical texts until the poor woman was dizzy. Finally, in a last, desperate attempt to win her over, Lewis claimed that he had his finger on the button that would set in motion the events that would inevitably ignite the fuse of the final battle. And what is more, he also said that in order to place his finger on the button, he had been forced to collaborate with a representative of the forces of evil.'

'Churbanov,' whispered Volsky.

'Yuri Churbanov,' reaffirmed the Chairman. 'The spider at the centre of the web. The common thread.'

'And yet what do Churbanov and Lewis have in common?' asked Volsky.

'Four years ago, do you remember, we allowed the American Baptist preacher, Donald Fallright, to come to Moscow?' Volsky nodded. 'He preached to a hundred and ten thousand citizens in the Dynamo stadium. A revivalist meeting Fallright called it.' Chebrikov arched his eyebrows. 'Jimmy Lee Lewis was one of Fallright's entourage. He was there at the stadium. And so was Yuri Churbanov.'

'Was contact established between the two men?'

'We believe so,' said Chebrikov. 'Do you know, Nikolai Sergeyevich, the title of the best-selling book of all time?'

The sudden change of direction caught Volsky un-awares. 'Er, no comrade General.'

'I have read it. And I believe you have too. It is the Christian Bible. And it was bibles that first brought Lewis and Churbanov together. Lewis brought the bibles to the Turkish frontier and Churbanov smuggled them across into Russia for distribution. Through his friends in the Pamyat.'

'And what did Churbanov get in return?'

'He brought Beluga caviar, sable and mink, icons, the stolen treasures from the Imperial Palaces, to the Turkish frontier and Lewis's networks smuggled them out to the West.'

ENGLAND

He strolled through Covent Garden, into St Martin's Lane, past Stringfellow's nightclub and into Monmouth Street where he entered the Two Brewers public house and joined the crush at the bar.

'Hiya,' said Rose the landlady as she dashed past, a clutch of dirty glasses in one hand, a dishcloth in the other. 'Won't be a minute, love.'

He was doling out the money on the counter when she returned with his red wine. 'Looks like another hectic night, Rose,' he said.

'It's Saturday night again,' she replied and picked up his cash. 'It's a must that the punters are out and about and seen to be enjoying themselves.' She winked at him.

'Know what you mean.' He thanked her and elbowed his way through the close-knit thickets of drinkers to the rear of the pub where humanity was usually thinner on the ground. The circular table next to the toilet entrance was empty. He shoved aside the overflowing ashtray and the empty crisp packets and sat down with his back to the wood panelling. It wasn't the best seat in the house but it provided an entertaining view of the frenetic antics and posturings of the assembled revellers. In an hour or two the pub would empty and the locals and regulars would be left to their own company and that of occasional, itinerant tipplers and topers.

Garner sipped his wine and allowed his gaze to roam over the congregation, and then over the photographs of screen and stage stars that were displayed along the higher reaches of the wall. Cobwebs of cigarette smoke were strung beneath the yellowed ceiling, stirring sluggishly in the breezes generated by the animated conversations down below, which reached his ears as a constant sawing drone.

He hadn't been near any of the customary Fleet Street watering holes for some time, and he hadn't missed them at all. He would never miss those days of the *wilderness*. He much preferred the relative anonymity of the Two Brewers. He knew most of the staff, could nod to the handful of regulars like himself, and nobody pried into his business or accosted him for favours. The pub was the nearest he had found to a local in this busy part of London.

Someone brushed against his shoulder, a young girl on her way to the toilet. She was followed by two men, and again Garner was jostled, this time with an apology. He shifted along the wooden bench out of the way, and, as he did so, a tall, broad-shouldered man dressed in a loud check jacket of red and green emerged from the crowd and stood in front of his table.

'My name is Arthur Piechler.' He held out his hand.

'I'll buy that,' said Garner, immediately on guard. 'But I think you've got the wrong guy.' He ignored the man's outstretched hand.

'Do you mind if I sit down, Mr Garner?' Piechler took a seat opposite Garner without waiting for a reply.

Garner took him to be an American from his dress rather than his accent which hinted strongly of England. 'Do I know you, Mr Piechler?' he asked suspiciously.

'No. We've never met,' he replied. 'But I have to admit that I know quite a lot about you.'

'I see,' said Garner warily. 'American?'

Piechler nodded. 'East Coast.'

'Is that where you learnt all about me? In those neat little files the CIA likes to collect?' He had had no contact with the CIA for a long time and he wasn't going to have them invading his private retreat. Mr Piechler was in for a rough ride, he told himself.

'Montclair, New Jersey, actually,' said Piechler with a grin. He unfastened his jacket and leaned closer to Garner. 'Don't worry, I'm not the bogeyman from Langley. Or anywhere else for that matter.'

'And I'm supposed to just take your word for it, eh?'

'I'm a Jew . . .'

'The CIA doesn't recruit Jews is that it?' he said sarcastically.

'White Anglo Saxon Protestants is more their line,' said Piechler. 'I work for the Contemporary Jewish Documentation Centre in Paris. I track down former Nazis.'

'Any ID?'

'Passport?'

'Good as anything.' Piechler produced it from his inside pocket and handed it over. Garner flipped through it, noting the name and photograph, the many visas, and the French Residence Permit, countersigned by the Documentation Centre. 'Seems okay,' he said as he gave it back. 'Could be a clever forgery though. You still could be CIA.'

Piechler smiled. 'A persecution complex is a useful attribute in your line of work, but I can assure you that it has been quite some time since you were favoured with the attention of my country's snoopers. I'm not CIA.'

'But you have a file on me?'

'Mr Garner, I understand your suspicion. Particularly after the incident in Diksmuide. I also knew Christian de Roos. We collaborated on a number of issues.'

His heart skipped a beat at the mention of his dead friend's name. The memory was still very painful. Nothing had come of the official investigation, which had not truly surprised him, and his own private inquiries had so far yielded nothing. But he was quietly determined to plod away at the case whenever he had the time and he was always on the look out for anything even remotely connected with de Roos. By mentioning Christian's name, Piechler had provided him with the best way of checking his credibility, for if he had worked with de Roos, then de Roos's colleagues would know about it. Piechler, he had to admit to himself, was beginning to intrigue him. 'I suppose you kept a file on Christian, too?' he asked.

'My organisation likes to keep tracks of its friends as well as its enemies. You and de Roos belong to the former category.'

'How nice.' Garner had the impression he had seen Piechler somewhere before. Recently. But he could not remember where.

Piechler took in and let out a long breath. 'Look. I need your help. You're a talented reporter and . . .'

'Was,' interrupted Garner.

'You do yourself a disservice. That community magazine you edit is very good. Excellent in fact. Your talents are obvious. We would like to employ them.'

'No. I'm no Nazi hunter,' said Garner, and he knocked back the last of his wine.

'Nazi. Fascist. New Right. Different names but the same doctrines,' said Piechler. 'Let them worry about the semantics, Mr Garner. You and I are fighting for the same cause, to expose what lies behind the rhetoric. And we both know what that is, don't we?' He drank his tomato juice in one swallow. 'Racial and social prejudice. Bigotry. The language of division, of the ghetto, of them and us. Articulated by politicians and pressure groups in the daily tabloids. And it all leads down the same path. To the gas chamber. But this time the Jews will have plenty of company: Asians, Turks, blacks, the poor, the dispossessed.' He toyed with his glass. 'I'm no Nazi hunter, either. I am simply a man who can see that history is about to repeat itself.'

'I understand,' said Garner. 'But . . .'

'Let me get you another drink first,' said Piechler. 'Red wine?' Garner said yes. Piechler gathered up the glasses and got to his feet. 'Hear me out. That's all I ask,' he added, and turned towards the bar.

Garner watched him part the crowd like Moses dividing the waters of the Red Sea all the way up to the counter where Rose served him without delay. His initial suspicion and hostility towards Piechler had evaporated. There was a time in the past when he could not move without feeling the CIA or DI6 on his back, and this experience told him that Piechler was not of that ilk. Still, he thought, the man was familiar. He knew his face.

'Here we go,' said Piechler, as he deposited the drinks on the table and sat down.

'Thanks,' said Garner. 'Cheers.'

'Mud in your eye.' Piechler contemplated his surroundings. 'Quite a place, eh? All those photographs.'

'Better than autographs disfiguring the walls.'

Piechler continued to look up at the walls. 'De Roos's death was a sad blow. The Centre will miss him very much.'

'Murder, Mr Piechler. Speak your mind. Don't hide behind euphemisms.'

'I can assure you I wasn't,' said Piechler. 'I brought up the matter of de Roos's death just to let you know that should you refuse my offer, I would understand your position.'

'De Roos's killers frighten the life out of me, Mr Piechler,' said Garner stiffly. 'But you can't kill ideas, you can't remove a person's influence and dedication simply by removing that person. I'm listening. Tell me about it.'

'Thank you.' Piechler sat forward. 'I came to Britain last week as part of a delegation to see your Home Secretary.'

Garner screwed up his eyes. 'That's where I know you from. I saw you on television. You gave a press conference.'

'That's right, Mr Garner.'

'What was it? Nineteen men, former Nazis living under assumed names in Britain?'

Piechler nodded. 'Correct. Nineteen men. Latvians, Lithuanians, Ukrainians, Byelorussians. But no Germans. We gave the Home Office their names, documentary proof of their true identities and the crimes they committed.'

'And what a waste of time it was, eh?' said Garner cynically. 'You handed over all that information and what did you get in return? A verbal runaround, I bet. Why reopen old wounds? Rake over the ashes? Why not let sleeping dogs lie? *Et cetera, et cetera.* Right?'

'Exactly right. Stonewalled, as we Americans say.' Piechler drank half his drink.

Garner stroked his chin. 'The interview on TV, the leader of the delegation, what was his name?'

'Abraham Hecht.'

'Well didn't he say that the names on the list would remain a secret until the Home Office had completed its own inquiries?' asked Garner. 'In fact, hadn't the Home Office made that a condition of accepting the delegation in the first place?' Garner continued to stroke his chin. 'That's it, isn't it? You want me to leak those names to the national press, don't you?'

'We could do that ourselves. We are not without influence in the media. But, no. You are on the wrong track altogether, I'm afraid.' Piechler smiled. 'Let me explain. You see, in a sense, our mission to see the Home Secretary was a diversion. Yes, we want the Nazis arrested and expelled, hopefully deported to Israel to stand trial for their crimes. But you will remember that I said there were no Germans on the list.' Garner nodded. Piechler paused momentarily. 'But there was a German we could have added to the list.'

'And yet you didn't?'

'Yes. And for a very good reason. Had the German's name been included, then the Home Secretary would have refused to have seen us, and would have probably refused us entry into Britain.'

'Don't you think you're exaggerating somewhat, Mr Piechler?' Garner sat upright and looked over Piechler's shoulder. The crowd had thinned out to a handful of drinkers who were now congregated at the bar. The din had subsided and the atmosphere was more relaxed and congenial. Rose was enjoying a cigarette with one of the customers. 'Don't misunderstand me,' he added. 'But what you have just said calls for some explanation.'

'A Home Office representative gave the delegation a name when we first applied to come to Britain. That official said if that name was included we would not be received by the Home Secretary. As simple as that.'

'And the name?' asked Garner.

'Treboven. Viktor Treboven.'

'Can't say the name rings a bell.'

'That's it exactly. His name means nothing to most people,' said Piechler. 'And yet it is a name that makes your Home Secretary shake. Viktor Treboven. A secretive man about whom very little is known. A man who is probably the prime mover in the rise of the neo-Nazis in Europe, if not the world.'

'Did he serve in the last war?'

'Yes. But almost nothing survives of his service record. But we know that he is one of the cold, detached variety. A manipulator, a puppet-master. You would enjoy a crack at him, wouldn't you?'

'You've recruited me already have you?' protested Garner. But both men knew the question was rhetorical.

'We would give you all the assistance you needed in ferreting him out. He has many protective shells around him. But we think there is a chink in his armour which we want you to exploit.'

'But what has he done exactly, you know, regarding war crimes?'

'I will supply those details later, Mr Garner,' said Piechler.

'I don't know,' said Garner reluctantly. 'From what you've said he sounds to me as if he's quite a powerful man.'

'Very powerful indeed. And very rich. He's probably one of the richest men in the world though his name has never figured in Fortune magazine's league table of the mega-rich. His business empire is controlled and operated through a series of trusts in Liechtenstein, whose commercial laws make the Swiss seem positive blabbermouths.'

'I see,' said Garner. 'You're using a feather to swat an elephant,' and he smiled. 'I think you are on to a non-starter.'

Piechler held up both hands. 'Don't be put off by that. He does have a weak spot, an indulgence which he allows himself. And that is where you can begin.' Piechler pulled a notebook from his pocket. 'When was the last time you were in Liverpool?'

AMERICA

I

'A warm Coors, please,' said Hamilton. The bartender was square and squat, with a row of chins resembling the thirty-nine steps. He stared at Hamilton as if he had two heads, then shuffled off into the back room to emerge a few seconds later with a heavy frown and the bottle of beer.

'Warm you said?' he queried, holding on to the beer like a man holding a grudge. Hamilton nodded. The barman sucked in air between his discoloured teeth to show his disbelief, before opening the bottle and depositing it together with a wet glass in front of his alien customer.

'Thanks,' said Hamilton, and he poured his drink. He did not like his beer cold: it gave him indigestion and marred the taste.

'Out of town, mister?'

Hamilton slowly quenched his thirst before replying. 'Out of the country, actually.' He accentuated his Englishness.

'Figures,' drawled the barman in disgust. He sauntered off to the end of the bar to resume his game of pinochle with the only other occupant of the bar, a tall, corpulent redneck wearing a straw Stetson.

The bar room was cool and dark, furnished in post-brawl American, and Hamilton was grateful for the relief it provided from the searing sun outdoors. He had more than an hour to wait for the pick up, and he had decided that outside the Post Office on Main Street, Alphine was not the ideal place to do so. Besides the heat and the suspicious, hostile looks of the locals, he had the impression that the dereliction and desolation which beset the town was still on the move, and was creeping up to envelop him even as he sat and waited on the boardwalk, so that after ten minutes or so, he had had enough, and he had scooped up his overnight bag and had made a dash for the refuge of the nearest, rusted beer sign which adorned the front of Frizzy's Cantina.

Frizzy and his friend continued their desultory game but Hamilton knew that he was the object of their attention, attested to by the frequent, surreptitious glances and stifled guffaws. The slovenly attitude and behaviour of the two men exactly matched the run-down appearance of the bar, and the town in which it was situated. But Hamilton knew it was all a sham.

Alphine so resembled many small towns in the southern States of America, marooned and poverty stricken, that an occasional visitor could be excused for believing that it was simply another example of the decline that afflicted small town America, as the young fled from the depressing boredom to the excitement of the cities, consigning the town to the elderly and the unimaginative. But a closer and more careful scrutiny of the inhabitants, a surprisingly good mixture of young and old, would show a well-fed populace dressed in rags whose demeanour spoke of hidden wealth and prosperity, so that a suspicion would arise that the men and women of Alphine were somehow engaged in an elaborate hoax, playing out roles in a meticulously rehearsed charade against a backdrop of ramshackle buildings and back-breaking dirt farms.

And the suspicion would be well-founded. For beneath the superficial poverty, there was a hard core of affluence: the citizens of Alphine enjoyed winters in Miami and the Bahamas, and sent their children to private, out-of-state schools. The secret of the hidden wealth, witnessed by the satellite dish on top of the Sheriff's Office and the wide, newly constructed blacktops which radiated from the town, was farming. In a semi-arid scrubland with a minimal rainfall, Alphine had made a success of fish farming, which accounted for the strange and esoteric manner of its inhabitants. Local people made no reference whatsoever to the fish farm. For the fish were all human, and they all spoke the language of international terrorism.

Every evening as the sun went down, in and around the town, English was replaced by Spanish, and the only barking came from a small band of mercenaries, instructors in the art of terrorism, who rattled out lessons and commands from the CIA bible, *Operaciones Sicologics en Guerr de Guerrillas*, to the eager troops of novice assassins and terrorists, who slept by day and trained by night. And two or three times a week, heavily laden CL-44 Turboprops rumbled down the illuminated blacktops, heading due south to the Contra camps inside the Honduras-Nicaragua border region, carrying arms and supplies, and the latest batch of graduated freedom fighters, to return the following night ballasted with neat, brown paper parcels of Columbian cocaine. Ten per cent of each cocaine delivery was for the people of Alphine for distribution up north on the streets of the devil's capital, New York.

Hamilton knew all this because he was one of the sponsors of the Alphine fish farm. The aeroplanes were his, part of his St Lucia Airways fleet, which he had leased to Southernair Transport, the front organisation he and his associates had set up to provide the lifeline for the Contras and their terrorist campaign.

Since the American Congress had vetoed military aid to the Contras, the President and his foreign policy advisors had determined to continue the struggle against communist infiltration on the American continent, despite the controversy raging over Irangate and the supply of armaments to the Contras which contravened the veto. The President's Private Sector Initiatives encouraged individuals, organisations and corporations to take up the funding and the fight against the red menace wherever it showed itself, and Southernair Transport was such an initiative. No governmental service or department was directly involved, though the CIA kept a friendly eye on the fish farm and ensured that snooping Federal men, from the Revenue Service, Immigration, and the other Agencies, were kept at arm's length so that the citizens of Alphine could do their patriotic duty in the defence of democracy and the American way of life, and receive their just rewards without undue interference from meddling officials.

But that was about to change very rapidly in the next few days, thought Hamilton, which was why he had rushed down to this part of the Texas-Mexican border. It was one of his planes, G-BDTE. This aircraft was about to become as famous as the Spirit of St Louis. Notoriously so. For G-BDTE had had the misfortune to stray too close to the Nicaraguan frontier, and the disingenuous Sandanistas had shot it out of the sky. But there was the consolation in that all on board had died in the resulting crash so there would be no survivors to tell the tale and cause embarrassment, which had been the case a couple of years previously when the CIA pilot had survived and had been put on trial in Managua after a similar incident.

It was time to shut up shop. But quickly. Alphine was now being prepared to disappear into the obscurity and poverty it had mimicked for so long. Hamilton surmised that the pinochle players would be gambling in cents rather than in dollars before the week was out. The place would be swarming with Senators and Federal men once the Sandanistas told the world that the plane had originated from the southern states of America. And the President would not survive an Alphinegate on top of the other scandals.

II

He left Frizzy's and strolled along to the Post Office, reaching the building at the same time as a silver-grey Chevvy Blazer cruised to a halt outside. A young man jumped out and beckoned to Hamilton, holding the door open as he did so. Hamilton glanced inside. 'Billy Joe,' he said to the driver, and threw him his bag.

'Good to see you again, Sir,' said Billy Joe. He placed the bag on the seat and waited for Hamilton to get in. 'Keys?'

Hamilton handed them over. 'I booked it through to Big Bend National Park.'

'Okay,' said Billy Joe. He threw the keys to his companion. 'Big Bend, Eddy. Take your time.'

'Right. Where is it now, Sir?' asked Eddy.

Hamilton pointed down Main Street. 'Tan Pontiac. Outside the garage.'

Eddy closed the door and Billy Joe let in the clutch and roared out of town in a cloud of dust.

'Take me to your leader,' said Hamilton. 'I take it Blackmore is still at Iron Mountain?'

'Yes, Sir. But he ain't standing still long enough for anybody to talk to him. He's running all over the show, pulling everything up by the roots. He sure is pissed.'

'Isn't everybody?' said Hamilton.

'By the way, all the planes got out. They all . . .'

'I know, Billy Joe. Heard last night,' said Hamilton. He settled himself against the door and rested his head on the upholstery, closing his eyes, feeling a sudden need to sleep. He had been on the move for over twenty-four hours, having flown in to Houston the previous day, then straight on the shuttle to Midland-Odessa where he had expected to confer with Blackmore.

William Birch Blackmore. Yes, he would have hit the panic button and would be running about like a headless chicken, shutting down the operation personally before the authorities and the media caught wind of what had been going on down at the ranch which was the headquarters for the Alpine fish farm. Only the elite were trained there. And there was some very sophisticated hardware, on loan from the CIA, that had to be moved very swiftly and secretively to a safe place before interested parties could question why and how it got to Iron Mountain. But that was Blackmore's problem, thought Hamilton. As long as his planes were safe in the

West Indies, that was all that concerned him. And he had learned in Midland-Odessa that they were indeed safe. So he could not understand why Blackmore had left the message that he was to follow him down immediately to Iron Mountain. He could only surmise that there was another problem.

Hamilton opened his eyes and gazed out of the windscreen. They were in the foothills, heading south, passing the town of Marathon on the right, the ranch at Iron Mountain some ten miles further on in the hazy distance. He yawned and stretched. 'Who else is at the ranch, Billy Joe?'

'Well, let's see,' drawled the driver, pushing his baseball cap to the back of his head. 'Your old buddy, Colonel Becksmith arrived first thing this morning. Johnny Heritage was with him. Then there's a couple of suits from Langley, the Director's personal representatives, so I'm told. Checking out the hardware. Don't look too pleased, either. Full of the jitters.' He winked at Hamilton. 'And that's about it. Except for the hired help and the trainees. But I hear they're all being shipped up to Baton Rouge.'

Blackmore's main operational base was just outside Baton Rouge from where he controlled his financial largesse and coordinated the crusade against the threat of world-wide communist influence. Any organisation that stood for the all-American apple pie received Blackmore's patronage, including those foreign-based movements, irrespective of colour or creed, that sought American help in establishing right-wing regimes in their countries of origin. 'That should be fun,' said Hamilton after a moment. 'Those Afghans he has up there are not going to take too kindly to their Contra cousins, are they?'

'The CIA have promised to sort that out for him. Their

main concern is to help shut down Iron Mountain before the shit hits the fan.'

III

They came over a low rise and the ranch lay before them at the foot of Iron Mountain, nestled among a stand of Pecan trees. To Hamilton, its setting appeared artificial, as if the house had been imported from Hollywood and deposited there in the most cinematically appealing location. Billy Joe drove into the car park and let Hamilton out. Their arrival had been unnoticed by Blackmore, who stood at the front of the house, a bundle of files stacked in his arms, shouting orders at the three men who were busy loading crates and packing cases into an armoured truck. 'Goddamn, Buster,' yelled Blackmore. 'Get that one in first.' He balanced on one leg and pointed with the toe of the other. 'That one. Then pack the smaller ones round it. Here Paco. Take these.' He handed over the files to a swarthy, muscular individual who dropped them into a nearby case.

Hamilton wound his way through the maze of boxes and crates without attracting attention, and stood and watched the men at work. Blackmore, arms akimbo, scrutinised the loading process. He was dressed in stylised cowboy clothes, which would have made Gene Autrey appear gaudily overdressed. The heels of his boots were stacked to give him added height, and his hair had been dyed since their last meeting so that his iron-grey locks had now disappeared under a sleek blackness. He looked ten years older as a result.

A Begonia creeper, bearing trumpet-shaped flowers of blue and red, had taken hold of the front of the house and its tendrils were climbing up on to the roof and dangling down across the windows and the main entrance, on either side of which stood a whitewashed tub of Bluebonnets, the State flower, next to a wooden rocking chair.

'You work them too hard, Bill,' said Hamilton finally with a grin.

'Alex,' said Blackmore after a two or three head jerks to locate the voice. 'Goddamn, Alex. Sneaking up on a man like that.' He too smiled, and clasped his breast with both hands. 'Gave me a shock, young man.'

Hamilton walked past the truck, his hand outstretched. 'How are you doing, Bill?'

Instead of coming to meet him, Blackmore retreated up the steps. 'Don't blame me, Alex. It wasn't my fault. If they'd told me beforehand, I'd have stopped him going.'

Hamilton stopped at the bottom of the steps. 'What are you talking about, Bill?' He let his hand drop to his side.

'Didn't they tell you at Midland when you called yesterday?'

He shook his head. 'Only about the planes.'

'Shit,' said Blackmore. 'Come on inside. The others are waiting for you.'

Hamilton followed the tall American up the steps and into the reception room. There was a smell of freshly percolated coffee and old leather, and Hamilton paused for a moment to savour a memory. Blackmore was already halfway across the room, heading for the hallway which led to his inner sanctum, a soundproofed box in which he conducted all his special business.

The walls of the room were adorned with the mounted heads of white-tailed deer and wapiti, together with two caches of hunting rifles, old and new, including a Kentucky Flintlock.

On his first visit to the ranch several years ago, Hamilton had been guided by Blackmore's wife, Eleanor, now deceased, and he knew the secrets of the place. The trophy heads, which Blackmore hinted were all his own work, had in fact been bought in bulk from a specialist store in Fort Worth catering to the needs of the armchair hunter. The Remington over the fireplace, *The Coming and Going of the Pony Express*, was a good copy and not the original as Blackmore boasted, and the furnishing was reproduction Federal Style after Duncan Phyfe; hand-made and carved, yes, but in a workshop in Idaho whose Armenian proprietor made copies from museum catalogues. Eleanor had betrayed her husband's secrets to him, including that most cherished one, when Blackmore had been unexpectedly called back to Baton Rouge.

'What's the hold-up, Alex?' asked Blackmore glancing back.

'Nothing at all. Just getting my bearings again.'

They marched down the long airy passage to the back of the house and reached a heavy double door which glided open silently in response to Blackmore's electronic key. This room had been grafted on to the back of the house by the CIA and Blackmore had furnished it with a conference table and bulky leather chairs.

John Heritage sat in a lounger sipping his usual Bourbon and branch water, while Roy Becksmith paced the room dressed as he always was in quasi military uniform of tan cotton. As Hamilton entered, Becksmith spoke. 'Just bad luck, Alex. I'm sorry.' He thrust out his hand and Hamilton shook it.

'From what Bill said outside, I take it you're not referring to the plane,' said Hamilton with a frown.

Heritage put aside his drink. 'Pagliai went down on the plane.'

'Shit,' exclaimed Hamilton. He dropped into the chair next to Heritage. 'What the hell was Stefano doing aboard? He was supposed to have been in Las Vegas on R and R.'

'That's what I thought, too,' said Heritage. 'But Roy had other ideas. Over to you, Roy.' He gestured with his free hand, palm upwards.

Becksmith glided to a halt. He bit his lip like a child steadying itself for a reprimand. 'I told Stefano to fly down to Tegucigalpa on a scheduled flight. But he insisted on going on the supply run.'

'Okay,' said Hamilton patiently. 'But why was he going to Honduras in the first place, Roy? John and I were keeping him under wraps for something special. You knew that.'

'Pedro Suarez,' whispered Heritage as he got to his feet. 'Gin and tonic, Alex?' he asked and went over to the bar. Hamilton nodded.

'We heard a rumour that Suarez was pissed off about something and that he was going to go to Washington and talk to Congress,' said Becksmith.

'I see,' replied Hamilton wearily. Heritage brought him his drink, and he took a long swallow.

Becksmith sat down on the arm of the chair. 'That would have finished off Stan Hardy if he could have testified about the drug runs and the arms deals with the Iranians. Suarez knew it all.'

'Stan Hardy is finished. Congress is reaming his arse. Suarez couldn't have hurt him anymore,' said Hamilton. 'Irangate. Contragate. It's all been said!'

'Hardy's an American patriot. And he's being crucified by all the commies in Congress and the media. He needed help, Alex. What's more Suarez wouldn't have stopped there, he would have spilled the beans on our fish farms.'

Hamilton was about to say something rude about American patriotism and the American dollar when he remembered where he was. 'As it is we're closing down Alphine anyway. For good. And not because of Suarez.'

Blackmore intervened. 'This is only a temporary set back. We'll open another farm when this has all died down. Don't go soft on us Alex.'

Hamilton rubbed his eyes. 'I'm not, Bill. Just tired, that's all.' He twirled his glass and yawned. 'Look, you've known for a long time that John and I, through the Miller Foundation and my principal in London, have been working on a highly delicate matter. The Foundation has backed you down here, but they are now pulling the plug because we don't want any connections made that could have people snooping around the Foundation. Not until, at least, this rather delicate matter is finished. Okay?'

'What about Baton Rouge?' queried Blackmore.

'Go ahead,' said Hamilton. 'But the Foundation, and John will back me on this, will keep you at arms' length.'

'For the time being, Bill,' added Heritage. 'And by the way, Roy,' he added, turning to Becksmith. 'Where was Bryant? He usually handles terminations for us on this side of the world, doesn't he?'

'He was up in the Ozarks somewhere, doing one of his survivalists training sessions. Couldn't get him.'

'So you poached Stefano instead?' said Hamilton wearily. 'That was bad, Roy. Fucking awful, in fact.'

Becksmith squared his shoulders and half closed his eyes. Heritage slowly shook his head in his direction, and the tall ex-marine allowed his aggression to subside before speaking again. 'Well, we've got Bryant now, and he'll take care of Suarez. He's hiding down in Santa Cruz. Bryant will take him out.'

'Let's hope he does,' said Hamilton. 'In the meantime, John and I are a man short.'

IV

After a dinner of cold cuts, which Blackmore served up personally, Hamilton and Heritage wandered outside while Becksmith and Blackmore remained inside, closeted in the safe room, no doubt, thought Hamilton, hatching up some other crusades. He sat down on the wooden rocker as Heritage went over to the car, returning moments later with a small transistor radio which he tuned in to a country and western station. He placed it on the ground to Hamilton's side, pulled over an empty crate and sat down.

The two men were of the same height, a hair's breadth over six feet, but there the resemblance ended. Hamilton, once the man of action, having seen active service in Oman and Afghanistan, was going to seed in his new role of organiser rather than perpetrator. His well-fleshed face was beginning to droop and sag below the eyes and beneath the chin under pressure from too much of the good life, which was further confirmed by a telling bulge above his belt-line. Heritage, on the other hand, whose only active service had been behind a desk and occasionally on top of it with one of his secretaries, was slim and fit, and never a day passed without a round of Canadian Air Force Exercises which gave him the air of a man of action, full of compressed energy. His hair was dark brown in contrast to Hamilton's which was thinning and sandy coloured, parted very low on the left side and swept across his forehead to hide the growing baldness.

'Goddamn,' said Heritage, mimicking a southern drawl. 'Sure do love that Merle Haggard.' He crossed his legs and gripped his knees with his hands. 'Not quite your cup of tea, eh, Alex?' he added, in his usual voice. 'More of a Beethoven or Brahms man, I think. This is not the kind of music that would go down too well in the officer's mess, eh?'

Hamilton glanced sideways at his companion. 'What's bothering you?'

'You shouldn't be too hard on Roy, you know,' replied Heritage. 'I know you SAS types look down your noses on guys like Becksmith. But he trained up the Delta Force from scratch, made them into a crack unit . . .'

'With a little help from me and some of my SAS squaddies,' interrupted Hamilton.

'Okay, okay. We're allies. Help one another. But he'd have pulled off the hostage rescue in Tehran but for the helicopter crash at Desert One.'

'Yes, I know. But he was judged a failure, shunted sideways and then out. Tough luck,' said Hamilton. He pushed the radio nearer to Heritage. 'I don't like all this garbage about patriotism.'

'The refuge of the scoundrel?'

'Never truer; Becksmith, and Blackmore come to that, all this patriot nonsense. Jumping in with both feet where one is more than adequate. I joined my regiment for Queen and Country. I fought to stay alive. Nothing patriotic about that. But that lot,' he inclined his head towards the entrance and sighed. 'They live and die for the bloody flag.'

Heritage grinned. 'You're tired, Alex. Those two guys are plenty tough. Becksmith has seen lots of action. Korea, Vietnam, and then Iran.' He leant in closer to Hamilton. 'And they say old Blackmore killed his wife. You remember Eleanor, don't you?'

Night had come and its shadow partially obscured Heritage's face. Hamilton could not see the expression on his face and his voice had betrayed nothing untoward. 'Yes, I remember her,' was all he said.

'A lot younger than old Bill. He knew she played around.' Hamilton shifted uncomfortably in the chair. 'Had her bedroom wired for sound and vision.' Hamilton swallowed hard. 'They said he used to get his kicks from watching Eleanor in action on video. It's rumoured that she used to join him and watch too.'

'They sound a right pair.'

'Old Bill didn't mind one bit, or so they say, so long as she confined it to the house.' Hamilton paused and looked up at the sky. 'Nice night. Plenty of stars. . . .'

'And?' said Hamilton impatiently. 'Let's hear the rest'.

'Oh yes. Yes,' said Heritage absent-mindedly. 'Yes. Then she took up with one of Bill's bright young men, all muscle and no brains. They went off to Mexico together, Eleanor and what was his name?' He scratched the side of his head. 'Wayne somebody. Maybe something Wayne. Anyway, they both end up dead. Car accident. Somewhere north of Acapulco.'

'I thought you said Blackmore had them killed.' Hamilton could feel the sweat on his brow despite the coolness of the evening.

'Both of them full of heroin. Over a cliff they went. I heard the ignition in the car wasn't even turned on.'

'I see.' He was relieved the tale had come to an end. He wondered what he looked like on video.

'I just wouldn't underestimate these guys, Alex,' warned Heritage. And Hamilton knew he knew about his fling with Eleanor. The story had been a warning.

'With errant wives I won't,' he said sharply. 'With deploying men such as Stefano without permission, they're a bunch of bloody redneck fools.'

'Point taken. And talking of Stefano, what are we going to do now that he has joined that great Italian opera house in the sky?'

Hamilton brushed a hand across his forehead. 'We'll have to use Bryant I suppose.'

'And you don't like that, do you?' Hamilton shook his head. 'Well, we did have him down as second man, eh?' argued Heritage.

'Yes, I know. But there wasn't or shouldn't have been any way we should have had to rely on our second choice. Stefano was our man. Ideal. Now we've Bryant. A religious freak. He's even worse than those two patriotic comedians in there.'

'Maybe,' answered Heritage. 'But he'll do the job. Look Alex, when it comes down to jobs like this, the motives of the man at the pointed end don't matter a flying fuck. The man will do his job. Why he does it, and for what reasons, are his concern. Stefano, an out and out killer;

74

Bryant a religious freak. In the final analysis either man would have seen ASH through.'

Hamilton got to his feet and shook the creases out of his trousers. 'I suppose so, John,' he said reluctantly. 'But the old man in London loved Stefano. He was his boy. There's going to be some shit flying when I tell him that Stefano is dead. It's all right for you, and Becksmith and Blackmore. None of you have ever seen the old guy cut loose when something upsets him or goes wrong.

'That's why he pays you big bucks, Alex my boy. And gives you all those companies to run. The rough with the smooth. And anyway he'll have to go along with Bryant. He's got no choice. Not if he wants to see ASH to fruition.'

ENGLAND

I

The flat was on the second landing. The smell of cat's piss, damp mortar and fried food permeated the dank corridor. Garner stepped cautiously through the scattered jetsam, the scuff of his leather-soled shoes echoing like whispers in a cathedral crypt, up to number seven tucked away in the corner on the right.

There was no bell. He rapped the knocker and the response was immediate as if Duffy had been waiting for this summons. Through the frosted glass of the door Garner could see the blurred form of the old man limping towards him. He heard the chain rattle and then the door began to open. Its progress was hindered by the frayed hall carpet which rose in waves as it became trapped beneath the edge of the door. Duffy prodded it with the toe of his boot, smoothing and flattening the ridges until it came free.

Garner waited patiently like an expectant salesman, arms behind his back, a half-formed smile on his lips, watching Duffy's antics. The old man was dressed in a dark grey, double-breasted suit which had, like Duffy, seen better days. The trousers, held up by belt and braces, were bagged at the knees, and the jacket hung limply on Duffy's sparse frame, open and loose like the untied flaps of a tent. He wore a grubby white shirt unbuttoned to the midriff which showed a strip of grey hair on the chest. His face was red and pitted and there was a tiny scar across the bridge of his nose. All that was needed to complete the picture, thought Garner, was a black tam to cover the balding pate. 'Cormac Duffy?' he inquired politely. 'My name is Peter Garner. I believe you are expecting me.'

'So I am, bonny lad.' He inspected Garner out of the corner of his eye. 'Aye, Peter Garner.' The accent was Geordie though there was a flavour of bronchial Liverpudlian in the background. 'You'd better come in then.' He stepped back inside.

Garner followed the hobbling figure down the short hallway, past the gloomy living room and bedroom and into the kitchen. A wide picture window overlooked a narrow balcony and the rest of the sprawling estate, and allowed the afternoon sun to brightly fill the room and dispel the pervading murkiness.

The kitchen walls were painted a pale yellow but were discoloured with brown splashes of grime and grease over the sink and antiquated cooker, upon which stood a blackened kettle. There were no worktops except for a spindly-legged table around which were gathered four matching chairs.

Garner looked out of the window at the concrete blocks and maisonettes, at the boarded dereliction, at the decaying, crumbling dumping ground for people and battered cars. He shut his eyes in despair.

Duffy pulled out a chair. 'Take a seat, bonny lad,' he said. Garner sat down. Duffy carried the kettle over to the sink and began to fill it with water. 'Tea?'

'Yes, that's fine,' said Garner. He took out his tape recorder and two blank cassettes and loaded one of them into the machine. He had contacted a friend, Philip Key, political editor of the *Liverpool Echo*, to arrange the appointment with Duffy, and Key had provided some details of Duffy's life. What particularly fascinated him was Duffy's prison record: six years for assaulting a police officer and twenty years for manslaughter.

'We don't choose to live in places like this,' said Duffy as he warmed the teapot next to the kettle. 'Though some politicians would have us believe we do. You know what, bonny lad, I was born in Newcastle at the end of the Great War, reared in a place like this. Oh, we didn't have the tower blocks then but the soul-destroying grubbiness and poverty was there just as it is today. My three grandchildren are growing up in the same conditions I grew up in. Nearly seventy years I've been knocking about and nothing's really changed. And they talk about progress.' He snorted in disgust. 'Progress? Change? Don't make me laugh.' He wrapped a cloth around the kettle handle and poured some hot water into the teapot. 'The propertied classes still have their property, the moneymen their money.'

'Do you want a hand?' asked Garner getting to his feet.

'Two cups is all we need,' said Duffy. He poured the water in the sink and spooned three heaped spoonfuls of tea into the warm pot. Garner placed the two stained mugs on the table. Duffy filled the pot with boiling water, and then struggled into a chair, positioning his damaged leg under the table with both hands.

'Does it still bother you?' asked Garner.

'What? Oh that?' He massaged his leg. 'Aye it does,' he said and grimaced. 'And thank God it does, too. This old leg of mine is a constant reminder, my own political weather vane. Without it I might have been seduced into thinking that everything was okay in the world.' He glanced slyly up at Garner.

'Should I pour the tea?' asked Garner, ignoring Duffy's inference.

'Aye, go ahead.' He watched Garner's every move as he poured the tea and added the milk. 'I know your work, Mr Garner. Your early stuff especially. Very good, too. Then you seemed to have forgotten it all, went off the rails, as it were. But you're back now, bonny lad. Otherwise we wouldn't be having this little chat now, would we?'

'Sugar?' Garner replaced the teapot on the gas cooker and picked up the sugar bowl. Duffy shook his head while continuing to rub his leg. Garner sat down.

'Yes, lots of people forget,' continued Duffy as he reached for his tea. 'Forget where they came from, forget who helped them, forget their enemies.' He warmed his hands on the hot mug. 'They go to work in blinkers, keep their heads down, afraid to look up. They come home in blinkers, not even knowing that places like this exist, and close their front doors, shutting out the world. They sit there in front of their television sets with their tabloid newspapers, and they soak up all that pap that passes nowadays for politics and social comment.' He pointed at the tape recorder. 'Aren't you going to turn that thing on?'

'Okay,' said Garner. He depressed the red button.

'When I was a lad,' continued Duffy. 'Aye, when I was a lad I had something about me, just as the other lads did.

We knew what was going on. We were out of work, but we knew why.' He rubbed his leg. 'We used to meet up at Carrick's café in Westgate Road in Newcastle.' Duffy sniffed and stroked his wide nose. 'Probably not there anymore. Politicians and developers have to demolish places like that, to disrupt communities, to dissipate and disperse the pressure. Know what I mean?' Garner nodded. 'I became politically aware then, found out why I couldn't get a job. It's the same reason today why the kids can't find work. There's been no change, no real fundamental changes in society for decades. The moneymen still rule.' Garner was about to speak, to ask about Carrick's, which in the thirties had become the main recruiting office for the International Brigades, but Duffy continued unabated.

'Your generation had the right idea, Mr Garner.' He prodded a gnarled finger at him. 'You were out on the streets in 1968. You showed them what for. But then you gave up when you had them on the run. You thought you'd made your point, and that everything was going to be okay from then on. And so you cleared off.' He shook his head sadly. 'You should have stayed on the streets, stayed until the changes you wanted had been made. Then we wouldn't be in the bloody awful mess we're in today.'

II

As he drove down the motorway to London, Garner could not get Cormac Duffy out of his mind. He had arrived in Liverpool under the misconception that he would be interviewing a tired old man, an opinionated bore cantankerous and unco-operative. Instead, he was driving home with the image of a man who was full of life, vigorous and alert, a man who, despite a painful injury and the tragedies which had beset him, still retained his faith in humanity and continued to struggle on its behalf.

Duffy was a born fighter, and he had fought all his life for his beliefs. He had not allowed himself to be misled or diverted, and in this he was luckier than his fellow man. For Duffy had a nemesis, a man who stood for all he hated and despised, a man who acted as a focal point, beside whom Duffy arrayed his beliefs in antithesis. As long as that man lived, Duffy would live. And fight.

Garner slipped the first cassette into the tape player on the dashboard and ran it forward to the point where Duffy had taken up the story about his joining the International Brigade. Garner only half listened as the memory of Duffy's vivid account was still fresh in his mind. . . .

III

'. . . There were no children. It rained constantly. The freezing January wind lay in ambush at every corner to snap and chafe at sagging damp socks and reddened ears. The inhabitants of Madrigueras, the hunched men in shabby suits, black hats and dark scarves which covered their lower faces, the stooping women in toe-length woollen shawls, sailed the streets, lost souls, solemn, grave bundles that existed on a diet of tortilla and wine, and muffled greetings to the foreigners in their midst. The

81

life had gone from the village, seemingly sucked out by the cloying green mud that the cascading rain made of the pathways.

'Not a tree broke the flat, featureless plain of Murcia upon which the oblong adobe hutches squatted in bitter isolation, and the only colourful relief to the drab landscape was the splash of vivid posters and slogans on the walls of the Casa del Pueblo which the Socialists had set up in the early days of the uprising. The poverty and hardship of the village was profound and depressing, frighteningly harsh, as old as time itself, and it ate into and destroyed any trace of humanity. It was a contagion that afflicted me from the first day I arrived, from the moment the protective tarpaulin hood was jerked aside, from the second that my feet were swallowed up by the icy mud as I landed from the rear of the rattling truck that had brought me and my comrades on the latest leg of our odyssey. Every night before I fell asleep in that dreadful place, shivering, hungry, wet, curled up in a ball on a smelly palliasse beneath a tattered army blanket, I would warm myself by the glow of memories which were barely a fortnight old. Memories of the windswept ferry trip across the Channel, of meandering on deck, head down, excitement supressed, suspicious of the other red-faced passengers, sworn to secrecy, as there were government agents on board who would turn back volunteers. To Calais. Abroad. Overseas. Solitary men dashing for the grimy night train to Paris, waking heavy-lidded in the hollow enchantment of the Gare du Nord that echoed with the clanking and roaring of the steam engines. Doors thrown open, the ringing of hobnailed boots and steel-tipped heels on the platform as the train, a splay-footed centipede, disgorged the men in baggy corduroys and flapping flannels. Trilbies and cloth caps with greasy peaks bobbing through the bustle of cardboard suitcases and porters' carts. The queue for the free taxi ride round to the Bureaux des Syndicats, exchanging covert glances with fellow travellers, still suspicious and taciturn. Then signing on as a volunteer. And with that signature came relief, came the release of pent-up excitment, came the smiles. Fraternal greetings from all about. Handshakes, rough and strong from the mines and the steelworks, long and thin from offices and lecture halls. French, Spanish, all shapes and shades of English, jabbering and laughing. The chance to speak, to share secrets of name, age and football team. Two days and nights sleeping rough, an eighteen-year-old Geordie among the sights and sounds of the sinful city. The smells: freshly baked bread, garlic. The traffic, the buildings, the people. Calvados, pastis, black coffee at the Dome. No politics, new friends, socialism. The Gare Austerlitz aboard the Red Train. The chiming, chanting choruses, garlands of paper flowers, the pert French lasses, forward and unafraid, who kissed goodbye with open lips. A clicking, clanking journey south to Perpigan, to sleep, to reaffirm new friendships. More celebrations. And at dead of night, the silent bus ride across the border to Figueras in Spain. Barracked in the ancient castle. By train to Barcelona. The bands, the marches, parades through the city, noisy, brash and colourful among the party banners, slogans and the purple and gold of Republican flags. Parcelled off in ones and twos into the homes of eager Catalans, dark hovels lit only by wide smiles. Strolling down the Ramblas, assailed by grinning children; long, exhausting nights in cafés, hesitant choruses of revolutionary songs, toasts to the Brigades. Sleep. The blur of Barcelona was quickly followed by the dazed ascent to Albacete, and then the crawl to Madrigueras.

'Madrigueras translates as the burrows, but a linguist was uncalled for to put into words what was evident to the naked eye. It was home to the 57th British Battalion, the training ground for the hundreds of raw recruits who were ready to die for the cause whose physical embodiment was the men and women of that bleak environment. They were an ever-present reminder of the soul-destroying drudgery that had been the lot of working people since time immemorial, a touchstone when spirits flagged in the withering drizzle, a hope for the future when tired limbs could not rise from the clinging slime.

'I made two good friends at Madrigueras: brothers, Tom and Peter Robinson, lively Cockneys who never stopped grinning. They had both been at Cable Street, and like me, had decided to volunteer for the Brigades as the only way to continue the struggle against fascism which we all believed would one day engulf the world in bloody conflict. Tom, the elder, was more afraid of what his mother would do and say for taking Peter with him, rather than anything that Franco could possibly have had in store for him. He was the most popular man in our barracks, and he never permitted any moaning or groaning. Ably aided and abetted by Peter, who was only sixteen, he was always there in the thick of it during training, always aware and ready to question during the nightly political harangues, ever willing to help fellow recruits no matter what the problem. But for the presence of the two Robinsons, there were many who might have succumbed to the numbing influence of that awful place. For a month we endured a debilitating training schedule under the disdainful watch of the battalion's commanders, most of whom had had no previous military experience though many of them pretended they had. We slogged through the mud on exercises and manoeuvres, we dug trench after trench after trench, we marched, we charged, we fell flat on our faces. And all that time it rained, and the wind, like our leaders, howled and barked at our heels. I was assigned to the machine gun company along with the Robinson brothers, and we were instructed in the use of the heavy Colt guns, which, like the rest of the battalion's armoury, was old, dating from the Great War. We learned basic tactics, were overburdened with demands for discipline and the need to give of our best, but, all in all, we were not what could be described as a well-organised fighting unit. We received a peseta a day as pay.

'And then, on the second day of February, merciful release. The Battalion received orders to move up to the front on the Jarama river south of Madrid where the fascist forces were preparing yet another assault on the capital. A stomach-churning tension swept the barracks at this news. The prospect of battle, the unspoken thought of possible death, of killing a fellow human being, were all shrugged aside in a riotous celebration of our liberation from the suffocating misery of the burrows.

'Laughing and joking we boarded the open railway trucks and stowed our gear. Despite the cold the good humour prevailed as we were steadily shunted northwards from town to village to marshalling yard and back again. We were joined by the men of the Dimitrov and Franco-Belgian Battalions, and henceforth we were known as the Brigada Mixta, the XVth International Brigade. After three days we finally reached our destination high upon the Madrid plateau, the small town of Chinchon, on the Madrid-Valencia road.

'The sun was shining as we detrained. We were in a new world of rolling hills and olive groves, and everyone looked and felt keenly optimistic. The fighting had already begun when we arrived, and as we were part of the reserve, we enjoyed two full days of respite as we casually unloaded our kits and equipment. In the distance we could faintly hear the noise of battle, but somehow it did not appear real.

'I knew nothing about military campaigning, but I did have a general idea of the current situation. The Republican forces, regular troops of the Spanish army, militiamen and the International Brigades, held the front along the Aranjuez road with their backs to the Jarama river. Opposing them, Franco's Nationalists, regular army units, Moroccan regulares, and the ground forces of the German Condor Legion under von Thoma. The Nationalists wanted to cross the Jarama and cut the Valencia road, to link up with the Italians who were pressing south, in order to encircle Madrid which Franco was determined to seize, no matter what the cost.

'Within days the fascists had punched a huge hole in the Republican centre, driving forward across the Aranjuez road right up to the river bank. But they could not cross the Jarama: heavy rain before our arrival had swollen the river into a raging torrent. There was a lull in the fighting. The British Battalion idled away hours in the sunshine among the olive groves, checking their weapons, writing letters, falling victim to the practical jokes of the Robinson brothers.

'And then disaster. At first light on a frosty cold Tuesday, a *tabor* of Moroccans sneaked up on the sentries of the Andre Marty Battalion guarding the railway bridge at Pindoque, and slit their throats. The Nationalists streamed across the Jarama and turned on the surprised Republicans with an animal fury. The northern sector of the front was in chaos. Then later that afternoon, in the southern sector, Moors stormed the vital crossing at San Martin and forded the river. The battle was upon us.

'Tom Wintringham, the Battalion's commander, was immediately ordered to move his troops forward into the breach. Despite the gravity of the situation, there was no sense of urgency among the men: we ambled through the groves and copses to take up our positions, smoking and laughing, enjoying the cool spring air. The machine gun company took the highest point, a grassy hillock on which was perched a large white house. Our maps showed it as the Casa Blanca, but it was to go down in history as Suicide Hill, the first of many which arose during the course of the war. Of the six hundred men of the British Battalion who took up positions on and around Casa Blanca, barely two hundred survived the bitter fighting on the Jarama river.

'We dug in on the hill and set up the Colt machine guns. Ahead we could see the river and the town of San Martin, and watch the Nationalists rebuilding for the next offensive. Desultory rifle fire came our way, bullets occasionally whinnied overhead or splattered harmlessly at our feet, but nobody was bothered, and this, combined with the relaxed atmosphere of the troops, made for an unreal, dream-like state which even the company commanders found difficult to penetrate or break. The German artillery managed to do so, however.

'A thunderous barrage descended on Casa Blanca and the other positions around it as we were completing our preparations. To a man, we shook and trembled with fear and fright, like the earth beneath our feet, and everyone found out at that moment that the colour of adrenalin was brown. The screaming cacophany pierced to the very depths of our souls. We also discovered the frailty of our bodies as whistling shards of white-hot shrapnel decimated our ranks. The shrill cries of the bloodied shapes that once had faces, names, family and friends, supplemented the roar of the exploding shells and we prayed to be returned to the clinging mud of Madrigueras.

'As the murderous salvos continued, those of us who were unscathed by the explosions and the scything hail, and, accepting that death was inevitable, came to our senses and looked to the fallen comrades. We scurried through the darkening mist of smoke and blood, covered in filth and dirt, to give what aid and succour we could to the wounded. Not a thought was given to returning fire for we knew that we were outgunned, so we suffered our fate, blessed our gods, rubbed the rabbit's foot, as we lay under that blanket of death for a day and a half.

'We did not hear the barrage stop. We felt it. It was the stillness of the churning earth which alerted us. A deathly hush. We waited. Silence. Even the pathetic, bleating whimpers of the dying and the maimed were stilled. We scrambled to the lip of the trenches and peered out. Not a flicker of movement from the enemy lines. We watched. And then we saw them.

'First one, two, then several. Difficult to pick out against the terrain. Jerking rolling dots that looked harmless from our lofty vantage point. As they moved up the grassy slopes, gaining shape and colour, the dots became recognisable as Moroccan regulares. The Moors were scaling the heights.

'When they came within range, we opened up with what we had left of our guns, but even after a few minutes it was obvious that we were dealing with phantoms. The Moors exploited every fold and niche in the hillside, finding cover from our raking fire where none appeared to exist, making themselves invisible before breaking out again to advance a further couple of yards. Rarely did we have a target to shoot at, and our ammunition was being wasted as we emptied belt after belt into the crawling hillside.

'The artillery resumed firing, finding our trenches once more with unerring German accuracy, giving cover to the advancing Moroccans, making us dive for cover in the ruins of the trenches. Within a few hours, the Moors were able to enfilade our lines with rifle and grenade, and here and there, small pockets of vicious, hand-to-hand combat developed. The slaughter was incredible. But the British Battalion stood its ground.

'I can remember seeing John Kerrigan, a Glaswegian docker, staggering through the clouds of cordite smoke, crashing through the piles of wounded and dead, his big hands clamped to his neck, trying to stem the fountain of blood that gushed out of a gaping tear below his chin. He collapsed at my feet and gurgled his last. He was one of many. I only gave him a cursory glance.

'Confusion reigned throughout the afternoon. We could not guess where the Moors would appear next. They ghosted in like phantoms out of thin air, among the ranks, in the trenches, below the earth banks, wielding their knives and bayonets, slashing and stabbing, only to disappear again before they drew fire. We tried to concentrate our volleys on what we thought was the direction of their primary thrust, but visibility was poor and we hardly knew whether we were on target or not.

'Then, towards evening, I was called to help with the evacuation of some of the wounded. The pace of the battle was falling off. I found myself alongside the Robinson brothers, who, like myself, had so far escaped unscathed. The three of us were lifting Taff Jones on to a makeshift stretcher. Poor Taff. Despite the carnage I had witnessed that day, my stomach was churning at the sight of this brave man who had lost the side of his face, and his right arm. He was babbling like a baby. I tried to cradle his head. I spoke to him to reassure him, but he did not seem to understand. Then, as we began to carry him away from the front line, the trench was suddenly lit up by a bright, searing light. I saw myself catapulted into the air which was full of choking dust and dirt, and my whole body shook with the tremor of the explosion. I was unconscious before I hit the ground.

'I vaguely recall coming to in the back of a truck. I was lying across Tom Robinson's lap. He had a big scab of dried blood on his forehead. Next to him, with his hands tied behind his back, was his brother Peter. Then I blacked out again.

'I have this dream. A scruffy Moor prods my broken leg with his rifle butt and forces up my head from my chest. We are in the courtyard of a dilapidated farm. I can see an old stone barn, its door hanging open on broken hinges. It is evening and a fire has been lit beside the barn, around which a group of Moors are warming themselves. I can hear them jabbering and laughing. Then a great cry goes up. The Moors are excited and start leaping about. Tom and Peter

Robinson are wrestled into the midst of the soldiers, both trussed up like Christmas turkeys. There is great hilarity and shouting. And the Moors castrate the two brothers and cut their throats. Viktor Treboven, idly smoking a cigarette, looks on from the sidelines . . .'

BOLIVIA

I

As he drank his coffee he once more rehearsed the plan for the next day's big event, going over the details from inception to execution and escape, until he was satisfied he had covered all contingencies. Then he refilled the cup, adding cream and two sugars, and carried it into the bedroom where he deposited it on the floor beside the bed. Kneeling down, he clasped his hands together, elbows on the bed, and began to pray silently to himself.

On the bed lay a .45 Automatic Calibre Pistol with National Match trigger and Bo-Mar adjustable sights. As he finished his benediction and got to his feet, he took up the pistol and weighed it again in his hands. It wasn't to his liking. The sights were superfluous to his needs as he had only asked for a pistol as back-up. Though the heavy 230-grain bullets had plenty of stopping power, he much preferred a weapon like his own 9mm Heckler and Koch P7 with its higher muzzle velocity and greater penetration. But this job, as he reminded himself, was a rush job, and he had to take whatever the local CIA had to offer.

He consoled himself with the fact that the rifle that had been supplied was much more his style, a custom-built Remington 40XB. He threw the hand gun back on the bed and dropping to his knees, pulled out the leather case from under the bed. He undid the buckle and strap, up-ended the bag, and allowed the rifle to slide out. From the side pocket of the bag he took out the Redfield telescopic sight and clipped it to the rifle.

He went to the open window and carefully placed the weapon on the wide sill, removed the bolt, then packed it firmly against the frame, using one of the pillows from the bed. He had not fired the rifle before and he would have to zero it by boresighting. He could not risk doing it by grouping on a target as the reports might attract the local police.

Bryant looked down the barrel through the breech and trimmed the rifle's position until he could see the small square of white paper he had affixed to the body of the dying pine trees a hundred metres away in the scrubland. Without moving the rifle he looked through the scope, noted where the cross-hairs fell and adjusted the windage and elevation until they coincided with the view down the rifle barrel. Then he replaced the bolt and made the final adjustment to the elevation, nine minutes for the four hundred metres range at which he would kill Pedro Suarez.

II

In the distance Bryant could see the highway and the steady stream of vehicles moving between the airport and the city. The sun had just risen behind him and already he could feel its heat on his back.

He lay on his stomach on the roof of the adobe shack, and used his binoculars to follow the track which forked off from the main road and descended as a dusty, snaking ribbon to the walled villa four hundred metres below him in a secluded hollow. At the foot of the high metal gates, which gave access to the compound, sat a man in the uniform of the local police. His chair was tilted on to its rear legs so that the back rested against the wall. The policeman had taken off his peaked hat, hung it over the muzzle of his rifle which was standing upright next to him and was busily gnawing through a lump of crusty bread. As far as Bryant could ascertain, this man was the only guard on duty. The house was empty, he knew, from yesterday's reconaissance, and he was surprised at Suarez's lack of security. Perhaps he felt truly safe here on the outskirts of Santa Cruz in the knowledge that the American Congress had guaranteed his safety. But the man should have known better.

Bryant put aside his glasses and sipped some water from his canteen. Overhead the faint boom of an airliner made itself heard, and he returned to his observations. The policeman, having finished his snack, was bored. He picked his nose and rubbed it into the grimy coating of his khaki trousers; then both ears were de-waxed; fingernails next, with special attention paid to the thumbs. He stood up, kicked a couple of pebbles into the drainage ditch at the side of the track, then sat down again.

It was getting warmer by the minute. Bryant rolled over on his back and dried his hands on the towel. He looked down the scope on the rifle, which was propped up on a makeshift tripod, and rechecked the elevation. He took out a cartridge from the cardboard box, and using his hunting knife, he cut off the tip of the slug and carved a deep cross in the lead. He repeated this process with three other cartridges before loading one into the breech and ramming the bolt home. He waited.

Bryant prided himself on being apolitical as his father before him had been. 'Never meddle in politics, son,' his father had told him. 'It is the work of the devil.' And so Bryant had avoided politics like the plague, and had followed his father in the worship of the Lord.

When he was sixteen his father had taken him up into the Ozarks to hunt, and while there, Bryant had learnt the other side of his father's life, and the sacrifices he had made for the sake of the Lord's work. At first Bryant junior had not completely understood what his father had told him, but that night as he had dozed, rolled up in his sleeping bag, the starry summer sky a ceiling, he had came to terms with his father's role of assassin. Though the Bible admonished against killing, there were times, Bryant junior decided, when killing was necessary, just as his father had explained. And after service in Vietnam, which he likened to the medieval Crusades, he took up his rifle in civilian life in the name of the Lord. *Exterminans*, the avenging angel, his father had named him on his death-bed. 'The Lord be with you,' had been his dying words. And so he had: forty-six missions in the name of the Lord, each approved and sanctioned by his great friend and religious guide, the most Reverend Jimmy Lee Lewis; and never once had there been any pursuit or hint of capture. And Bryant had no doubts that this mission would pass without a hitch. 'The Lord be with you.'

Suarez arrived just before noon in a battered Mercedes driven by a big burly brute who dwarfed his employee.

Bryant had seen them leave the airport highway in a cloud of dust and he had followed their progress down the track. As they pulled up outside the villa, the policeman was ready for them, at attention, his rifle by his side. The driver had got out first, spoken a few words to the man, glanced around suspiciously, before opening the rear door for Suarez. They made his work very easy for him.

The bulk of the man partially obscured Suarez from the probing eye of Bryant. Suarez was short and thin, a weasel of a man, with black hair and a pencil moustache. He stood behind the driver for a moment, but then stepped into the open to talk to the policeman who saluted before he replied. Suarez appeared deeply interested in what the man was saying. The driver meantime climbed back into the car.

Bryant brought the cross hairs to bear on Suarez's temple, the most prominent target on offer being the head. Slowly he squeezed the trigger. The rifle kicked against his shoulder, the sound of the shot echoed a reply to a departing jet, and Suarez's head ballooned and disintegrated into a bloody swirl of red, grey and white, which engulfed and drenched the gawping policeman.

Bryant shot the driver through the head where he sat in the driver's seat; the policeman, prancing and dancing, wailing and screaming, caused Bryant to waste precious seconds as he drew a bead on him. He settled for a chest shot which opened up the unfortunate man as if he had been torn apart by a gigantic can opener.

Leaving everything as it was, Bryant nimbly descended the ladder at the back of the shack and went inside. Its owner was sprawled on the earthen floor, just as dead as when he had left him some hours before.

He stepped over the corpse and went to the table upon which sat a square of C4 plastic explosive into which had been placed a timer. Bryant set it for five minutes, went out again, jumped into the car, and roared off, taking the back road to the airport.

ENGLAND

I

There was someone in the room.

Garner lay still, trying to control his breathing, his head buried beneath the duvet.

Suddenly the duvet was pulled from the bed. He shouted and sat bolt upright, blinking rapidly at the morning sunshine, his arms raised to defend himself. He caught a glimpse of a woman leaving the room.

'Masturbation and narcissism go hand in hand,' she chimed as the door slammed shut.

'What the hell is going on?' exclaimed Garner. He leapt out of bed and put on his robe. 'Veronica?' he shouted. 'Is it you?' He thought he had recognised the woman's voice. His legs turned to jelly.

As he came cautiously into the living room, he heard her crashing about in the kitchen, and saw the shoulder bag on the coffee table. It was open. He peeked inside and took out the passport. Ms Veronica Joan Sinclair it said on the first page. The black and white snapshot did not do her justice, he thought, as he replaced the passport.

'Bloody mess in here,' she called from the kitchen. Garner tiptoed forward. 'And stop creeping up on me.'

'What are you doing here?' asked Garner as he came into the kitchen, trying to keep his voice even, despite the tension gripping his stomach.

'Cleaning up after you by the looks of it.' She stood at the sink washing the dishes. The kettle was boiling. 'And next time you have tomato soup, try and keep it in the bowl and the saucepan.' She turned to face him. 'God. What a slob.'

Garner raked his hair with both hands. 'Sounds like your parting shot to me five years ago.' His reply was intended to be offhand, casual, but it came out with an edge to it.

'Three and a half to be precise.' There was a hint of an American accent in her voice. 'Go and put some clothes on. You look positively indecent.'

The cord on Garner's dressing gown had slipped its knot and the robe hung open, partially exposing his nakedness. He pulled the cord tight and retreated to the bedroom in some confusion where he found his jeans in a pile beside the bed. He dressed quickly, pulling on a creased sweater and slipping his feet into a pair of old leather sandals. As he came back into the living room, Veronica emerged from the kitchen carrying two cups of coffee which she put down next to her bag. She sat down on the settee, took out a packet of cigarettes and offered one to Garner.

'Given up,' he muttered. 'The drink too.' Her presence was confusing him. He didn't know how to react to her.

'Ha,' she exploded. 'Don't try and tell me you've changed. That face of yours says at least a two-day drinking spree.' She lit her cigarette with a Zippo lighter, clicking it shut with her thumbnail. 'I called in at the so-called editorial offices of your rag. Your

99

assistant said you hadn't been about for two days.' She took his front door key out of a pocket of her skirt and threw it to him. 'You're asking for trouble leaving that under the doormat.' He slipped the key into his jeans.

'So what are you here for, then?' asked Garner. He picked up his coffee and went and sat in the armchair opposite her. 'Use the saucer as an ashtray. I don't think there's one in the place.'

She flicked her ash into the saucer. 'This is a real dump,' she said. 'I suppose it's compulsory to wipe your feet before going outside on to the street.'

'God almighty,' sighed Garner, shaking his head. 'All the time we were together you never stopped moaning. You go away and come back years later and you just pick up where you left off. Moan, moan. Don't you ever stop?' he said defensively.

'I've no intention of picking up where I left off, Peter Garner.' Her voice was hard, though Garner noticed the hardness was absent in her slate-grey eyes, which, in the bad old days, usually radiated anger whenever she was upset.

'It wasn't meant as an invitation,' he said indifferently, staring her straight in the face. A lock of strawberry blond hair fell across her face and she brushed it away behind her ear. Her hair was longer than he remembered, untied and almost shoulder length, and she was wearing make-up, a touch of lipstick and a hint of rouge about the the cheeks. Gone was the pinched and bitter look, the hair pulled back from the forehead into a bun at the back of the head, which she had adopted along with the feminism she thought would bring her happiness. 'But I'm sure you haven't travelled all this way just to tell me I live in an awful place,' he added.

As he spoke, she sat back on the settee and crossed her legs. Her skirt rode up above her knees, exposing her thighs. He shifted his gaze to her face again, to her eyes and gently sloping cheekbones, to her full red mouth and rounded chin. He followed her neck to the wide, square shoulders, then down to the short-sleeved white blouse which failed to conceal the fact she wasn't wearing a bra.

'What happened to the house in Putney?' she asked.

Garner concentrated on his coffee as he felt a vague stirring in his loins. 'Sold it and bought the newspaper. And this place.'

She glanced round the room. 'You were robbed,' she stated.

'The Putney house was too grand for you. Now this one isn't good enough for you,' he retorted acidly.

'Half the money was mine, remember? I don't think you have invested it very well.' She sat forward and stubbed out her cigarette into the saucer. 'Look, let's not argue, eh?' she said, but her attitude conveyed just the opposite.

Garner let out his breath in a short sigh. He was about to say something but decided against it. Instead he stood up and carried his cup through into the kitchen. 'Let's not argue, she says,' he whispered to himself as he rinsed the cup and placed it on the draining board. He stood in the doorway with his hands on his hips. 'So that's it, is it? You want your share? Got the divorce papers in your bag?' For some unexplained reason Garner found himself holding his breath while he waited for her answer. He had tried to push Veronica from his mind over the years but had been unsuccessful. She did not figure as prominently now as she had done in the months immediately following the split, but she was still there, on the periphery; and from time to time he had to mentally pull himself up short as she occasionally slipped into view to disturb his peace. Looking at her now he doubted whether she would ever be out of his life.

She lit another cigarette and squinted her eyes at him through the cloud of smoke. 'The divorce? No, I haven't given it a thought. Have you?' She stared at him. 'I came over to see Gerda actually. Among other things.'

Garner let out his breath slowly. 'Oh. How is she?'

Veronica shrugged. 'Difficult to say really. I don't think she's over it yet. Probably never will be. But she's coping. She sends her love and her thanks for staying with her.'

After the *Rijkswacht* had interrogated him for three days in Belgium, he had flown to The Hague, and had spent a week with Gerda de Roos in the flat in the Zeerstraat. He had tried to comfort her; she had clung to him, not letting him out of her sight, except at bedtime. And even then she had been loath to let him go. All the funeral arrangements were left to him as her only thoughts were on the last few minutes of Christian's life about which she questioned him remorselessly, as if she were attempting to fix every detail forever in her consciousness.

In a way he had been glad to get back to England; he had never felt comfortable with other people's grief. He had enough problems simply dealing with his own. And it had been a very wearing week with Gerda. 'I keep promising myself to write to her. But I haven't got round to it yet,' he said to Veronica.

'And if you keep on drinking the way you do, you never will write to her,' she said, the hectoring tone back in her voice once more.

'I've told you I've given up drinking,' snapped back Garner. 'If you must know I was out celebrating.'

'Celebrating your reconversion, your return to the straight and narrow, to your old ideals and beliefs.' She laughed at him.

'I've done that already. I was celebrating a dear old man I met on Wednesday. Or rather what he said and told me.' He rose from the chair. 'You know, I truly envy people who know what they want out of life, who know where they're going or should be going, who never have doubts about it all.' He prodded himself in the chest with his forefinger. 'Me, I'm just a miserable slob who's not sure, who's had his doubts, who strayed and went wrong. I know because everybody I meet tells me so. Now I think I've got it together and I'm trying to make amends for the past.' Garner could sense he was going red in the face. 'So you don't like this flat. So what? Nobody asked you to come here. You walked out on me because you couldn't stand the life I was leading. Great. Now you come back, you don't know what I'm doing, and all you can do is ridicule.' He stormed off into the kitchen to the sound of Veronica's slow handclap.

He ran the cold water tap and doused his face, drying it on the teatowel. He remembered he had not brushed his teeth so he rinsed his mouth and gargled with salt and water before returning to the living room. 'You still here,' he scowled as he passed through into the bedroom. The duvet was still on the floor and he kicked at it.

'Stop sulking and come back in here,' he heard Veronica shout.

'Bloody bitch,' he mumbled quietly under his breath.

'I need your help. Honestly. Come on, Pete.' She paused when he did not reply. 'Look, I'm sorry for what I said. Truly I am.'

'Should be,' Garner said and kicked the duvet again. He felt the tension inside begin to subside.

II

He had sat and listened to her without any effort. Heritage. John Heritage. She had mentioned the name almost from the start, and despite the intrusion of the painful memory of himself and de Roos in Belgium, he found it easy to listen.

She worked for *The Nation*, a New York radical journal, and she was in hot pursuit of those on the periphery of the Contragate and Irangate scandals which were currently occupying the attention of every American, all the way up to the White House. Heritage was involved. What was more, he had an English connection, Alex Hamilton, whom she was now investigating.

Garner allowed the names to wash over him, allowing her to make the running, and to make a connection for him: Alex Hamilton, according to the brief file on Treboven that Piechler had given him, was Treboven's man, body and soul. And now Hamilton and Heritage.

'Let's go,' she had said finally. 'I've something to show you.' And so they went. To Victoria.

'That's the National Iranian Oil Company,' said Veronica.

'I can read,' said Garner as she pointed out the sign next to the main entrance of the building. Then walked on.

'And on the second floor is the Iranian Arms Procurement Agency, which does business with the occupants of . . .'

'Okay,' said Garner. He watched her out of the corner of his eye.

She linked his arm. 'Not this building,' she said, pulling him along. 'But this one.' They stopped outside a tall concrete and glass edifice. 'Top floor. All the businesses there are tied in with Hamilton. Glenridding Holdings Limited is legitimate as far as I know. Tobacco Importers. Then there's Venroyal Limited, again legitimate, I think. But there, three names down.' She pointed, and as she did so Garner noticed the uniformed doorman heading towards the foyer. 'KMS.'

He led her away. 'You'll never make a spy, you know, exposing yourself to the enemy like that.' He held her arm tightly, but she didn't seem to notice the pressure.

'I told you Hamilton is in Paris,' she said. 'Anyway, KMS, Kingston Manpower Services. One of the largest recruitment agencies for mercenaries. Ex-SAS, ex-Rhodesian Light Infantry, former Green Berets. Anyone who has been trained to kill. And they are in Nicaragua, Sri Lanka, Angola, in all the trouble spots, and Hamilton is the recruiter.'

They walked towards Victoria Station. It was a bright sunny afternoon and flocks of tourists clogged the pavements being shepherded by exasperated guides in the direction of Westminster. 'So he recruits mercenaries. And I take it that his arms deals are done through KMS also. Britain is breaking its own self-imposed arms embargo on Iran by using Hamilton to supply the Iranians with weapons through the back door. Right?'

Veronica now clung to his arm to prevent herself being separated from Garner by the milling crowds. 'That's right. Hamilton has overseas companies dealing in shipping and airfreight. And that's something for you

105

to follow up. What I'm after is Hamilton's dealings with Heritage and Colonel Stan Oliver. Apparently Heritage and Oliver used Hamilton as middleman to try and purchase some Blowpipe missiles from Belfast for the Contras.'

'And that hasn't come out in the Contragate hearings yet?' Walking arm in arm together was bringing forth memories from happier times and he found it difficult to concentrate on what she was saying.

'No, not at all. Congress is only challenging Oliver's role in illegal arms deals that emanated from the National Security Council. They are not bothered with any of the other deals done by the various maverick organisations in the States, the so-called independents, who have no direct connection with the White House. Heritage runs them through the Miller Foundation.'

'So Hamilton's in the clear as far as that is concerned?' he asked, glancing down at her, wishing she would return his gaze. But she looked straight ahead, intent upon her story.

'Yes. Unless I can pin something on him here. Dickson is looking into Hamilton's contacts in the States to see if there's a positive link with Heritage and thus Oliver.'

'Dickson works for *The Nation* I take it?'

'We're a team. A very good one. He used to work for the *Washington Post*.'

'Can't say I've ever heard of him,' said Garner quickly, to hide a sudden pang of envy that overcame him.

'You will if this story breaks right.' She stopped outside the Four Seasons travel agency and looked in the window. 'This is where Hamilton buys all his tickets.' She shielded her yes against the reflection. 'No, she's not in.'

'Who?' asked Garner.

'Alice Ormowe. She does all Glenriding's airline bookings.' They strolled on again.

'How long have you known this Ormowe woman then?'

'Since I arrived here six days ago.'

Garner looked down at her with a quizzical frown. 'And you've already got her working for you? Who does she think you are?'

'A Private Investigator,' replied Veronica with a Bogart lisp.

'You must be joking.'

'Why?' she protested. She patted her shoulder bag. 'I've got quite a few identities in here. She's a divorcee, needs the extra cash. I told her I was working for Hamilton's wife on their divorce. She jumped at the chance to help. Solidarity among women, you see.'

'God help us,' said Garner, and shook his head.

'God help you men, you mean.' She pulled her arm free. 'You need it.'

They reached the station forecourt. 'So that's how you knew where Hamilton was today, in Paris?'

'I know every place Hamilton's visited in the past six months. From Paris to New York, and then back to London. That's his present itinerary. He's a very busy boy. Hey, why don't we take a bus?'

'Where to?' said Garner, a quizzical expression on his face. Why?

'Back to your place, of course. We've still got things to talk about.'

Garner bit his lip. 'Such as what?'

'Lots of things. Hamilton and Heritage for instance. Come on. I bet it's ages since you've been on a bus.' She tugged his shirt. 'Come on, Pete.'

Garner had to smile at her youthful enthusiasm. 'Okay, then.'

'Which one then?'

'The number eleven, the Liverpool Street bus, the one that's just pulling out.' As he pointed, Veronica was already into her stride, sprinting to meet the red double-decker.

III

Gold Cup Day is traditionally Ladies Day at Royal Ascot. The race for the Cup over two and half miles, instituted in 1807, used to be the most prestigious event at the Royal meeting, and one of racing's most prized ribands, second only to the five Classics. Nowadays, because of the pressures of the breeding industry and the explosion in prices of racing stock, the thoroughbred stayer, an animal that can gallop resolutely for more than two miles, then present its opponents with a devastating turn of foot to sprint home to the finishing line, is currently out of fashion as investment-conscious owners and trainers aim their charges for the more lucrative middle-distance races which can bring near instantaneous financial returns and rewards. As a result, the Gold Cup has lost much of its kudos, and the very few top class entrants in training for the event usually find they are competing against plodding handicappers whose parvenu owners are looking for a place in the record books and the chance to mingle with Royalty should their handicapper fortuitously upset the odds laid against the classic stayer.

Another factor which has contributed to the fall from

grace and favour of the Gold Cup, and which was currently exercising the mind of Sir Michael White, head of Her Majesty's Secret Intelligence Service, D16, was the decline since the War of the great stable and stud empires of such men as the seventeeth Earl of Derby, the old Aga Khan, the Lords Roseberry, Glanely and Astor.

As he stood in the paddock at Ascot on a sunny afternoon in the middle of June, the Director of D16 even lamented the break up of the Jewburg thoroughbred dynasties whose owners, the nouveaux riches of the commercial world, had entered racing at the turn of the century in order to better their social position, and had built up their breeding stock despite the opprobrium of the aristocrats and the hostility of the racing fraternity. 'Money was not a consideration for them. Their only concern was the development of thoroughbred lines,' expounded White. 'And even the Jewburgs, once established among the peerage, maintained their racing and breeding empires to that end.'

'How very interesting,' said Sir Robert MacKenzie, White's opposite number at D15. 'Fascinating.' He looked across the ring at the gaping circle of racing aficionados and had the impression that he was an animal in a safari park, engaged in some instinctive ritual, which the visiting public found particularly appealing.

'Indeed, Robert,' continued White. 'Sprinters, stayers, Classic winners. They were all the same to those old men of the turf. The bloodline was everything. But the bloody socialists and their crippling death duties put paid to all that. The empires were dismantled and the bloodstock dispersed.' He leant forward on his shooting stick. 'And in their place we have these little dark-skinned creatures with their vast wads of oil money, with their shady managers and so-called bloodstock advisers, searching for a quick return, distorting the market and the breeding industry to the detriment of such races as the Gold Cup. They can't be bothered with a good, old — fashioned stayer. Not their cup of tea. No money in it for them.' He chuckled quietly to himself when Mackenzie failed to respond. 'Perhaps the only consolation is that the parade ring for the Gold Cup has become a sanctuary. It's the only place at Ascot where you don't have to rub shoulders with the grubby little men of the desert.'

Mackenzie had ceased to listen but White continued unabashed in the same vein. Mackenzie's attention was focused on Sir John Goodison, a few feet away to his left, who was chatting amiably to his trainer and jockey. Like White and Mackenzie, he too was dressed in a morning suit, and wore a tall grey topper. But unlike Mackenzie, Goodison and White wore their suits as uniforms in common with their fellow elitists, and their bearing and demeanour placed them in a class apart from the rest of the racegoers who were compelled to don morning attire for the sake of outdated propriety. Goodison's trainer gave the jockey the leg up and once installed in the plate, his feet in the irons, the reins comfortably but securely gathered in one hand, the jockey touched his cap with his riding crop, and Goodison nodded his dismissal. The trainer led off the quiet chestnut, whose muscled sheen provided a vivid contrast to the green, beige and red of the jockey's silks, and he joined the parade of the four other entrants for the race. Goodison joined his two guests.

'Should turn into a bit of a procession, eh?' said White.

'The ground's a little too much on the firm side for his liking,' said Goodison. 'Still, he hasn't got too much to beat.'

The three men stood in a circle while the onlookers left the rail to place their bets and take their seats. Goodison was the tallest by a short head from White, with Mackenzie in third place by a neck, and it would have been obvious to even the most casual of observers that Goodison was the centre of attraction. His two companions inclined their bodies towards him, and they seemed to be hanging on every word he uttered.

'I have decided, Robert, to leave Cormac Duffy to the tender care of Alex Hamilton,' said Goodison. Mackenzie had his hands clasped behind his back and his chin thrust forward as if standing at ease on a parade ground. 'Duffy is an old friend, as it were, and I would sooner deal with him personally than have your plodders marching all over him.'

'As you wish,' replied Mackenzie with relief. 'And Garner?'

'A different kettle of fish altogether,' said Goodison. He held his gloves in his right hand and he slapped them down on the side of his thigh. The left hand, the one with the three fingers missing, was, as usual, concealed in a trouser pocket whenever he was on public display. 'I know of him, of course, and he will bear watching.' He glanced across at White. 'Have you anything?'

White was at attention. 'We put a trace on the Jewish delegation from Paris and they are all bona fide employees of the Centre. One of them, Arthur Piechler, is the probable source of Garner's sudden interest in Duffy. Piechler telephoned Garner from Paris last week.'

Before Goodison could ask the obvious question, Mackenzie supplied the answer. 'That was before we tapped his 'phone,' he said. 'So we do not know what transpired. They haven't spoken since.'

'My man in Paris learnt of the call from the switchboard operator at the Centre,' said White quickly. 'He has a way with the women, if you know what I mean.' He smirked.

Goodison surveyed the two directors, deep in thought. He was older than both by at least ten years but he appeared much younger, and it was the bright sparkle in the diamond-blue eyes which heightened the illusion. Finally he spoke: 'That would seem to suggest that their probing is relatively overt rather than covert. More importantly, it is probably rooted in Duffy's dim and distant past. Hmm. Is the Turkish route organised, Michael?'

'Yes,' said White. 'All under control. But Conville wants your people over there.'

'Good. Very good,' replied Goodison. He considered for a moment. 'There's a meeting of The Room next week. The final one before we become operational.' And with that he turned rapidly on his heels and strode off across the paddock with White in hot pursuit, and Mackenzie, caught unawares by the sudden change of pace, bringing up the rear. 'Both of you keep an eye on Garner and Piechler,' he added. 'I want to know if they get within five years of the present.'

IV

'. . . Treboven saved me from the Moors. He saved me for himself.

'A German doctor reset my leg as best he could under the circumstances, and for two months I lay in a tiny cubicle in the farmhouse while the battle for Madrid raged on. Every day, Treboven would visit me.

'He taught me German and Spanish, and he even used to correct my English. A Rhodes Scholar he claimed, even though he was in the German Army, and he had only just come down from Oxford when the hostilities had broken out. Treboven was Prussian, from a military family, and he was everyone's nightmare of the typical Prussian bully. He did not appear to possess any human qualities.

'His concern for me had nothing to do with any humanitarian impulse. He had this theory about society that it was simply a giant organism under the control of men such as himself who were its brain. And society could only be stable if the lower orders, as he called them, were docile and obedient, conforming to the commands from the brain. But from time to time, the lower orders became uncontrollable, were led astray by agitators and trouble makers, and so it was the task of the brain to restore an ordered equilibrium. The agitators, the non-conformists, the thinkers of the world, had to be eliminated, extirpated like some diseased part before order could return. And war was the chosen instrument for this clumsy surgical process. Whole nations would have to perish to allow Treboven's perfect society to continue.

'Treboven saved me because he believed I could be useful. One or two of the non-conformists would always be needed, he said, to be held up as examples, to act as reminders to the subservient masses, of what a rebel looked like, how he thought and behaved, and, most importantly, how he was to be dealt with. I was Treboven's pet. I was his example. When I could walk again, Treboven paraded me all over Spain. This is the enemy, he would announce to the Nationalists, and pat me on the back. A tame enemy, but dangerous nevertheless. I had characteristics which set me apart from them. Me and my type. And we had to be put down without mercy whenever and wherever we were encountered.

'If Treboven was fortunate enough to have any Republican prisoners to hand during his lectures to the troops, he would have them executed, or murdered rather, right there and then in front of everybody. I remember after the fall of Zaragoza, he personally garotted two Germans from the Thaelmann Brigade in front of the Seo, the main Cathedral. But that was a drop in the ocean really when you consider that seven and a half thousand Republicans were later slaughtered in the city and buried in mass graves.

'Treboven was quite mad. He wasn't human.

'He was an Intelligence Officer under colonel Erich Kuhlenthal in Foreign Armies West. That was the third branch of the Troops Department, the Truppenamtr, which was a front for the Great General Staff of the German Army which had been forbidden and supposedly disbanded under the terms of the Versaille Treaty. The world wanted to believe at that time that there was no German Army, just as it wants to believe today that there is no threat from a resurgence of Nazi and fascist ideals and beliefs. So there were no Germans in Spain in 1936, no German armour or aircraft. But Treboven was in Spain to report on the effectiveness of the nascent German war machine. He and I were among the first to enter Guernica after the Condor Legion's aircraft had bombed the town out of existence. Treboven gushed with excitement at the destruction and havoc the Legion had wrought.

'Later he reported on the poor showing put up by the Panzer Mark I against the Russian T-26 tanks, and how supreme the German 88mm guns were against anything that the Republicans could muster. You can understand now why military historians argue that Spain was the proving ground for the *blitzkrieg* tactics of the German forces that later engulfed Europe.

'And as the Nationalists went from strength to strength in the war, Treboven and I travelled throughout Spain. He tortured and tormented me daily with details of my own execution once Madrid had finally fallen and Franco was installed as *Caudillo*. I attempted suicide on one occasion but his Moorish bodyguard stopped me, and from that day forward, two Moors were constantly at my side, day and night, watching me, reporting on me, saving me for the day when Treboven would slip the thin metal band of the garotte around my throat and turn the screw slowly to choke the life out of me.

'But it was not to be. As the Nationalists entered Madrid, Colonel Kuhlenthal ordered Treboven to hand me over to the Red Cross. Treboven naturally objected: I was his, he had saved me so he could do as he pleased with me. Kuhlenthal insisted, and I was duly handed over to the Red Cross officials. Treboven's parting speech to me was that he would see me in England one day, the day the British Government formally surrendered to the Fuhrer.

I returned to England in the autumn of 1939 and I sat out the war in Newcastle, at home with my parents when I wasn't in hospital having my leg re-broken and reset It never did mend properly, and I suppose, in a way, neither did I. The horrors I had witnessed have never left me. We talk of the atrocities of the last War, and forget about Spain where the Germans first practised the art of murder. And we fool ourselves into thinking that it will never happen again. But it has. And it will.

'I used a stout hazel wood stick, my grandfather's, to help me get about, and in '43 I was sufficiently mobile to take a job at the shipbuilders, Swan Hunter's, as a clerk in the Drawing Office. And I joined the union, eventually being elected Branch Secretary.

'Now Swan Hunter's were building submarines for the government, as were Vickers-Armstrong across the country in Barrow-in-Furness. About a year after the War ended, I heard from a union colleague in Barrow, Harry Verity, that a group of German scientists, all of them former Nazis, were being employed in a top secret research programme at Vickers-Armstrong. It wasn't until many years later, after the Americans had put a man on the moon aided by former Nazis such as von Braun and Heinz Habe, that the world heard of Operation Paperclip: the Allied conspiracy at the end of the War which saw Nazi scientists, economists and the like, spirited away from retribution to the safety of research establishments and universities in Britain and America, but mainly America. A paperclip affixed to the front of the Nazi's dossier meant that he or she was under the protection of the government, and beyond the reach of the War Crimes Tribunals.

'Such were the Germans in Barrow-in-Furness. They had been captured as a group by British troops in 1945 at Kiel, the main German submarine research depot. They had been working on a new submarine propulsion unit, fuelled by Hydrogen Peroxide. The Americans allowed Britain to keep these Germans as their share of the Paperclip Conspiracy, leading the British government and the Admiralty into believing that Hydrogen Peroxide was the fuel of the future. Meanwhile the Americans had another group of Germans who were far advanced along the road to producing a nuclear-powered propulsion system; and while Britain wasted time and money with the Hydrogen Peroxide unit, the Americans were able to develop nuclear powered units. Such was the trust and co-operation between America and Britain.

'But when the people of Barrow heard that they had Nazis in their midsts, they took to the streets. The local Mayor and Harry Verity organised and led a series of protest marches through the town which culminated in the shipyard being besieged by its own workforce. Eventually the Vickers-Armstrong management had to let the Germans go. In fact they left Barrow pursued by the locals.

'But through my contacts in Barrow, word came that the Nazis were coming to Swan Hunter's. In secret. And that special facilities were being set up for them at the yard. The union and the workforce were alerted. Everyone in the shipyard outside of the bosses was a spy. We knew everything about the plans, and in June, early on a Sunday morning, Swan Hunter's was surrounded by the workers in anticipation of the Germans' arrival. Police were called in to keep the gates clear. The Germans arrived in a bus with a police escort but it could not reach the gates. The Nazis were told to get off the bus and to walk the gauntlet of protest up to the gates.

'We watched them get off the bus, each one of them carrying a suitcase, each of them with their heads down, scurrying to the safety of the gates. Except for one of them. He was the last off the bus: he took his time; he stared back at the ranks of the bawling workers with a mixture of amusement amd contempt on his fine Nazi face. He sauntered towards the gates.

'Viktor Treboven.

'A red haze swam before my eyes. I pushed forward. I struck out with my stick at the hands that tried to restrain me. I raised that stick above my head and brought it down

117

with all the force and strength I could muster, down, down, down. . . .'

V

Garner switched off the tape-player.

'God,' exclaimed Veronica. She stubbed out her cigarette and immediately lit another. Garner crossed the room and pushed open the rest of the windows. A light summer breeze rippled the curtains and carried with it the hum of late-night traffic.

They had spent the entire afternoon and most of the evening travelling about London by bus, going from terminus to terminus, and visiting parts of the capital neither of them had seen before. It had been Veronica's idea: from the initial hostile encounter that morning, through her request for his assistance, she had gradually relaxed, as he had, and reverted almost to the woman he had first known and loved, and married. And he, not wishing to spoil or interrupt the transformation, had gladly acquiesced to everything she had asked of him.

When they had first met, she had had a simple, eager and energetic approach to life which was ruled by her concern and compassion for others; and she was unfettered by any complicated expectations. But she did not seem to have any direction, nothing concrete in which to channel herself. He was writing and making his mark; she seemed to drift. She was constantly wanting a push, wanting assurances and reassurance; she needed a task, a cause, with which to be involved. He had tried to help, made suggestions, introduced her to friends, to groups, to organisations, all of which had offered her the opportunities to be involved. But she had always started only to end unfinished; there were projects, but none that she ever saw to completion or fruition. She just did not know what she wanted. And as his path carried him into the *wilderness* the first barriers had been thrown up between them. She began to envy his success, to criticise it, to compete with him. He often wondered whether his move into the *wilderness* would have been so complete had it not been for Veronica and the comparisons she had conjured up. She had been quite correct, but her motives had been wrong, to remind him that their formerly shared political beliefs were being sacrificed along the road into the *wilderness*. She reminded him to hide her own inadequacies.

The house in Putney had been a disaster. His work took him abroad frequently; drink became his friend, and the soul-destroying argument the norm. They had both slipped into brooding contemplative silences whenever they were together, the slow fuse which one day had ignited and caused the final explosion: and they had torn one another apart. Having made strangers of one another they had both been surprised and shocked at the barbs the strangers had inflicted. Veronica had decided that there could be no way back. Garner had returned from Moscow to find the house empty. Packed her bags. Gone. Gone from London. From England. Only a letter.

'Have you any more tapes?' asked Veronica. Garner drew the curtains and returned to the settee, deep in thought. 'Duffy's story can't end there, can it?'

'No,' he said as he unplugged the tape-player and ejected the tape.

A few weeks after her departure, a mutual friend had

phoned to say that he had helped her to find a job on *The Nation*. He had called her a couple of times but she had refused to speak to him. His letters went unanswered, sometimes returned unopened; what he had said in his earlier missives he could not remember but he guessed it had not been very nice – a written continuation of their final, abusive fight. He had even tried for a response with the divorce papers, but she had ignored them. In the past year he had written twice more, gentle inquiring letters, with no mention of the past or of what he was doing now, how he had changed. And though she had not replied, he somehow formed the impression that he had succeeded in getting through to her. However, he was not sure why he had tried.

When she had arrived at the flat that morning, they had fenced with one another, he defensively, she offensively. And he supposed that he had unconsciously tested the extent of her thrusts when he had stormed off into the bedroom. She had called him back and apologised. And he had sensed that there was more to the apology than the need for his help in investigating Alex Hamilton. Much more. And he had responded positively. The silly, inconsequential jaunt through London had followed.

They had forgotten why she was in London, had dismissed Hamilton and Heritage from their minds; they had simply lost themselves in each other, chatting about nothing in particular, relaxed, comfortable, in each other's presence, home-bred tourists in their own land. The late night delicatessen in the Strand was just closing as they leapt from their last bus ride, and the proprietor kept it open long enough for them to purchase some cheap wine, a stale French loaf, a wedge of solidifying Brie and a roll of garlic sausage.

Back at Garner's flat they had enjoyed one of their picnics on the floor of the living room; one of those picnics they used to have indoors in the winter to remind them of the summer, in front of a roaring fire, in the dark, the two of them, alone except for their flickering, dancing shadows on the walls, uninvited guests who were always welcome. Cormac Duffy had been the guest this time.

Garner opened the last bottle of wine and brought it through into the living-room. She sat on the floor, her legs tucked beneath her, back against the settee, chin resting in her hands. He sat down, filled his glass, and then filled hers.

'Duffy served six years for the assault outside Swan Hunter's,' said Garner, taking up Duffy's story again.

'But I bet he thought it worthwhile,' said Veronica.

'Not at all. He broke a policeman's shoulder with his stick. He never reached Treboven: he was unharmed by all accounts. He didn't appear at Duffy's trial. Duffy was charged with assault and causing an affray. Treboven wasn't mentioned once.'

'That's amazing,' said Veronica. 'Didn't Duffy try . . .?'

'The Establishment protects itself. Duffy was stitched up. Six years in Walton gaol in Liverpool.' Garner went on to tell how Duffy met and fell in love with Kitty Hanlon, a prison visitor, and how they married and set up home in Liverpool upon his release. 'But even the gentle Kitty, a Quaker, could not halt the march of ghosts within Duffy. He couldn't hold a job down, he brooded, became bitter, twisted. Only with the arrival of a son, Patrick, did Duffy begin to come back to life. But that didn't last long.'

'Why, what happened then?'

'He found Treboven again.'

'How? Where?'

'In the library. In a newspaper. A photograph of Sir John Goodison, financial wizard.' Garner paused to collect his thoughts. 'This was in the early sixties. And it must have come as a shock to Duffy: Treboven was now Goodison, successful businessman. He set off for London, Kitty couldn't stop him. He tracked Treboven or Goodison down through the companies he ran.'

'You're going to tell me something awful now,' interrupted Veronica. 'I know it.' She clasped her arms about her knees, hugging them to her body for comfort.

'You're right,' said Garner. 'Poor old Duffy. His anger ruled him, as did the frustration and bitterness. He had not planned what to do once he had cornered Goodison. He just charged in with that stick.'

'Again?'

'Yes. This time there was a fateful outcome. Goodison's chauffeur, struck a glancing blow by Duffy, fell down the stairs leading to Goodison's office in the City. He died a week later in hospital without regaining consciousness.'

'Oh God,' said Veronica.

'Manslaughter. Twenty years. The trial was held *in camera*.'

'What?' exclaimed Veronica. '*In camera?*'

'Security reasons, reasons of State and all that good nonsense,' explained Garner.

Veronica thought for a while before replying. 'Does that mean that Treboven, or Goodison as he's known now, was somehow involved with the government or something like that, secrets, secret service?'

'Exactly.'

'But how? I mean, if Duffy's story is correct, he was a Nazi.'

'Oh Duffy's story is all true, don't worry about that. And how Treboven came to be mixed up with the government and possibly the Secret Service I intend to find out about tomorrow.'

'Who from?'

'A man I used to know some years back.'

'Can I come with you?' asked Veronica.

'Well, not to see him. He's a little, how should I put it, er, retiring. Shy. But you can drive down to Guildford with me. That's where his office is.'

'Thanks,' she said. She got up from the floor and sat next to him on the settee. 'Is that the end of Duffy's story?'

'Almost,' said Garner, and yawned.

'Do you want to go to bed?'

'I may as well finish the story,' said Garner, and then realised what Veronica had asked him. She reached down for her glass from the floor and turned her face away. The moment had passed. 'Well,' he continued, gathering his thoughts once more. 'He served his time in Walton again. His son had grown up without knowing him. On his release, he tried to put Treboven behind him. Kitty had worked hard all the time he had been in prison and had put Patrick through university. Duffy tried to give him a father's love, tried to live in the present for his sake. But like father like son. Patrick, after graduation, moved into local politics and made a success of it. He married a nice young girl, Marie, and they had three children, a girl and two boys.'

'It sounds like a happy ending,' smiled Veronica.

'Just over two years ago, Patrick told his father that he had been making inquiries about Treboven–Goodison. At first Duffy was irate. But Patrick persisted and in a way

Duffy was proud that his son should take up his fight. Marie was pregnant with their third child. Patrick went out one night to celebrate his election to the Liverpool Council. He never came back.'

'What? He just disappeared?'

'No. He was killed in a car accident. Run down. The driver never stopped.'

'Was that the official verdict? Accident?'

'Something like that,' said Garner. 'Duffy of course insists it was murder, what with the way his life has been haunted and destroyed by Goodison.'

'He has every right to believe it was murder,' said Veronica getting to her feet.

'Murder or not, the boy Patrick is dead. Kitty died a month later of a broken heart. She had stood by her husband for all that time, brought up a son single-handedly, only to see him die so tragically before Duffy had had a chance to get to know him properly.' There was sadness in Garner's voice as he spoke.

Veronica leant over him, taking both his hands in hers. 'That's enough for today,' she said. 'You're tired. And so am I.' She stood and stepped back and pulled his arms. Garner got to his feet. 'Do you mind if I stay here?'

'No. Not at all,' he said, a little unsure of what she meant exactly.

'The settee will be fine.' She walked towards the kitchen. 'Off you go. I'll clean up in here.'

'Okay,' he said, somewhat crestfallen. 'See you in the morning. I'll be going to Guildford about ten.'

She stopped at the kitchen door. 'That's fine. I'll have time to get back to the hotel and change.' Their eyes met.

'Right,' said Garner, breaking the eye contact and going

through to the bathroom to brush his teeth.

In the bedroom he undressed quickly, switched off the light, pulled back the curtains and hopped into bed. He listened for the sounds of Veronica moving about, but there was only silence, and he began to drift off to sleep. He caught his breath as he came fully awake with a start. There was someone in the room; he had heard the door creaking open.

There in the moonlight cast through the windows stood Veronica. She was naked. 'Are you awake, Peter?' she asked.

'Yes,' he said hoarsely. He could see her breasts rising and falling.

'Then move over,' she said and took a step nearer the bed.

He pulled the duvet up under his chin so that only his face and the tips of his fingers showed. 'Be gentle with me,' he whispered as she climbed on to the bed.

'Pig,' she said, and dug him in the ribs.

VI

'What are you thinking about?' she asked.

'Nothing. I'm asleep.' He had his back to her, lying on his side, staring at the wall.

'What are you dreaming about then?' Her voice was still husky from their long and passionate bout of love-making.

He sighed loudly. 'You. You and me. You and me together.'

'It's not a dream you know.' She pinched his bottom.

'Ouch,' he cried and turned over onto his back.

'See, I told you. It's not a dream.' She giggled and climbed on top of him, placing one hand across his mouth. 'Don't talk,' she said. 'Don't analyse, either. It's early days and I don't think either of us knows what's happening. So just let it happen.'

His reply was partially muffled by her hand. 'Is that the best way?'

'It's the only way,' she said. She didn't know why she was in bed with him and she doubted whether he knew either. There had been something in Duffy's story and something within herself which had prompted her forward into Garner's arms. Why, she didn't know.

He lifted her hand away. 'Remember the days on the barricades? We had something in common then. But then I became settled into my work while you were still searching. We began to grow apart. We . . .'

'And now we have something in common again: Heritage, Hamilton, Duffy?'

Garner stroked her hair. 'Could be,' he said. He felt a lump in his throat. 'I love you. I suppose I have always loved you. I used to hate arguing with you because it hurt us both. That was why I used to sulk. And I was lonely, even when we were together during the wilderness years because I would remember all those long, intense hours of discussion and debate into the early hours of the morning, how we both loved them. And then they were gone. I had no one to talk to, you know, the way we used to talk.'

'Don't talk, Pete,' she whispered. A warm teardrop, quickly followed by another, trickled down his chest.

She quietly sniffed away her tears as they lay together in silence. Soon she heard Garner's gentle snoring and she tried to make herself sleep, but her mind and her body were too active as thoughts and feelings threw themselves at one another.

When she had left for New York she had been determined to make a success of her life, to be a somebody just as Garner was. She soon realised that this could only be accomplished by hard work: nobody was going to hand it to her on a plate. So she had worked hard day and night at *the Nation* until she had a by-line of her own and she made the occasional television appearance. But, despite her success, there was a void in her life. She had taken several lovers, Dickson, her colleague, being the latest and longest-serving, but she was not truly happy. She shared her success with them all, each one of them being a success in their own right, but she found it unfulfilling. Sharing success was simple, if not downright boring, she discovered.

Then one day it had dawned on her: she was living in a self-imposed cocoon. She had her fame, her lovers, but she was shielded from the real world about her which was populated with the very people she was supposedly trying to help. She had no contact with them whatsoever and she had never given a thought to the effects, intended or unintended, which her words might have upon those people. She had broached the subject with Dickson, and, like all the men she had known in New York, he believed that success was an end in itself. Not one of them, and she was just as guilty, gave a thought to the responsibility that went with the fame. And she firmly believed, after a great deal of soul-searching, that they went hand in glove.

Garner had not wanted success: his political beliefs and his talent for writing had made him a figure within the protest movement and he had assumed responsibility for all those dissenting voices and had articulated their views. From that had grown his success. And he had wanted her to share, first and foremost, the responsibility with which he had been burdened: he had wanted her to become involved in something, anything, in order to shoulder some responsibility of her own, for like success, responsibility was difficult to share with someone who had not taken up the onus of responsibility for themselves.

He had needed her help in a sharing partnership but she had rejected all his offers and refused to share his burden. And so he had let it go when it had come under increasing pressure from the divisions that had grown up within the protest movement. All he had been left with was the success and he had refused to accept any more responsibility. The **Establishment** had then stepped in, and the road into the *wilderness* opened up before him, and he did not resist its call. She had seen that her own success in America was hollow, without meaning or substance. And so was New York. Commitment from the outset, responsibility, should have been her starting point, and not the chimera of success which had led her to America and away from the only person she had ever trusted. They had hurt one another deeply and she doubted if either of them truly knew the reason why.

At one point, she was greatly depressed and but for the arrival of two letters from Garner – soft, undemanding notes – she had felt as if she was about to go under. But she had survived, just as Garner was now surviving, and so she had decided that one day, when the time was right, she would return to England and look him up. Perhaps she was totally wrong, perhaps her conclusions were widely astray, but she had the urge to see him, an itch to scratch. She had no idea of what kind of reception she would get from him, or how she, in turn, would react to him. She would just let it happen and see what resulted.

And it was happening, she told herself. It was, and it was good. She slipped from his chest and moulded herself against his side. She was asleep.

AMERICA

I

The Room was established on the first day of December, 1917, in the wake of the Russian Revolution, by a group of Anglophile Americans, who were among the richest men in the world. Names that would have graced and enhanced any social, commercial or industrial gathering of the time – Astor, Doubleday, Mellon, Morgan, Rockefeller, Roosevelt – met in secret on a monthly basis at 34 East 62nd Street, New York, in a private, unoccupied apartment with an unlisted telephone number. The apartment block was owned by John Davison of Rockefeller's Standard Oil Company and leased to the Western Union Cable Company of Vincent Astor; and the erstwhile, listed tenant, Judge Frederick Kernochan, a close personal friend of President Woodrow Wilson, resided with his wife and family on an estate on Long Island.

The main objective of this secret society was to assist Britain in maintaining her colonial empire by providing intelligence on those groups, both national and international, which sought to disrupt and dismember it. The belief was that what was bad for British interests was also bad for American. The two paragons of capitalism stood or fell together, a notion that persists even today.

The Room had no official standing at first though it maintained working contacts with the Federal Bureau of Investigation and Britain's Secret Intelligence Service through the old boy network. Some of the society's members had seen service in the intelligence departments of the American Armed Forces; others had engaged in commercial and industrial espionage through the conglomerates they directed and controlled; and the remainder had dabbled through a romantic curiosity stimulated by popular fiction.

When President Franklin D. Roosevelt entered the White House in 1933, he took The Room under his wing as the second arm of his own private intelligence gathering network, the other being the Office for Trade and Development, which was financed by special, undeclared funds. In the days immediately preceding Pearl Harbor, The Room, had reached the zenith of its activities and involvement in clandestine operations, and from 1942 onwards, with the creation of the Office of Strategic Services, the forerunner of the CIA, The Room was bypassed as the OSS assumed responsibility for American Intelligence collection and collation.

After the War, an attempt was made to revive the fortunes of The Room, but it was discouraged by the CIA which had appointed Allan Dulles, a former operator, its first Director. From time to time, the few remaining, living members of The Room would gather, not in the apartment which had finally taken a real tenant, but in hotels, at Country Clubs, in private residences, to relive some of the escapades of

131

bygone days. These tired old men witnessed the rise of another secret society similar to the one they had known, and they viewed its birth and development with a mixture of envy and alarm. This society, the Ares Club, named after the Greek God of War, had a very restricted membership: it was open only to the chairman and chief executives of those companies who appeared on the Pentagon's list of Approved Defence Contractors. Alternatively known as the War Club to insiders, the Ares Club set out to ensure that America would always lead the world in weapons research, development and production. Regardless of whether a Democrat or Republican ruled from the White House, the Ares Club, through its highly paid lobbyists, ensured that it always got its way.

In 1987, with the death of the last surviving member of The Room, the Ares Club, in its one and only democratic vote, decided to change its name and adopt that of The Room. With the change of name came a change of character: membership was relaxed to include like-minded individuals not only from America but also from the rest of the free world. The first to sign up under the new charter was an old friend and ally of the Ares Club, Sir John Goodison, who, for as many years as anyone could care to remember, had assisted the club both as a private individual and as a paid consultant of DI6. And it was in Sir John's apartment in New York's Park Avenue that The Room came to life once more on a monthly basis.

II

'. . . The Soviet Nuclear Arsenal. The Human Rights issue. Afghanistan. They were our weapons. We used them as rods to publicly chastise and castigate the Russian Bear. They were the pointers we used to demonstrate to our reluctant allies the insidious, unchanging nature of the Evil Empire in order to win acquiescence to our policy of nuclear escalation.'

Hamilton adjusted the sound level as Sir John's voice steadily rose in a controlled fury. Before him lay the text of the speech which Sir John had prepared a week earlier, and as far as Hamilton could see, he had not deviated from it by a single word despite the fact he was speaking without a prompter.

'. . . But now we have lost those weapons. The Russian Premier has disarmed us. His diplomatic initiatives in Afghanistan have given us the spectre of a peaceful solution and the withdrawal of all Soviet forces. On Human Rights, he has pulled the rug from beneath our feet. Detainees are being released in their hundreds, with thousands more to follow. And what has hurt us more than anything is that many of the former dissidents, rather than taking up residence abroad when offered, are choosing to stay on inside the Soviet Union to actively assist the Premier with his programmes of glasnost and perestroika. Furthermore, gentlemen, the Premier has seized the question of nuclear disarmament by the throat and paraded it all over the world, a gesture which has convinced the world that he is determined to see an end to nuclear weapons . . .'

The top left hand screen in the bank of television monitors suddenly blurred and faded. Hamilton lifted off his earphones, stretched out, and thumped the monitor with the flat of his hand. The screen came to life again. He glanced at all the other monitors which showed the splendid meeting room from a variety of different angles, and checked that the video recorders were still functioning before donning the earphones again.

'. . . And as a result we have been forced to take the first step on the slippery slope to disarmament. The Intermediate Nuclear Forces accord, which will see the removal of all such weapons from Europe, has been signed. And we are powerless to prevent a helter-skelter of further treaties which will bring deep cuts in the strategic arsenals, and the eventual cancellation of Star Wars and similar, parallel areas of research and development. We have nothing left to use against the Soviets, nothing with which we can publicly justify our not continuing the disarmament process. The cupboard is bare. We will slide uncontrollably down that slope to peace and harmony, and we will be left financially, politically, and morally bankrupt . . .'

Hamilton leafed through the remainder of the script. Not long now, he thought, and stifled a yawn. He doubted he would see his bed much before the opening bars of the dawn chorus as he was sure Sir John would have some final, off-the-cuff remarks to make to The Room; and then he would want to go over the final plans for the operation. Hamilton yawned widely and settled down as comfortably as he could in the captain's chair.

'. . . It is not the President's fault. He is one of us, a cold warrior. But his hand has been forced: he had to negotiate the accord. And we need him to ensure that his Vice-President follows him into the White House when his term of office expires. The Kennedy solution to our predicament, the predicament of our continued survival, cannot be applied to the President. Gentlemen, we cannot survive without a return to the Cold War. Which leaves us with one option only, one that involves collaboration with our sworn enemies, but one that will ensure that we can go on as before. That option, gentlemen, we are calling ASH ...'

III

The whispering air-conditioning in the Russian Room kept the temperature permanently low and Hamilton shivered at the unaccustomed cold. He poured himself a stiff brandy and kept on the move, wandering among Goodison's accumulated treasures which adorned the walls and covered the floor. His leg brushed against an elaborately carved table in gilt wood with a Siberian malachite top, in the centre of which stood a silver bowl decorated inside and out with a floral design in enamel. He looked closely at the bowl and noted that the enamel was edged with twisted silver to match the rim and base of the bowl, and he concluded that an Ottoman influence had been at work in the design by the choice of tulips rather than roses.

He paid scant attention to the icons gathered on one wall, shrouded in individual glass cases; twelve in all, some bright and vivid, others dark and faded. But he did recognise the Byzantine icon, The Virgin of Vladimir, in which the child Saviour nuzzles tenderly against the cheek of his Mother, and the icon of The Saviour of the Fiery Eye.

However his interest lay in the opposite wall among the creations of Repin, Serov, Malyavin and Vrubel. His eye was caught by Repin's portrait of Alexei, the only son of Tsar Nicholas, the last ruler of the Romanov dynasty, and for some minutes he perused the features of the young boy as he sat on a garden bench in the grounds of Tsarskoe Selo, the fairytale palace on the outskirts of St Petersburg, where he and his family were later to be confined by the Bolsheviks prior to their executions. Hamilton tried to guess at what was in the mind of the Tsarevich on that idyllic summer's day, living in a world of privilege which cushioned and divorced him from the grim realities which one day would descend upon him in a whirling fury.

'Morbid,' Hamilton told himself, and he set off again upon his peregrinations. Beneath the curtained window was a seventeenth century carved table in plain wood, and he remembered clearly the day it had arrived at the Park Avenue address. Goodison had fussed and clucked over it as it had been carried inside.

Hamilton knew something of its history, that it had been carved in the village of Tikhvin near Novgorod and that it had been stolen from the Cathedral of Hagia Sophia in that city during the War. On top of the table rested a gold snuff box encrusted with diamonds and signed by Ador, one of the great goldsmiths of his day. Next to it was a splendid angular *kovsh*, a wine-taster, in gold and enamel, far grander than the one Hamilton himself owned from the same period, that of Peter the Great. He put down his brandy and picked up the *kovsh*, holding it up to the light to try to read the inscription.

'*In 1702 in December*,' said Goodison. He stood in the doorway, watching Hamilton. '*The Great Lord and Grand Duke Peter Alexeivich presented this kovsh to the Novgorodian Mikhail Sereishikov for his devotion when he was burgomeister in the Liquor Tax Collection Department, and who collected as against the preceding year the sum of 18 thousand 929 roubles, 20 altyn and 2 tengi.*'

Hamilton returned the wine-taster to the table. 'More or less as I read it,' he said with a grin.

'Quite a sum of money in those days,' said Goodison, walking across the room. He took out a clean white handkerchief, picked up the *kovsh* and polished it where Hamilton had held it. 'It shows that the Russians have always had a propensity towards, and a tremendous capacity for, the demon drink.'

Hamilton was bemused as he observed Goodison replace the dish and then carefully polish and adjust its position so that it lay exactly where it had been before. 'I don't remember having seen it before,' he said.

'It only arrived last week, in the Reverend Lewis's latest consignment. A beautiful piece, don't you think?'

'Splendid,' confirmed Hamilton. Goodison sat down in a Chippendale-style chair which had once seen service in the Hermitage theatre. 'Can I get you anything?' added Hamilton as he moved to the drinks trolley.

'No, nothing for me, Alex,' he said, waving his clawed hand. 'I will be going to bed shortly. The red-eye back to London,' he explained.

'Me too,' said Hamilton. 'But not that early.' He remained standing. 'So, do we . . .?'

Goodison's eyes were hooded and he smirked as he interrupted. 'If I'd told them I had put the world on a collision course with the sun, they would have agreed to it. Provided I gave them the monopoly on suntan creams and lotions.' His eyes were closed now, as if he were reminiscing on some event far back in the past. 'Their only concern, Alex, is to see that the nuclear monsters their scientists dream up are turned into practical realities for deployment so that they can continue to loot the Pentagon. And they will go to any ends, as they have always done, to ensure that the money rolls in.'

'If it rolls in for them, it rolls in for us too,' said Hamilton and immediately regretted it as he saw the eyes of his employer open with a start.

'Money, my dear boy, is of no consequence to me. It has served its purpose,' said Goodison with a sneer. 'And that reminds me, Alex, I still haven't forgotten about Stefano. I hold you personally responsible for his loss.

'Yes, sir,' said Hamilton contritely. He had hoped this particular thorn had been forgotten.

'This Bryant fellow, Stefano's replacement.' He closed his eyes again. 'I want a final update on him. I want to be sure, certain beyond doubt, that he is our man. Understand?'

'Leave it to me, sir.'

'See to it personally. And Duffy too.'

'I will arrange that as soon as I get back to London.'

'Personally. We have neglected Mr Duffy for some time. We need to show him that our interest in him has not declined.'

'As soon as I get back to London.'

Goodison appeared to have fallen asleep; he did not speak for several minutes. But Hamilton knew from experience that the interview was by no means over. Finally Goodison cleared his throat. 'We won't be using

138

any of our trade routes through Turkey, in or out.' Hamilton raised his eyebrows quizzically. 'Century House, with Sir Michael's blessing, will provide the routes.'

'Why is that?' Hamilton was annoyed. He did not like working with the stiff, upper-crust lips of DI6. 'Surely ours will be more secure?'

'Perhaps. Then perhaps not,' said Goodison. 'But you have to take an all-round view.' He faced Hamilton. 'One has to look at the possibility, however remote, that things may go wrong. Wouldn't you agree, Alex?'

Hamilton recognised the implied reprimand over the death of Stefano, but he also saw Goodison's second line of thought behind his cautious reasoning. And he marvelled at the temerity of the man. 'I see,' he said.

'Should things go wrong, I would not wish to jeopardise the Reverend Lewis's Bible routes. Better to lose a DI6 route than any of ours.'

'I agree,' replied Hamilton. No mention, he thought, of the treasures which Lewis brought out of Russia on the Bible routes, the best of which ended up in Goodison's Russian Room. Even if ASH was a failure, Goodison still wanted to maintain the status quo; and the steady supply of Bibles to the atheistic Russians, of course.

'I suggest you pay a visit to Turkey. With Heritage. Just to finalise plans. White's man out there is a chap called Conville. He is expecting you. A week to ten days' time, I would suggest,' said Goodison, and he dismissed his minion with a curt nod of the head and a wave of the hand.

IV

Goodison couldn't sleep: the meeting with his associates, the worry over Hamilton's competence, the prospect of an early-morning flight, all combined to make him restive. He moved across the bed to the edge, away from the curled, sleeping form of his young blonde companion, and lay on his back, staring up into the dark recesses of the ceiling.

Hamilton. A fool, he thought. Money was a means to an end. And that end was power. Power over people and their destinies. He had the power; he had built it up over forty years. His power could not be bought with money. Hamilton and his grubby friends worked, lived, for money. They did not understand the power it could produce, except at the very basic level of bribes and expenses.

His own empire was truly world-wide now: he would be firmly entrenched in Russia in a few weeks' time. And Russia would one day collapse, both socially and economically, just as it had done under the weight of the Fuhrer's tanks. The economic pressures forced upon Russia by the continuing arms race would prove an unbearable burden in a very short time. Gorbachev had given the people a hint, a flavour, of freedom. They would want more and more. But the government would be unable to provide the changes the people wanted. They would rise up. Chaos would ensue. And from that chaos would rise, phoenix-like, the New Order, spearheaded by the Pamyat, whose allies throughout Europe and America would ensure its survival.

Goodison smiled smugly to himself. His Empire would survive. He yawned but knew that sleep would not come.

His mind was too active with the thoughts of the future. He turned on his side and reached out. He touched the young man's shoulder, gently at first, and then, when there was no response, more demandingly, shaking him and saying: 'Wake up little one.'

The youth sighed deeply and straightened his body. He put out his hand to Goodison.

ENGLAND

I

G arner sang as he showered, his gruff baritone wounding the delicate melody, his tongue twisting on the unusual poetic phrasing of *La Barca de Guaymas*. But he persisted with the tale of the young boatman who set sail with a song on his lips, his boat full of hopes, only to be overwhelmed by the raging seas to return to Guaymas with death in his soul. '*La muerte en el alma*,' he chanted against the splash of the gushing water.

It had been his mother's favourite and she had sung it to him as a child, as a warning, he now realised. She in turn had learnt it from her own mother, Dona Isobel, a dark-haired Catalan beauty, who had discovered it in Mexico where she had lived for several years as the wife of a minor functionary at the Spanish Embassy.

To Garner, the song summed up the past few years of his own life: his hopes had been dashed, his soul had died, and he had wandered off into the *wilderness*. But, unlike the boatman in the story, he was alive again, and had already relaunched his boat on the seas. De Roos and Duffy had said so. And now Veronica had confirmed it. She was back; they had forgiven one another.

He soaped his body vigorously and allowed the warm water to cascade over his shoulders and down his back, and he took up the song again, whistling it tunelessly while his thoughts returned to Veronica.

They had met on the barricades in 1968, he in his final term at Magdalene, she about to begin her first year at the London School of Economics. She had literally fallen into his arms: he had caught her as she stumbled when the crowd had suddenly surged forward, and she had been squeezed off her feet. Throughout that day they had stayed together, and when night fell, he had taken her to Carlisle Street, to the crash at the Black Dwarf, where they had slept together on a smelly mattress in one of the back rooms.

That weekend he had arranged to go home to Falmouth to see his father, who was suffering with the initial effects of the cancer that was eventually to kill him, and Veronica had insisted on accompanying him. She had been fascinated by his parents – Irish father, Spanish mother – and had diverted everyone's attention from the illness with her questions about the family, tracing the relationships through the framed photographs of stern patriarchs and bustled matriarchs which hung in every nook and cranny of the cottage.

When he came down from Cambridge, he moved to London rather than return home, and Veronica lived with him in a seedy flat in Kentish Town until she graduated, when they had married and set up home in Kilburn. By that time he was establishing himself as a radical journalist of some repute, writing on a freelance basis. He even made a couple of appearances on television, one of the many alternative voices, interviewed on the streets, or brought into the studio for discussions and debates.

But Veronica had drifted: she did not complete her post-graduate studies, nor could she settle on a job, a career. She had said right from the outset, and Garner had agreed, that children were out of the question for some years ahead. Perhaps, thought Garner, had they had a child early on in their marriage they may have been happier. Perhaps, he speculated, and not for the first time, that her restlessness grew from the decision not to have children.

He in turn had grown more and more away from his former friends and their beliefs until the time arrived when he was, in all honesty, a defender, or at least an apologist, for the status quo. His work became syndicated not only in Britain but also in Europe, and occasionally in America. He had in fact come full circle, from left to right. The home in Putney, the large salaries and fees, expense accounts, were the trappings that this transition had brought. And briefly he had enjoyed the fruits, particularly when he was away from Veronica.

He had enjoyed the company of self-important, self-seeking politicians in smart restaurants and at chic parties who had sought him out to indulge their particular bias; he thrived on the press junkets to the major capitals and rubbing shoulders with Super Power negotiators, bolstering the Americans, decrying the Russians; he loved the cut and thrust of the grasping, acquisitive society he lived in; and nothing gave him greater pleasure, nor such a feeling of power, than the clandestine contacts with CIA, DI5 and DI6 officers who used him, with suitable remuneration, to plant disinformation in his copy to discredit the Russians and the Peace Lobby. And all the while he and Veronica were pulling away from one another.

The years in the *wilderness*, as both he and Veronica described that period of his life, were a drunken orgy of self-deceit and betrayal. His earlier hopes had been dashed and he had wandered off into a nightmare of despair until he had been forced back to his sense by the message in the mirror, the image of Guevara during his last moment on earth. The man's memory had deserved better. And he, Garner, knew better, and deserved better also.

II

He turned off the shower and stepped out of the cubicle. Veronica was in the kitchen: he could hear her bustling about, stacking away dishes and pans, and the smell of freshly brewed coffee was creeping into the bathroom. He dried himself quickly and wrapped the towel about his waist before going through into the living-room. 'Would you like some music?' he asked.

She stepped out of the kitchen to answer him. 'If I'd known about all that ugly fat earlier I wouldn't have come within a mile of you last night.' She pointed at his midriff.

'Fat?' he said pulling in his stomach. 'Pure muscle.'

'Which can't support itself. Must be very tired.' She went back into the kitchen. 'Do you want some coffee?'

'Please. And do you want some music?'

'No thanks. My heads still fuzzy after last night's wine.' She poured two cups of coffee and brought them through.

Garner was standing in the middle of the floor, deep in thought. 'What's the matter?' she asked as she handed him the cup.

'Something you said yesterday. It reminded me of something I had to ask you.'

'What about?'

He shook his head. 'Never mind. Look, you'd better get a move on if you're coming to Guildford with me.'

'I'm ready now. I'm not going to the hotel.' She looked at her watch. 'What time will we get there?'

'About ten. Why?'

She pursed her lips. 'I said I'd phone Alice Ormowe at half nine.'

'Half an hour won't make that much difference,' said Garner. 'She'll . . . Hey, that's it.'

'What is?'

'What I wanted to ask you. Remember you said you knew every place where Hamilton has been for the past six months?'

'Yes. Alice supplied me with a list of all his itineraries.'

'Have you got it with you?' Veronica nodded. 'Can I have a look please?'

'What are you up to, Pete?' She put down her cup on the table and picked up her bag, rummaging through it until she found her small notebook.

'Here, let me have a look.' He almost snatched it from her in his eagerness. He flipped through the pages.

'Near the back,' suggested Veronica with a frown.

'Got it.' He studied one of the pages, turned it, then turned it back again, going over the page from top to bottom, his lips moving silently as he read the notes. Finally he closed the book and handed it back to Veronica, a look of sadness on his face.

'What's the matter?' she asked.

'Remember me telling you that Heritage was in Bruges when Christian was murdered?'

'Yes,' said Veronica.

'Well, so was Hamilton.'

III

'Mr Garner for you, Mr Tamer,' announced the secretary. Garner walked past her into the room and immediately felt himself sink into the deep pile of the beige carpeting.

'Thank you, Lucy.' Dereck Tamer rose from behind a desk the size of a snooker table and advanced on Garner with his hand outstretched. 'Good to see you again, Peter.'

'You too, Dereck.' Garner looked up into the broad, tanned face of Dereck Tamer as they shook hands quickly.

'Do you mind, Peter?' asked Tamer, and he gestured to Garner's midriff.

Garner shrugged, took a step back, and raised his arms above his head. 'I'm not wired, if that's what you're after.'

'Didn't think you would be,' said Tamer as he ran his hands expertly over Garner's body. 'Just a precaution.' When he had finished, he retreated rapidly to the confines of his desk. 'Pull up a chair. Make yourself at home, Peter,' he invited. Tamer folded himself into his seat.

Garner placed his chair directly opposite his host, wondering as he did so whether his eyesight and hearing would cope with the separation imposed by the polished bulk of the oak desk. 'Nice place you have here,' he said.

Tamer nodded his head slowly. 'Yes. Not bad at all.' He pushed himself back in his leather chair. 'Did all the soundproofing myself. False windows, of course. And I personally sweep the room a couple of times a day. Nothing gets in or out that I don't want to. Makes the clients feel safe and secure,' said Tamer, as if delivering a precis of his own glossy advertising brochures.

'Big business, now, security systems,' said Garner. 'And nothing too big or too small for Tamer Associates I hear.'

'That's right, Peter. Everything from dogs and personal bodyguards through to total secure strategies.' He toyed with a paperclip. 'We handle the lot.'

'Very lucrative, too,' prompted Garner.

Tamer closed both eyes momentarily then concentrated again on the shape he was making of the distorted paperclip. 'Certain people come to us and ask us to ensure that certain other people don't interfere with their lives, as it were.' His eyes were hooded as he spoke. The paperclip snapped into two pieces. 'We do our best.'

'I'm sure you do,' said Garner brightly.

'However,' he continued. 'I would not place you among that group of certain people, Peter.' He raised his eyebrows and smiled at Garner.

'True, true,' said Garner wistfully. 'Don't have the money for a start and even if I did, I don't think the enemies I've made in my life would go out of the way to see me dead.'

'You think not, eh?'

'You've heard something, Dereck?'

'I've heard lots of things in my line of business.'

148

'Such as?'

Tamer carefully placed his elbows on the table and joined his hands together. 'You wanted to talk to me, right? I'm listening.'

'Well, let's see,' said Garner, stroking his chin, sounding as if he had a whole range of topics to discuss and was unsure of where to begin. 'You might have had dealings with the man I'm interested in. Viktor Treboven?' He pushed back in his chair. 'He's also known as Sir John Goodison.'

Tamer grinned. 'You know, Peter, you are a bit of a disappointment to me.'

'Why's that?' said Garner cheerfully.

'Is this what you've come to see me about?' He picked up another paperclip and tried to straighten it. 'Treboven is Goodison. Goodison is Treboven. Schoolboy stuff, Peter.'

'But isn't that the way the system is supposed to work?' replied Garner. 'The majority, the schoolchildren, are kept in the dark about what a minority, the teachers, know but keep to themselves. And the teachers treat their pupils with contempt whenever they learn something the teachers haven't taught them.'

Tamer shrugged his broad shoulders. 'The same thing applies with parents and children, don't you think?'

'The difference being, though, that people have a habit of dying under your system.'

'Not my system, old boy. Used to be, but not any more,' replied Tamer.

'Don't give me that, Dereck,' said Garner. 'You may have left DI5 but the system remains intact.'

'Left DI5. Me?' asked Tamer. 'Did I leave or was I pushed? Or had I seen enough, or had enough, of being a teacher?'

'You tell me,' said Garner.

Tamer got to his feet and turned his back on Garner. 'You know, what with all the controversy over former officers writing their memoirs about DI5, I thought for a moment that you came here to talk me into writing mine.'

'Maybe I will one day,' said Garner. 'I'm sure you've got lots to tell.'

Tamer shuffled back in his chair and dropped into it amid a creak of protesting leather. 'Lots to tell, eh? You don't know the half of it. Sometimes, Peter, I get the urge to put it all down on paper and really blow the whistle on those bastards in Curzon Street. And Century House, too!' He glanced up at Garner who witnessed the cold anger in the man's features. 'Yes, the other mob as well. They were all in it together. Bastards.'

Garner felt that he was losing his direction, that he was getting away from Viktor Treboven. He tried to steer the conversation back to his subject. 'I understand,' he said. 'But . . .'

'Remember Georgie Todd, the freelance reporter?'

'Yes. Of course. We . . .'

'And did you ever come across a guy called Joe Mercer?'

'Mercer? Yes. I think I did meet him once or twice. Didn't he work for . . .?

'DI6,' interrupted Tamer. He became silent suddenly after his bout of interruptions.

'Okay,' said Garner. 'And . . .?'

'They both died on the same night,' said Tamer finally and with finality.

'Well I knew about Todd. Read about it and went to the funeral. But I didn't know about Mercer. Wasn't he on the Russian Desk?'

'He ran the Russian Desk,' said Tamer. 'He and Todd were good friends. Very close friends, if you get my meaning.'

'A bit like you and I?' Tamer had been one of Garner's chief sources for disinformation and general lies in the days of the *wilderness*.

'More so,' replied Tamer. 'I liked Todd. And I also liked Mercer a lot,' he added with a trace of nostalgia. 'Mercer took no nonsense from the Peterhouse Mafia. And they did for him in the end.' Again he shrugged his shoulders. 'And because Todd knew too much. Well. . . .'

The Peterhouse Mafia, so called because they had all studied at Peterhouse College, Cambridge, were a right-wing clique within both DI5 and DI6. Over the years, from the mid-sixties onwards, they had come to dominate both organisations, ruthlessly removing all those who would not accept their view that Russian spy organisations had infiltrated all aspects of the security and defence establishments. The Peterhouse Mafia applies a very simple Catch-22: if a serving officer did not believe that Russian spies were everywhere, then he must be, by definition, a Russian spy himself as only a spy would deny the existence of spies.

Garner had been aware of the group. Besides Tamer, he had had many other contacts within the Security and Secret Services, and he knew how and why they operated as they did. 'Are you honestly suggesting . . .?'

'I'm not suggesting anything, Peter. I'm telling you,' said Tamer firmly. 'You don't know what those bastards are like. And I'd love to tell the world about them, too.'

'But you won't, will you?' said Garner. 'If you really felt as strongly about it as you say you do, then you would have spoken out about it right after you left DI5.'

'Would I now?' asked Tamer. 'And as I said earlier, I was pushed. I didn't leave. I knew what would happen if I made trouble. So I let them push me out.'

'And that's what stopped you speaking out, the fact that they may come after you?'

Tamer was angry. 'Don't be sanctimonious with me, Peter,' he said sharply.

'Whoa, hold on Dereck,' protested Garner. 'I'm being nothing of the sort. I'm just trying to absorb and understand all you've told me. It's been a bit of a shock, that's all, hearing what you've told me. I'd no idea of the extent . . .'

'Yes, well,' said Tamer, somewhat mollified. 'You yourself were tied up with it all. On the periphery, admittedly. But you must have seen what was going on.'

'I knew some, guessed some. But I never thought it had sunk to killing off serving officers and their contacts,' protested Garner.

Tamer grinned slyly. 'You should be grateful to me for getting out when I did. Had I stayed and fought it out with the Peterhouse Mafia as Mercer did, then you and I would have ended up as a double act with Todd and Mercer. Think about it.'

'I am. I don't like what I'm thinking. Or hearing.'

'And you can thank Viktor Treboven for it all.'

Garner screwed up his eyes. 'How do you mean?'

Tamer paused for effect, gathering his words about him, before replying. 'Viktor Treboven, for over thirty years, was a paid consultant to both DI5 and DI6.' As the look of surprise came over Garner's face, Tamer grinned broadly. 'You didn't know that either, eh? Well, well.' He continued to grin, showing his pearly white teeth. 'How do you think he managed to become Sir John

Goodison? How do you think he got to be so fabulously wealthy?'

IV

Garner sat on the settee cross-legged, an A4 pad on his knee, scribbling furiously, pausing very occasionally to stare at the wall opposite as if for inspiration, a glass of flat beer at his elbow.

Veronica came in from the bedroom holding up two odd socks. 'I thought this kind of thing only happened when I was around,' she said. Getting no response, she crossed the room and stood in front of Garner waving the socks under his nose. 'Look. Odd socks.' He glanced up at her, his expression remote and uncomprehending. 'Remember the arguments we used to have about your socks? You were always accusing me of losing them.' She smiled.

'Hmm. Probably got another pair just like that somewhere,' he answered. 'In the wash bag.' He tried to look round her at the wall, as if searching for the thread he had lost with her interruption.

She shook her head. 'Want me to pack them like this?'

'Yes,' he said and resumed his writing.

'Anything in particular you want packing? Alice said Hamilton had an open ticket so we could be there a while. Your bed, or that settee, for example?'

Garner put aside his pad and sipped his beer, pulling a face at the warm, flat taste. 'A few shirts and some jeans. If it looks like a prolonged stay I will have to come back. I've still got to get out this week's edition you know.' While he had been talking to Tamer, Veronica had contacted Alice Ormowe and had found out that Hamilton was flying to North Carolina that day. She had contacted her partner, Tony Dickson, in New York, and alerted him to Hamilton's imminent arrival, and then had decided to follow Hamilton. Garner had agreed to accompany her. She was busily packing for him while he made notes on his meeting with Tamer.

'Okay,' said Veronica with a sigh. 'I'll leave you to it.' And she did. 'The same old Garner,' she said to herself as she went back to the bedroom, smiling.

Garner returned to his notes and began to read what he had written.

The Rat Line. That had been Tamer's starting point. 'The Americans set up and operated the Rat Line.' Tamer had said. 'It was an underground escape route to South America for wanted Nazis, their reward for co-operating with the Yanks in identifying communist agents in Germany and the rest of liberated Europe. Klaus Barbie was the most celebrated beneficiary of this American largesse, and the Americans have always maintained that very few Nazis escaped this way.'

Garner had heard the story before and had taken little interest in what Tamer had said until he dropped his bombshell. 'But think of the matter this way, Peter,' Tamer had continued. 'The Yanks were propping up Banana Republics in Latin America, the economy of South America was in ruins and Mexico was leftward leaning. That whole continent was about to explode in 1945 and be engulfed in communist takeovers. The Americans could not possibly police all the trouble spots on their own back porch while facing off the Russians in Europe and financing the European reconstruction. So what did they do? Simple, really. They allowed literally thousands of Nazis to escape to South America; the worst kind of Nazis, the murderers, the sadists, the supremists. And they added a very welcome bit of spine to the quivering dictatorships out there, ensuring the survival of American-friendly regimes and the destruction of the nascent liberation movements, most of them communist inspired. The Nazi escape routes were inspired, organised, financed and executed by the Americans. The Nazis were America's unofficial policemen in her own back yard. And to hide American involvement, organisations such as Odessa, supposedly financed by Nazi plunder, were invented.'

Garner had found it a struggle from then on to keep up with Tamer as the stories flew from his lips. Once open, Tamer's floodgates could not be closed. When the meeting was finally concluded, Garner had felt physically drained as if Tamer's revelations had absorbed him rather than he absorbing them. Tamer had detailed Operation Paperclip which Garner had first heard of from Duffy, but Tamer's detail far surpassed that of Duffy.

Treboven had fought the Second World War in the eastern theatre, under General Gehlen of Foreign Armies East. Gehlen set up and led the greatest espionage network the world had ever seen and at the end of the War, the Americans simply took it over lock, stock and barrel, and used it as a weapon in the Cold War. But Treboven had not been taken over by the Americans. In the closing days of the War he had been wounded and sent to recuperate in Kiel where he was involved in trying to root out a suspected spy in the Naval Research establishment there. And it was at Kiel he had been captured and brought, along with the scientists, to Britain to continue the research.

'The British were pissed off with the Americans because they had taken over Gehlen's spy network and refused to share its intelligence. And it was Kim Philby, under orders from his boss at DI6 to ferret out what he could about the Gehlen networks, who uncovered the fact that Treboven was in fact a highly decorated officer of Gehlen's Soviet network, and not the security officer attached to the Naval Research team, a role he had played since coming to Britain. From then on, Treboven's future was secured.'

Tamer had then described Treboven's rise to power, his consultant's role in British operations in Latvia and Albania and Poland throughout the height of the Cold War in the fifties and sixties. 'Even DI5 used him inside Britain to spot communist agents who were infiltrated into this country as bona fide employees at eastern bloc embassies. And all the time he was playing the spy master he maintained his contacts with his Nazi chums in South America, in Europe, even inside Russia itself. His business interests expanded rapidly and provided a convenient front for his espionage activities. Klaus Barbie, Otto Skorensky, Doctor Mengele, were all partners of his, and there was never a question of anyone putting the reins on him. His power became so great that he virtually ran British Intelligence for more than two decades. Then when he tired of it, he ensured that his protégés, the Peterhouse Mafia, were in place before he finally retired.

'Did Hamilton ever work for British Intelligence?' Garner had asked.

'No. Never. Hamilton runs Treboven's business enterprises. He's not too bright is Alex Hamilton. Too many years in the army. And it is men like Hamilton that are Treboven's, or should I say Goodison's, Achilles heel. Treboven is not a man to underestimate. He's highly intelligent. And cunning. But like all intelligent men, he cannot work with men of the same ability. So he hires men who are his inferiors, men who have to have their thinking done for them most of the time. And it is these men who make the mistakes which Goodison has to remedy. Hamilton's probably the best of a bad bunch. But he's lazy.'

AMERICA

I

Three tiny holographic figures appeared on the left-hand side of the frame, the smallest of the shapes sandwiched between the taller pair. All three began to move slowly across to the right.

Bryant sighted down the scope, imposed the cross-hairs on the smallest target and squeezed off a shot. He snapped back the bolt on his Remington 40XB, ejected the cartridge, rammed another into the breech, and fired again. By the time the holograph images had marched off the right hand side of the grid, he had put five shots into the head of the central figure.

In the soundproof control room deep in the basement of the Administrative Centre the Reverend James Lee Lewis reset the programme as the printer clacked out the results, and Bryant once more lined up on his target.

'Pretty neat shooting,' commented Heritage, and he tore off the printout and handed it to Hamilton.

He examined the five traces and saw that Bryant had scored five direct hits to the target's head. 'Yes,' he confirmed as the printer started up again with the second round of results.

Lewis swung round on his seat. 'It's set for five hundred metres,' he said. 'That's why we can barely see the target.' He pointed out of the window. 'The bars around the frame are fitted with sound sensors which pick up the vibrations from the supersonic waves created by the bullet as it passes through the grid. The computer then fixes the point on the target where the bullet intersects the frame and we get the printout.'

'Five on five again,' laughed Heritage. 'He's sure on form today.'

'Once more,' said Hamilton, as he examined the second printout. 'Speed the images up if possible.' He had to be sure as Goodison would want to know.

'Can do,' replied Lewis. His fingers flew over the keyboard and the programme ran again.

Hamilton watched Bryant in action. He was lying on his stomach ten metres in front of the grid with the Remington supported on a tripod. He fired smoothly and rapidly and Hamilton counted four shots.

'Full marks again,' shouted the delighted Heritage.

'Again,' ordered Hamilton without turning round. 'Faster.'

This time Bryant managed only three shots and Heritage reported that they had all been on target.

'Ain't no use going any faster or else they'll break into a sprint,' said Lewis. 'We could change the angle if you want.'

'Leave the angle as it is,' said Hamilton. 'But get him to change position. Put him over to the right.'

Lewis switched on the microphone. 'Move over to your right, Lenny,' commanded Lewis. Bryant scooped up the rifle and cradled it in his arms, stood, and walked off centre.

Len Bryant did very well indeed. Thirty-four direct hits from thirty-four shots. Hamilton was pleased, Heritage was impressed and Lewis was hoping to fit in a trip to Baton Rouge in the not-too-distant future: he had seen Bryant too many times on the electronic firing range and was bored by his prowess.

'Where do you keep the liquor round here, Jimmy?' asked Heritage as he rumaged through the cupboard in the corner.

Lewis shook his head. 'We'll have to go upstairs.'

'What's this Church of the Aryan Nations?' asked Hamilton. He was looking through Bryant's file.

'One of those white survivalist groups,' said Heritage. 'They go out into the back of beyond and pretend they're being chased by Ruskies. They have all the gear and weapons for a twenty-year siege.' He laughed.

The Reverend Jimmy Lee Lewis was not so amused. 'Their time will come. And there will be many a despairing soul who will be grateful for the likes of Len Bryant and fellow worshippers. They train here once a month on the range and I can guarantee that they all can, men and women, shoot the eyes out of a Russian at three hundred metres.

Hamilton stared out of the window at the stocky figure of Bryant as he dismantled the tripod. His movements were steady and sure, unhurried, casual almost, but they were underlined by a deftness which suggested a man completely at home with the tools of his trade. His swarthy complexion was an added bonus. 'Okay, Jimmy, we get the message,' he said in a conciliatory tone. 'Quite a guy is old Lenny. Quite a shot, too.'

'Runs in the family,' said Heritage as he put on his jacket. Lewis shut down the terminal and the printer.

'So it would seem.' Hamilton turned the page and read on. 'Is this true, about Kennedy?' he asked in surprise.

'Yes indeed. His daddy took out Kennedy, and he was getting ready to take out his brother when that Arab beat him to it,' replied Heritage.

The father had married an Armenian girl of sixteen when he was well into his forties. Len Bryant had been the result. Not only did he speak Armenian but he was also native competent in Spanish and French. Bryant's father had been a great believer in education. Hamilton continued his research. 'Why did Bryant change his modus and use a handgun on the Swedish Prime Minister?'

'Doesn't it tell you there?' asked Heritage.

'Uhuh,' said Hamilton.

'It was a night hit,' explained Heritage. 'He was using one of those infra-red Starlight Scopes and he somehow managed to damage the lens. So, he waited until Palme came out of the cinema and then just walked up to him and shot him dead. Cool as ice, was old Lenny.'

Hamilton closed the files. 'Neat too. The Swedish authorities are still looking for a Kurdish assassin.' He smiled across at Lewis. 'Right, let's go and find that drink. Ask Bryant to join us will you Jimmy?'

Lewis looked surprised at the suggestion. 'He's a good Christian. He doesn't drink or smoke.'

II

They had flown in to Douglas Municipal Airport at Charlotte just before noon where Tony Dickson had

161

met them. He and Veronica had hugged and kissed, and then chatted animatedly to each other, ignoring Garner who was consigned to the periphery where he had sombrely witnessed the exchanges, shuffling his feet, not knowing which way to look. Finally, Veronica had disengaged herself and introduced him to Dickson who had shaken his hand firmly, staring him straight in the eye, challenging him to remember that they were all sensible adult human beings and that this was America in the latter quarter of the twentieth century where personal relationships were light years ahead of those in Britain. Garner had taken an instant dislike to him.

Dickson was as tall as Garner and appeared to be the same age, early forties, but there the resemblance ended. Dickson was balding and the remains of his wispy black hair clung to his shiny pate about the temples. His forehead was freckled and tanned as was the rest of his face which was partially obscured by a large pair of horn-rimmed spectacles fitted with Reactolite lenses. He was extremely thin except for the rounded paunch which balanced precariously on the waistband of his jeans. On noticing it, Garner had immediately straightened and flattened his own stomach.

Driving south, with Veronica in front and Garner in the rear, they had crossed from North to South Carolina on Highway 21, heading for Rock Hills where Dickson had tracked Hamilton the previous day. Garner took no part in the conversation, pretending to watch the scenery, but all the time casting sly, jealous glances at his wife and her lover in the front.

That they were lovers he had no doubt. Although neither he nor Veronica had mentioned their sex lives during the separation, having been too busy rekindling their own affections, she would have needed the virtues of a saint not to have taken a lover in the past three and a half years, and Garner knew that Veronica was far from saintly. But the questions about her celibacy, or lack of it, had begun to prey on Garner's mind from the moment Veronica had suggested they follow Hamilton on his latest visit to America. He was jealous. And why not, he told himself.

After the meeting in Guildford with Tamer, Garner had resolved to throw in his lot with Veronica and *The Nation*. He wanted to unmask Goodison as Treboven the Nazi for Cormac Duffy's sake, but he appreciated the difficulties and, much more, realised the dangers of such a task. De Roos's death still haunted him. However, he believed, and Veronica had concurred, that if he was able to tie in Goodison with some underhand dealings of Hamilton, particularly in relation to the Irangate and Contragate scandals and the neo-Nazi conspiracy, and publish an exposé in his own broadsheet, then Fleet Street, which knew a good story once the stink became unbearable, would sink its usually lackadaisical teeth into Treboven's ankles. And Goodison's past would be certain to come to light in all its gory detail. And perhaps de Roos's death would not then have been in vain.

He could not help wonder, as he sat in the back of the car, whether Veronica had deliberately engineered this meeting between them by suggesting he should accompany her. Was she comparing the two of them? Was she about to make a choice between them? Was she so involved with the pursuit of Hamilton that she did not appreciate the feelings she was arousing? Or was she simply playing one off against the other? Whatever the reasons behind the meeting, Garner was not going to spoil his own chances of retaining Veronica's affections by any overt show of jealousy or mulishness. After all, he reasoned, as the car turned off the highway and took the road to Rock Hills, he was assuming that Dickson and himself were the only two men in her life. For all he knew there might be several others. He would have to guard his feelings and hope that Veronica would continue the rehabilitation they had begun a few days ago.

The first sign flashed by, a huge square of red on blue: Interfaith World Mission USA, it said in large letters, and gave directions and the distance to the centre for Religious Renewal. 'I'm Worth Millions is how the cynics usually translate the IWM movement,' said Dickson over his shoulder. 'Rock Hills is the spiritual, administrative and financial capital of the whole tele-evangalist undertaking. A legal con trick, robbery with intent to do spiritual harm, extortion by scripture, are other phrases often used to describe IWM.' He guffawed loudly. Garner noted that Veronica gave a perfunctory grin.

'So what's Hamilton doing here?' asked Garner sitting forward and resting his arms on the back of Veronica's seat. 'Buying tobacco for Glenridding?'

'Heritage is here,' replied Veronica. 'The Terrible Twins again.'

'Heritage is tied up with this lot through the Miller Foundation so if there's something going down somewhere along the line, then it's only natural that Hamilton puts in an appearance.'

'But you don't know what they're up to?' persisted Garner.

'Well, rumour has it that they were involved in Blackmore's fish farm in Alphine. That's in Brewster County, Texas,' said Dickson.

'Yes. I know all that. Veronica told me. And I also know about the attempt to buy Blowpipe Missiles.'

'Oh. Well, er, there's all that,' said Dickson. 'They may be preparing to open another farm. But at the moment we're just following them, chasing whatever leads come our way in the hope that something will break'.

Garner stared at the back of Dickson's head and shook his own. Out of the corner of his eye he noticed that Veronica was smiling to herself.

On the outskirts of Rock Hills, Dickson took the left fork in the road and within minutes they were queueing on a slip road to enter through the grandiose portal of the IWM Theme Park. 'All your spiritual needs in one location,' announced Veronica in a drawling American accent. 'Disneyland without the laughs.' She turned in her seat and winked at Garner. Dickson guffawed again. 'The shake-down commenceth herein, brother Peter. Hallelujah. Have your dollar bills ready.' She held out her hand and he took it. She squeezed his hand.

Dickson paid for a Day Visitor's ticket at the Welcome Centre and refused the offer of a guide, explaining that he was a regular visitor. They drove on along the main avenue through the complex keeping to the snail's pace speed limit, and Dickson pointed out some of the salient features of the Park. 'We've just passed Donald Fallright's boyhood home on the left. The two tower blocks are hotel accommodation, and over there, down in the dip among the trees, are log cabins for those wishing to relive the lives of their forebears.

'Fallright was in England recently,' interrupted Garner. 'On tour with Lewis.'

'He's the nearest thing to a saint the IWM and America have,' said Veronica.

'You'll see pictures of him everywhere,' added Dickson. 'That's a restaurant complex there. There's about thirty or forty eating houses in the Park.' As they drove on pedestrians waved at them and Garner waved back.

'Friendly lot,' said Garner.

'That's the television and radio station up ahead,' said Dickson. 'We go left here. Yes that's right. To the Administration Centre.'

'Is that where Hamilton and Heritage are?' asked Veronica.

'Yes. You can't get in there without a special pass. And I assume there are sleeping quarters inside because they took their bags in yesterday.'

'Anyway, Sonny should be able to tell us,' said Veronica.

'Sonny?' asked Garner.

'One of my legmen,' said Dickson with a hint of authority. 'He stayed overnight.'

'There he is,' said Veronica, pointing.

'Car park in the rear,' said Dickson, and swung the vehicle into a tight turn just past the roadside café.

From where Sonny sat, Garner reckoned he had a clear view of the comings and goings at the Administrative Centre.

III

'The First and Second Epistles of John,' said Bryant. 'The Antichrist shall rise up to power before the Last Judgement, and he will oppose Christ in the battle between good and evil.'

166

'And he shall bear the mark of Cain,' added Lewis in a cheerless monotone.

'That's true. Amen,' said Heritage with a look of pure innocence.

Hamilton stared at the floor, not wishing to be a part of Heritage's sudden and rapid conversion. 'That's all very interesting, gentlemen, but . . .'

'Mr Hamilton, my daddy used to say that the Spirit of the Good Lord works through his chosen people,' said Bryant. 'Jesus Christ set many tasks for the faithful, some small, some large. It is the large burdens that need the most spiritual strength if they are to be accomplished, and it is the Elect who have the strength because they continually pray to God for guidance. And he guides them for the Elect are his chosen few. They work according to God's Law and not the man-made laws of the politicians who are the devil's slaves. I, like my father, am above man's law. I work to bring about the Kingdom of Heaven.'

'Amen,' said Lewis.

'Whatever paths have brought you to me, whatever motives set you off on the search for me, they do not have any relevance, Mr Hamilton,' continued Bryant. 'The Good Lord has spoken to me and I know what has to be done. My name is *Exterminans*, the Angel of the Lord, armed with sword and shield. I will cast the devil out. I will cast him down to the fiery pit from whence he came. My story was written centuries before in the Old Testament.' Bryant looked from Hamilton to Heritage. 'I will not fail for it is the Good Lord who will guide my arm. Armageddon is nigh. The battle will commence and good will triumph over evil.'

'Amen,' said Lewis.

'We should take a walk through these holy grounds and feel the contact of the Lord. He will confirm what I have said.'

IV

'So,' said Dickson. 'What have we got? Peter's dead friend in Belgium.' He held up one hand and began to count off his fingers. 'We know both Hamilton and Heritage were in Belgium at the same time. Number two, we have the old man Duffy who has been chasing this former Nazi, Treboven or Goodison, who is Hamilton's employer.' He moved on to his third finger. 'And we know that Hamilton and Heritage have both been involved with colonel Stan Hardy, on the periphery as far as we can ascertain, in Irangate and Contragate.'

'And now there's this meeting about which we know absolutely nothing,' added Veronica.

'On the steps, now,' said Sonny urgently. 'Don't turn around.'

Dickson, Veronica and Garner all turned round to face the Administrative Centre. At the top of the broad sweep of stairs, four men stood in conversation. 'Hamilton, Heritage and Lewis,' said Dickson, squinting through his spectacles. 'Don't know the fourth, the short one.'

'Neither do I,' said Sonny. 'Here.' He picked up his camera. 'Put down your hamburger, Pete, and stand over there with Veronica.' Sonny pointed to a spot which would place the Centre in the background of his proposed snapshot.

Veronica and Garner stood side by side on the grass verge. 'Put your arm round her, Pete,' suggested Dickson with a grim smile. Garner obliged and Veronica snuggled in close to him.

Sonny adjusted the lens, checked the light setting, and fired off several quick takes. 'Go and join them,' he told Dickson. He positioned himself on the other side of Veronica but he did not put his arm around her. Sonny snapped away at the four men as they descended the steps and took the woodland trail into the back of beyond. 'Let's follow them,' he suggested.

They ambled down the trail in pursuit of Hamilton and his coterie, never getting too close, mingling with the other walkers, but allowing Sonny to casually add to his collection of photographs.

In the late afternoon, Garner and Veronica found that they had lost sight of Sonny and Dickson, and they took the opportunity to stroll along together without the intrusion of having to explain why they were there. It was warm and pleasant as they walked through the leafy glades and hilly copses, crossing the railway line that circled the Park, fording trickling, crystal-clear streams, avoiding the main thoroughfares and the beaming, waving visitors from all over America.

They had not spoken for some time, being content in the silence of their own company and the peaceful tranquility of their surroundings, when Veronica broke the spell and spoke. 'What are you thinking about now?'

'Oh, just something that Christian and I were discussing that morning. You know, a few hours before he was killed. I suppose it's all tied in together.'

'What is?' She pulled him on to a grassy knoll and they sat together arm in arm.

'Well, he was a man of the sixties just as I was. He was saying that nothing is inevitable in the field of politics. You hear people say that the Left was in the ascendancy but that now the pendulum has swung the other way it's the turn of the Right. It's destiny. And it's destined that the pendulum will swing back from Right to Left and back again.'

'That today's Rambo Conservative consumerism is the inevitable outcome of what went on in the sixties, now that the Right has come to power.'

Garner smiled. 'I like that phrase, Rambo consumerism.' He plucked a piece of grass and began to chew it. 'No, Christian didn't believe in inevitability. Neither does Cormac Duffy. People who do are deluding themselves, they are resigned to inaction. Why do anything? they say; just sit back and enjoy life, everything will turn out okay because some time in the future there will be change. But there's no logical reason why there should be change, why Left should follow Right. Because that has happened before in the past it does not mean that it will do so in the future. Why not Right being followed by further Right, by fascism, for example?'

'Or by the end of the world in a nuclear holocaust?'

'Exactly. But because it's never happened before, people think it never will. Look what's happening in Russia. They are moving away from totalitarianism while we in the West are moving towards it. That's what Christian was saying and why he was so interested in the rise of the neo-Nazis. He believed they are creeping back into power. Like Cormac Duffy, he thought we came off the streets too soon in the sixties without securing the basic changes that brought us out in the first place. Duffy said that while we were out protesting, the forces of reaction simply bided their time until all the demonstrations died down. Now the new Right is on the march again and most people are ducking the issue by saying its inevitable.'

'And that it's okay because soon it will be the Left's turn again,' said Veronica. She stretched out on the grass with her hands behind her head. Her breasts rose and fell as she talked. 'So we do nothing and let it happen. We are digging our own graves.'

Garner lay down beside her on his side, supporting himself on his elbow. 'Duffy never gave up the fight. He's been fighting to expose Treboven for most of his adult life, never accepting for one moment that Treboven would inevitably be exposed.' His right hand rested on Veronica's stomach. 'When I remember the rubbish I was paid to write about the Russians, making them out to be monsters with two heads and six legs almost, it makes me cringe. Me, and others like me, shaped people's perceptions of the East and prolonged the Cold War and encouraged the Arms Race. We've done untold damage. We've got to set the record straight.'

Veronica stroked his cheek. 'Never mind, Pete. We'll keep bashing away to make amends, eh?'

'You know, politicians and governments don't rule the world. They are all just cyphers, the errand boys of big business, the multi-nationals. When the Spanish Civil War started, when the fascists attacked the Republican government, companies like Ford and Texaco refused to give the Republic any credits. They were given to the fascists. When Mossadeg, the Iranian Prime Minister, nationalised the oil industry, the oil companies got the CIA to bring down his government and the Shah was installed.' He paused to gather his breath. 'Now look at Iran. And the same thing happened in Chile: the multi-nationals brought down Allende, a legitimate, popular government, because he was bad for business, their business.'

'And you can bring it closer to home,' she said. 'Goodison, or Treboven, has his tentacles everywhere. He's rich and powerful and controls many people and politicians through his business empire. It could only have been Goodison behind Christian's murder.'

'I know, I know,' Garner said.

She reached across and kissed him, once, twice, on the lips. 'That's enough for now,' she whispered.

He kissed her on the lips while his hand moved up to enclose one of her breasts. 'That's nice,' he said huskily. 'I need you. I need to be inside you.'

'Take it easy,' she replied gently. She knew his need, knew what he wanted for she wanted the same for herself.

'We are married, aren't we?'

'I don't think the people who run this place encourage public shows of marital affection. And you'd probably need to produce the marriage certificate to do it in private as well.' She was breathless as she finished speaking.

And he wasn't listening. He cut off her protests with his lips, as he knew she wanted him to.

ENGLAND

I

Cormac Duffy died because he had become soft.

His entire life had been one continous struggle, a never-ending battle against the evil that he saw all about him, the evil which sought to deny him, and so many of his fellow citizens, the right to a dignified human existence.

Until the day he had met Garner.

Whilst still maintaining his belief and commitment to the struggle, he had allowed himself the luxury of adopting a spectator's role: he had not thrown in the towel and surrendered; rather he had given up and relinquished his starring part, bequeathing the lead to Garner, a younger man with better access to the information which was essential in taking the fight to the oppressors. But the fact that he had passed on the lead led to his death, for with its passing, Duffy relaxed for the first time in his life. He lost his edge, that keenness of instinct, that wariness, which had kept him alive and well through so many years of tribulation. Without the fight to sustain him, he became soft, he became old.

And when he stared death in the face on the blustery rainy night on the Dock Road, it was not his gammy leg, it was not the alcohol he had consumed in the Irish Club, it was not the poor street lighting that was responsible for his death. He had become suddenly old; old in mind, old in his reactions, where once he had been alert and cautious. And when the speeding car loomed up in front of him as he crossed the road, pinning him like a biological specimen on a dissecting board in its blinding twin headlights, Cormac Duffy paused and waited, stood his ground unmoved, and unable to move, watched and witnessed his own murder.

The hurtling car scythed across his path, striking him at the knees, then the hips, and flung him skywards, twisting and turning in limp, ragged loops, until finally he dropped in a crumpled heap into the oblivion of a smelly gutter.

II

'Stand up straight, Paddy, for fuck's sake.' The policeman propped up the drunk in the shelter of a wide doorway.

'My name's not Paddy. It's John,' slurred the sot.

'Come on, Paddy. Let's hear it again,' cajoled the police officer.

'John. It's John,' shouted the drunk as he slid down the wall. 'I've told you that already.' He pushed himself upright again. 'Not drunk, either. So leave me alone.'

'Just tell me once more what you saw, Paddy.'

'Told you already,' said John Kinsella. A gob of thick saliva adhered to his chin like a transparent wart. 'Saw nothing. Nothing at all. Heard a bang as I came out, that's all.'

'You were in the club drinking with him, weren't you?'

The Irishman half closed his eyes and cocked his head to one side. 'Drinking? Me and Duffy? Not drinking, me. Bar's been shut for hours. Against the law to drink after hours, officer.' He hiccoughed and spat out to one side. 'Just having a chat, me and Duffy. It was his birthday, see. No drinking, though.'

'Then how did you get in this state, eh?' demanded the policeman.

'What state, officer?' Kinsella's legs buckled and he fell down on one knee. 'Nothing the matter with me.'

The policeman looked down on the drunken Irishman with a mixture of scorn and pity. 'Go home, Paddy. Beat it. We've got your name and address. We'll be around in the morning when you've slept it off.'

Kinsella struggled to his feet. 'Weren't drinking. He went out first. Then bang.'

'Straight home, Paddy. Or it's a night in the Bridewell for you.'

Kinsella's face twisted into a lopsided grin. 'Been there before you know. I like the Bridewell. Got my own room there. You ask Inspector Ball. They all know me down at Dale Street. Cup of tea in the morning. Very nice, officer.'

'On your way, Paddy.'

Kinsella lurched forward a couple of steps and then stopped. 'Hey. Is he dead? Is Duffy dead?'

'He wasn't made of rubber so he didn't bounce. Now beat it.' The officer watched Kinsella for a few moments, reeling down the street in the withering rain, before crossing the road to join his partner.

'Ambulance will be here shortly,' said the sergeant. 'Any luck with the Irishman, Bill?'

'He was as much use as mudflaps on a bloody tortoise,' replied Bill. 'Too pissed to know what's going on. Club steward heard and saw nothing. Nobody saw anything.'

'Except him,' said the sergeant. He pointed at the contorted remains of Cormac Duffy. 'No skid marks on the road. No attempt to stop. Hit and run, I'd say. Dead as last year's Christmas turkey.' He frowned and stroked his chin.

'Always the same on Saturday night. All the fucking maniacs pissed up behind the wheel and thinking they're Nigel fucking Mansell.'

'Maybe.' The sergeant turned and pointed back down the road. 'There's a dry spot back there. Found it while looking for skid marks. A car's been parked there for some time. Since before the rain started.'

'What do you mean, Ron?'

'Rain started about half-ten, so whoever was parked there must have been there before that time. And the Dock Road is not where you'd normally park if you wanted to keep your car all in one piece. So, whoever it was could have been waiting, eh?'

'Hey Ron, let's not . . .'

'What time did Duffy get to the club?'

'Look, Ron. That's not our problem. That's CID's. We report, they speculate. So let's leave it to them.'

'Just seems funny, that's all. A car parked there at this time of night. Could have been waiting for . . .'

III

As Hamilton headed north on the motorway, his ears were still ringing with the scathing, acid abuse Goodison had heaped upon him. The man had lost all control and at one point in the tirade he had thought that the old man was having a heart attack: his face had coloured a deep red verging on purple and the veins in his forehead and neck had stood out and almost pushed through their thin, epidermal covering. He had screamed and sworn, pranced and stamped, spat and snapped, striking the air with his clawed hand, spittle flying from the corners of his mouth like bullets from a machine gun, his viper's tongue stabbing at him with acerbic descriptions of his parentage, his competence, his future. Despite his many years in the army and the SAS, Hamilton had never been more afraid for his life as he was forced to sit there, mute and quaking, under Goodison's deadly assault. And never before had he heard the English language so foully used.

'Fucking Molloy brothers,' he cursed as he drove along, his eyes peeled for the exit signs for Manchester. 'I'll fuck those two,' he promised. 'And Riggin. The bastard. Whole fucking bunch of useless pricks. Twats.' He took a deep breath and continued. 'A simple fucking job, put the frighteners on the old man, let him know that it was known he was digging up the past again, and that would have been it. Simple.' He glanced down at the speedometer and saw that he was still within the speed limit. An encounter with the boys in blue would not have gone down very well. For the boys in blue, that is. 'I should have seen to it myself. But I'm busy. So I tell Riggin to arrange it. On past experience he's an okay guy. But then he passes it on to two flashy

Liverpool thugs who know jack shit, who want to show the fucking world how fucking clever they fucking well are by trying to scrape Duffy's arse with the car.' Hamilton was breathless. 'Bastards,' he huffed and sank into an angry volcanic silence.

He made good time, leaving the motorway at twelve-fifteen, and by one o'clock he had reached Princess Road and was turning into the mean streets of Mosside, cruising past the man-made dereliction towards the rendezvous with Allen Corbett. He passed the ruined cinema, latterly a Bingo Hall, which still advertised Wednesday evening as Bumper Prize Night above the boarded entrance. He turned left then right and parked behind the building, dousing the lights and switching off the engine. He sank down in his seat and rested his head against the lower half of the window.

Ten minutes later a car with two men drove slowly by and turned the corner, only to reappear a few minutes later in Hamilton's rear-view mirror. The car drew up behind him and parked. Hamilton opened the rear door and Corbett, tall and slim, Riggin, paunchy and reluctant, scrambled into the back seat.

'I'm awfully sorry about all this, Mr Hamilton,' whined Riggin as Corbett closed the door quietly. 'It wasn't my . . .'

'Shut your fucking mouth,' hissed Hamilton, his anger still to the fore.

As if on cue, Corbett leant forward and quickly slapped the now silent pimp once, twice, backhand, forehand, across the face. 'I've been wanting to do that ever since I picked up the slimy little bastard,' laughed Corbett. He pushed Riggin into the far corner of the car. The man began to sob.

'Saves me the trouble,' said Hamilton. 'Stop your blubbering.'

'Again?' asked Corbett.

'No, leave him alone. It's not him we want, it's the Molloy brothers.'

Riggin tried to sit upright but Corbett pushed him down. 'Tell him to stop, Mr Hamilton. It wasn't my fault. Anything you want. Anything,' he blubbered.

'Where are they?' demanded Hamilton.

'I've told him already,' protested Riggin. 'He knows. I've told him.'

'You tell me.'

'Folkestone Street. Number 34. It's just round the corner. Second floor flat.'

'Okay,' said Hamilton. 'Are they alone?'

Riggin nodded his head rapidly. 'I spoke to them about an hour ago. They'd been out for a few drinks. I told them what Corbett told me to tell them, that someone would be round with their money and that they had to stay put. On their own.'

'Are you sure no one's with them?' prompted Corbett.

'Positive. My girls have all been warned off.'

'Good,' said Hamilton. He leant across into the rear and patted Riggin's shoulder. The man jumped, expecting to be hit again. 'Take it easy,' he added. 'I told you it's not you we're after. Sorry about the rough stuff, but I've been very angry.'

'I understand, Mr Hamilton. It wasn't my fault, honest.'

'Okay. Is it far to walk?' asked Hamilton.

'No, no just a couple of minutes,' said Riggin, eager to please.

'Come on then,' said Hamilton. He opened the door. 'Let's go and give the Molloys a lesson they won't forget.'

'They deserve it,' agreed Riggin as he slid across the seat and followed Corbett out of the car. 'This way. Short cut through the entry.' He set off in front. Behind his back, Corbett passed Hamilton a pair of thin cotton gloves. Corbett was already wearing a pair: Hamilton slipped his on.

'Who's in the bottom flat?' asked Hamilton as he caught up with the plodding Riggin.

'No one. Been empty since last month.'

They emerged from the darkness of the alleyway. A mangy cat, perched on a broken wall, watched their passing. 'Have you got a key?'

'Front door'll be open,' said Riggin, somewhat breathlessly as he maintained his hurried pace. 'But the door to the Molloys' flat, they'll have it locked no doubt.'

Corbett kept to the rear as they marched along Folkestone Road. 'What number?' asked Hamilton.

'We're here,' said Riggin, coming to a sudden halt.

Hamilton held him by the shoulder. 'Tell them you've come with their money. And you're alone. Okay?'

Riggin nodded and passed into the dark hallway. 'No light,' he reported in a whisper. Hamilton pushed him forward towards the stairs.

Up the stairs the three men crept. Two of the stairs creaked loudly, causing Riggin to pause, but Hamilton urged him on with a hiss to the top which was partially lit by the bare bulb to the side of the Molloys' flat.

Hamilton prodded Riggin towards the door, and as he knocked, Hamilton and Corbett took up positions on either side of the door. Corbett drew his Colt Woodsman fitted with a standard silencer, holding it down the side of his leg.

There was no reply to the first knock; the second brought forth a muffled, incomprehensible reply. 'It's me, Corbett,' he answered impatiently.

The sound of footsteps preceded the next reply. 'What the fuck do you want?' demanded a thick, Liverpudlian voice.

'I've brought your money,' said Riggin in an exasperated tone. He glanced at Hamilton and smiled thinly.

A pause. 'I thought you were sending someone over?' said the man on the other side of the door.

'Couldn't find anyone I could trust with all this dosh.'

'You alone?'

'Since when do I need a bloody bodyguard?' retorted Riggin.

A bolt was thrown back and a key turned. The door swung open. Riggin stepped inside. 'About bloody time,' he said. He left the door open, facing Eamonn Molloy in the short hallway.

Corbett dashed through the open door. He struck Riggin in the back of the neck with his forearm. Riggin stumbled into Molloy, and then Corbett kicked both men in quick succession, forcing them from the hallway and into the square living room. Christy Molloy, half asleep, half drunk, stretched out on a moth eaten settee, raised his head at the sight of the swirling commotion. Hamilton stepped inside and quietly closed the door.

Corbett kicked Eamonn again in the side of the head and he spun and fell across his brother. Hamilton pulled Riggin to his feet and away from Corbett, who now levelled the **Colt** at the Molloys. 'Sit tight boys. Just want a word with you.'

'You fucking twat, Riggin,' cursed Eamonn Molloy.

'Shut it,' warned Corbett.

'Do you know me?' asked Hamilton.

Neither of the Molloys spoke.

'Answer,' ordered Riggin, letting the Molloys know whose side he was on.

Hamilton put out a hand across Riggin's chest to quieten him. 'You were supposed to do a job for me. Scare an old man.'

Eamonn Molloy dropped his head into his hands. 'It was pissing it down. Couldn't see properly. The old guy just stopped in front of the car.'

'No excuses,' said Hamilton. 'You're in the big league now. And you have to pay big prices for failure.'

The younger Molloy struggled up into a sitting position. 'What d'you mean?'

'You went over the top,' replied Corbett, watching their every move.

Christy Molloy swallowed hard. 'You can't,' he whined.

'They're going to teach you a lesson you won't forget,' chimed in Riggin. And he grinned nervously.

'You lot should know all about knee-capping, eh?' said Corbett.

'Bastard,' said Eamonn.

'Argh 'ey,' said Christy. 'Not that, mate.' He began to cry.

'You don't want knee-capping. Okay,' said Corbett and he shrugged his shoulders. 'How about this, then?' He shot Christy neatly between the eyes, the **plop** of the silencer almost lost in the sound of his sobbing.

Eamonn Molloy's eyes opened wide in disbelief, and he turned to watch his dead brother slump backwards. Riggin yelped and tried to speak, but horror twisted his tongue.

Corbett shot Eamonn behind the right ear. As he slid to the floor, Corbett stepped forward a pace and administered the coup de grace to both men.

'No,' cried out Riggin, and he began to shake. Sweat broke out on his forehead and he reached out with both hands to Hamilton, his mouth open wide as if to roar in protest. Hamilton brushed him aside and walked down the short hallway.

Riggin staggered a step after him. But Corbett caught him by the arm and swung him round. 'Sorry about this, Riggin. But no loose ends.' And so saying he placed the silencer in the man's gaping mouth and pulled the trigger. Riggin dropped to the floor like an empty sack. Corbett followed Hamilton into the hall.

Outside, Hamilton returned the gloves to his companion and they walked back to the cars in silence, Hamilton handing over an envelope containing Corbett's fee.

'Thanks, Alan,' said Hamilton. 'Sorry about the short notice.' They stood by the cars.

'No problem, Alex.' He checked his watch. 'Should be back in Edinburgh by six. At the latest. Flight's not 'til ten.'

'Where are you going?'

'A little place just across the French border. San Martin. Small fishing village, no tourists. Nice and relaxing.'

'Alison will enjoy that.'

Aye, and the kids are old enough now to make their own fun.'

'Well, have a good time,' said Hamilton as he got into his car.

'Will do,' said Corbett. 'See you. Take care.'

'Same to you,' replied Hamilton.

IV

'Sshh. There now,' comforted Marie Duffy. She held the young girl close to her breast, gently rocking her to and fro. 'She loved her grandad and can't understand why she can't see him again.'

Garner patted the child on the head. 'It's always hardest on the young.' She shrank away from his touch. He smiled and shrugged his shoulders. 'Again I'm sorry I couldn't get here any sooner, but . . .'

'That's alright, Mr Garner. Your office told me you were in America. I understand. And I'm glad you came anyway.'

'Is there anything I can do for you now?' Anything, you know, money to tide you over until . . .' He didn't really know what to say. He felt inadequate, much the same as he had felt with Gerda de Roos.

Marie shook her head firmly. 'We're fine. He was insured. And there's still some money left over from . . .' Her eyes clouded and her bottom lip quivered. 'From Patrick's accident.'

'Okay, I'll see you then. I'll keep in touch and let you know how I'm progressing.'

There were tears in Marie's eyes. 'Is there any point, Mr Garner?' she said bitterly. 'What good will it do me? What good will it do you? You could end up being killed. In a road accident, just like them. They're all dead. There's no point going on with it.' Her tears were flowing down her cheeks and running into her daughter's hair. The child whimpered and clung to her mother's neck.

'Treboven isn't,' said Garner with more anger then he had intended. 'He isn't dead. Yet.' As he looked at her, he realised that there was indeed murder in his heart.

'And that's going to make a difference? Him dying is going to stop the tears, is it? Bring them back?'

'No, but it may prevent others having to cry,' he said softly.

She wiped away her tears on the back of her hand. 'You silly men will always fight and leave us women to weep. But my two lads won't. I'll teach them not to fight.' At that moment, a neighbour came out of her house and stared across at them as they stood at the front step. Marie averted her head and stepped back inside. 'I'm sorry, Mr Garner. Don't take any notice. I'm a bit upset . . .'

'Don't worry, Marie. I understand.' He fingered the slip of paper.

'You've got Kinsella's address?'

'Yes,' he replied, reading it again, avoiding her eyes, her sorrow, her accusations.

'Try and see him today. He collects his pension tomorrow so he'll be broke and sober today.'

'Right.' He turned away as she slowly closed the door.

V

Kinsella's hair was shoulder-length, grey with streaks of brown and it had not seen a comb for a day or two. He wore a greasy gaberdine mackintosh, buttoned to the neck despite the temperature, and ragged strips of its lining gathered at his knees. He was clean-shaven, and his face was gaunt and yellowed, but his eyes were alert and his nose was sharp. 'Yes, indeed. A fine spread young Marie put on. You missed a treat.' Kinsella measured the creamy head of the pint of Guinness with a practised eye. 'Old Tommy keeps a fine drop of the black stuff. Cheers.'

'Cheers.' Both men knocked off the head.

'Did old Cormac proud. Proper traditional wake, like we used to have. Can't wait for my own. It's the keening I love the best.' He licked off the white moustache about his lips. 'It's a pity they have to spoil it all by having to bury them.'

'It's a pity they have to die in the first place,' said Garner.

'Aye. You've never said a truer word. Take Cormac for instance. A fine man. Gammy leg and all. A helpful soul, generous too. And clever. He'd read books you know. Thick ones with no pictures either. I've seen him, at home, or in the library. Aye.' Kinsella sank the remainder of his pint and held out the empty pot to Garner. 'He could smell broken glass, could Cormac.'

Garner went to the bar and came back with two pints which he placed in front of Kinsella. His own drink was hardly touched. 'Both for you,' he said.

'Ah, you shouldn't have done that now,' replied Kinsella as he gathered them closer. 'You'll have me singing in no time.'

Garner caught the twinkle in the old man's eyes. He had an air about him. Of cunning? wondered Garner. Everything the man said seemed to have two meanings. 'Singing?' asked Garner.

'Well, you know what I mean?' said Kinsella. He swallowed down a gulp of stout. 'Cheers, again.' He wiped his lips with the back of his hand. 'Now where was I? Ah, yes. Old Cormac. Clever man. Loved his reading. Particularly his history. Names and dates and places. Knew them all.'

'You sound as if you don't approve. Of history I mean.'

'I do, do I? Well, I'll tell you.' He stared at Garner. 'History is a nightmare from which I am trying to awake.'

'What if that nightmare gave you a back kick?' replied Garner, returning the Irishman's stare.

'As it did poor Cormac?' He finished off the remains of the pint.

'You know your Joyce, Mr Dedalus,' said Garner.

'And so do you, Mr Deasy,' said Kinsella. 'I had a chance as a young bucko to glance over the works of Mr Joyce. Just like yourself, I suppose.'

'And a memory to remember them too.' Kinsella was a good actor, surmised Garner, playing the role of the fool. In order to survive.

'And now you'll be asking what happened the night Cormac was killed. You know, Mr Garner,' he said, eyeing the third pint. 'The Liffey water is a wonderful drink. I wouldn't insult my stomach by drinking anything else.'

'Marie says you'd both been drinking heavily that night and that you didn't see anything of the accident. At least, that's what you told the police.'

'Accident is it now?' And his eyes gleamed as they fixed on something beyond Garner's shoulder. Garner glanced over his shoulder but there was nothing there. It was early evening and the Jawbone was empty except for themselves. Even the barman had disappeared. 'But you never tell the scuffers anything,' continued Kinsella. 'They're a waste of skin. Always have been. They called round to see me a few times. Particularly that Sergeant

187

Heslop. But I wouldn't tell them a thing. If my old man was alive today, God rest his soul, he'd turn in his grave if he knew I'd told the scuffers anything.' He made the sign of the cross and grinned inanely at Garner. 'The sergeant kept after me, but all that passed my lips were the lies. Honest to Christ.'

'So tell me what happened, then,' said Garner.

'That was what I was about to do, Mr Garner. Sure, we'd been drinking but we weren't langers or bevvied. The old Guinness doesn't attack you up here.' He tapped the side of his head. 'It's the legs that take all the aggravation. They go to sleep after five or six pints. That's why everyone thinks you're drunk.' He winked. 'But the old noggin stays as clear as a bell.' Kinsella screwed up his eyes. 'I saw it all, Mr Garner. Saw that car deliberately run him down. Ran down old Cormac, it did. Now why should anyone want to kill old Cormac?'

VI

He came out of the Jawbone and crossed the road to his car.

'Mr Garner,' said a voice behind him. Garner froze, stooped over, having just inserted the key into the door-lock. 'Peter Garner?'

Garner straightened up and turned. A tall man with thinning sandy hair and broad shoulders faced him. 'Yes?'

The man held up an identity card. 'Sergeant Ronald Heslop.'

Garner read the card slowly. 'I thought you were uniform?'

'Day off,' said the sergeant.

'Unofficial?'

'And off the record,' came back the policeman. 'We'll use your car.'

A surge of excitement ran through Garner's body. It was a long time since he had been involved in a similar exchange: unexpected, short and to the point. The last time was years ago when he had been approached outside his hotel late at night by a CIA agent who had fed him with some very clever disinformation about Soviet arms supplies to Grenada. He didn't expect that sort of information from Heslop, but he wondered all the same, as he unlocked the car, what exactly the man wanted.

'Been following me around, have you, Sergeant?' asked Garner, as the policeman climbed into the passenger seat. His plain clothes looked shabby and forlorn and his chin was covered in a day's growth which was darker than his hair and made him look unclean.

'Just turn left at the top and carry straight on,' said the sergeant.

Garner set off. 'Well?'

'I'd called round to see Marie.' He turned his head to watch for Garner's response. Garner watched the road ahead. 'First her husband, then her father-in-law. I called round to see how she was. We're not all . . .'

'Insensitive brutes in blue uniforms, eh?'

Heslop nodded. 'Something like that.'

'I understand, Sergeant. Tell me, you knew that Cormac's son had also been killed in hit and run?'

'Heard of it. So I looked up the file after the old man's death.'

As Garner slowed at the lights, he faced Heslop. 'What made you do that?'

189

'Straight on,' he said. 'What did Kinsella have to say?'

'What do you think?'

Heslop smiled thinly. 'He used to be a teacher at a boys' Grammar School in Crosby. Just down the road a ways. The drink got him. Went downhill after he was retired. But he's sharp. He's not fooling me.'

'I don't think many people could fool you, Sergeant,' said Garner. 'Which way now?' he added as they came to a T-junction.

'Left and straight ahead,' said Heslop. 'Funny thing. There was little follow up when young Duffy was killed. Nobody seemed interested in pursuing the case.'

'Were there many leads?'

Heslop shrugged. 'I'm not CID. I wouldn't really like to go out on a limb.' There was a bitterness in his tone which Garner detected immediately.

'And what about Cormac's death? Kinsella told me it was a deliberate hit and run.'

The sergeant rested his head on the back of the seat. 'Thought as much. It was raining that night. But there was a dry spot where the car had been. Whoever it was had been waiting for some time for Duffy.'

'And they must have had a good idea of him to pick him out in the rain at night, even with the street lighting.'

'There's that. And the cigarettes.'

'Cigarettes?'

'Five of them. Stubs really. On the pavement next to where the car was parked. But the rain got to them before the forensic boys could do anything with them.'

'Who's handling the case?'

'Nobody. Nobody at all. Go left at the next lights and left again.'

'Why are you telling me this?'

'Marie told me you'd been to see her. That's how I knew you'd be in the Jawbone with Kinsella. She said you worked for a newspaper in London, a community paper.'

'That's right. I own it in fact.'

'So I ask what are you doing all this way up here, asking about Cormac Duffy. You're the first newspaperman to show any interest. And then Marie says you were up not so long ago talking to Cormac.'

'That's right also,' said Garner.

'So I begin to ask myself why,' said Heslop.

'Again, why are you telling me all this?'

'Because there's something going on,' said Heslop sharply. 'Otherwise you wouldn't be up here.'

'And there should be a lot more CID activity. Am I right, Sergeant?'

'A lot more,' said Heslop slowly. 'A hell of a lot more.' He paused for a moment as if making up his mind to go further. 'And then two Liverpool thugs, the Molloy brothers, end up dead in a flat in Manchester owned by one of the biggest pimps in the North.'

Garner gripped the wheel tightly and tried to sound casual. 'And nobody sees the connection?'

'Right. And there is one. You mark my words. But no one bothered to look.'

'Except you.'

'Me. I'm uniform not CID. I can't do anything.' He shook his head. 'Twenty years next month in the force. Sergeant for ten. And I'm a good copper. But a sergeant I'll stay until I retire.' His tone was bitter again.

'Maybe if you follow up on Duffy's death, turned in some new evidence, there may be a promotion for you. To CID, perhaps.'

Heslop snorted. 'I'd probably end up being sacked if I chased up this case. If I cracked the Jack the Ripper case I'd probably still stay a sergeant.' He looked across at Garner. 'You seem a bit naive to me, Garner, for a newspaperman. I'll go no further in the police force no matter what I do. You see, I'm not a Mason.'

VII

'Where are you?' asked Garner.

'At the Barbican,' said Veronica. 'How did it go?'

'Missed the funeral. But I saw Marie, his daughter-in-law, and his friend Joe Kinsella. And the policeman who reported the accident.'

'So it was an accident?'

'No, it wasn't. It looks like he was deliberately run over. And that the men who did it were themselves killed.'

'Honestly?'

'Yes. Look, I'll be back tomorrow, about lunchtime, so I'll fill you in on the details. And don't forget, keep off the phones in the flat and my office. Okay?'

'Okay. And I've got something for you, too.'

'What is it?'

'Hamilton is on the move again. And Heritage is in London. I saw Alice earlier today. They're both booked out tomorrow on a Turkish Airlines flight to Ankara and then on to Diyarbakir.'

'Diyarbakir? Where's that?'

'South-east Turkey. Apparently Hamilton's been there before. It's not far from a town called Bitlis which is the centre for tobacco growing in Turkey.'

'So it could be a business trip?'

'Could be. But can we afford to assume that?'

'No, not really. By the way, have you heard from Dickson about the fourth man in Carolina?'

'Still working on it. He'll let us know as soon as possible. So what are we going to do about the Turkish trip?'

'I'll take care of that. Don't worry. Anything else?'

'No, I don't think so. Except that I love you and miss you.'

'I can't remember how long it is since you said that.'

'If that's all you can say then it'll be even longer before you hear it again.'

Garner laughed. 'Anyway you know I love you. And miss you.'

'A girl likes to hear it from time to time.'

'Love you millions. Look, I'm going to have to go. I'll see you tomorrow. Take care. And be careful. Watch your back.'

There was a pause on the other end of the line. 'You really think they're watching us?'

'They were watching Duffy. They must know about me seeing him so they'll be after us next.'

'Be careful, Pete.'

'And you too. Love you. Good night.'

'Good night.'

He waited until Veronica hung up before doing so himself. His dinner, which the waiter had brought to his room, was cold and he pushed it to one side. He hated hotel food. It was usually just about palatable when hot, but decidedly unfit for eating once the grease had settled and congealed. 'Ugh,' he said and dropped onto the bed.

Deep down inside he was angry and confused over Duffy's death, and he felt an overpowering sensation of guilt, blaming himself for Duffy's death. He could not help believing that his meeting with Duffy and what he had learnt subsequently had been responsible. And what made matters worse was the sense of inadequacy and futility that fuelled his guilt, for he realised that all his efforts to date could be dismissed as speculation, the overactive imagination of a has-been trying to make it back to the big time. He had nothing really of substance, nothing concrete, that could be substantiated by corroborating witnesses. Tamer would never go public on what he knew and even Veronica was working in the dark trying to make connections between America and Europe. And Piechler? He hadn't heard from him in ages.

De Roos's death should have alerted him to the ruthlessness of the opposition. He should have taken more care of Duffy. But in a sense, de Roos's death was not unexpected: he had worked for many years in the pursuit of dangerous fanatics with the knowledge that one day those same fanatics might strike back. Duffy's death, on the other hand, was entirely uncalled for. He was an ant attacking an elephant and now the elephant had stepped on him.

But there was one thing that Duffy's death told him, and it was the only consolation he could draw from the whole affair: someone, somewhere was afraid of what he and Duffy had been collaborating on. The elephant must have had a reason for crushing the ant.

And because of that he had to press on. There could be no going back now. De Roos and Duffy, their causes, were crying out for justice. Someone had to ferret out injustice, dishonesty and murder, and he, Garner, had had the mantle thrust upon him. It would be easy, he told himself, to pass it on and rely on others to do the donkey work and expose themselves to danger. But one day the world might wake up to find that everyone was relying upon everyone else to fight the good fight and that nothing was being done by anyone, and injustice and deceit had become institutionalised. He would see it through to the end because he owed it to his friends, to those he had wronged in the *wilderness* years, and, just as importantly, to himself, even if it meant putting his own life at risk. It was always easier to give up than to continue and he had had enough of throwing in the towel.

He got off the bed and collected his jacket from the back of the chair. He took out his address book from the inside pocket and looked up Nihat Sargin's telephone number in Ankara.

DIYARBAKIR, TURKEY

I

The names tumbled through his mind in quick succession, marching past on parade, coming to life as armies of dark-skinned warriors with black beards, tramping the sands of time. Hurrites, Midianites, Medes, Macedonians, Urartians. Name from legend, from the Bible, from ancient history, from well-thumbed texts, from the lips of Mr Freely in a stuffy classroom on a warm spring afternoon. Tiny Freely, a huge hulk of a man, whose prodigious memory for obscure facts was matched by an inordinate talent to render his pupils as rigid as the wooden desks at which they sat.

As he dozed in the small cubicle inside the arrivals hall, Francis Conville could feel the ghost of a smile haunting his lips as that memory of his schooldays stabilised and played back at normal speed. 'The kingdom of Uraru rose to power in the ninth century BC,' warned Tiny Freely as he prowled the aisles, eyeing his heavy-lidded students sprawled at their desks, heads firmly planted in their hands, their attention drooping during his cautionary pauses. 'Uraru is corruptly preserved in the Old Testament as Ararat,' he continued slowly, before twisting rapidly on his heels to swipe at Crompton's ear. 'Pay attention, laddie,' he roared above the noise of Crompton's whinge-ing protest. 'Right, then. In Latin, Ararat becomes Arme-nis.' He prodded Robinson in the ribs. 'And according to Genesis, Mount Ararat was where Noah docked his boat after the biblical version of a typical British summer.' He paused to scowl at the sniggerers. 'Mount Ararat is in eastern Turkey, which in some quarters is still known as Armenia. And it was there that the Urartians ruled, just south of the Mount, on the shores of Lake Van.'

The image faded away. The Urartians came as far as Diyarbakir, thought Conville, and he awoke with a start, wide-eyed, as if expecting to find himself face to face with a band of the louring invaders. Instead he found himself staring into the face of a young woman advertising the delights of a holiday in New York. A moment later a muffled announcement, first in Turkish, then in broken English, informed him of the arrival of Turkish Airlines flight 252 from Istanbul.

He stood, stretched, palmed the creases from his trousers, then strolled through to the customs exit. The modern-day descendants of the warlike Urartians, dressed in two-piece suits and armed with nothing more lethal than leather briefcases or rolled-up newspapers, crowded round the exit, jostling for a view of the incoming passengers. Conville positioned himself well away from the heaving throng, slouching against a dusty wall, arms folded across his chest.

Francis Conville was a couple of inches over six feet, athletically built, with short brown hair and fleshy features that were showing the effects of recent exposure to the blistering sun that June had brought to the region. The tip of his nose glowed a shiny tomato red where it had peeled, and flaky white strips of dead skin decorated his nostrils. His whole demeanour was one of calculated nonchalance and indifference which contrasted with his usual approach to work and life in general when he typified the young, ambitious, briskly efficient career officer that DI6 was keen to have on its books.

He had spent six days so far in the Diyarbakir area and was looking forward to his return to Ankara where he lived. He had not slept well since his arrival; his hotel was noisy and disagreeable, the service slovenly and sullen, and the food was awful. He suspected there were rats in the kitchen and in the darker recesses of his room which he avoided assiduously. On previous visits to Diyarbakir, he put up at the American monitoring base next to the airport, care of the base's CIA chief, which provided all the comforts of home, even surpassing those available to him in Ankara. But on this occasion, he had been instructed to avoid the base and any contact with the cousins so as to obviate any explanations as to his presence in Diyarbakir. Officially he was not there.

And therein lay the problem that had irked him for days and which accounted for his disinterest. He was being used as an errand boy, which, from time to time, was all part of the job. And this he did not mind so much. But what he resented was acting as dogsbody to independents such as Hamilton and Heritage in their maverick operations.

When he saw the two men finally clear customs, he did not go across to greet them. Instead he stood his ground, waiting for them to approach him and, as they neared, he pushed off the wall and walked outside without a sign of recognition.

II

Conville skirted the centre of the decaying city, driving through the slums stacked like broken egg boxes on the river bank, past the university, heading east on the Bitlis road, a two-laned blacktop that snaked through the cultivated hills of the Tigris valley. He had taken off his jacket, loosened his tie, and with the air-conditioning on full, he was at last feeling drier and more comfortable. His two passengers in the rear had not seemed bothered by the intense heat inside the car, which, after standing for over an hour in the unshaded car park, had been as hot as a baker's oven when they had set off.

'Did you notice the wall?' shouted Conville above the noise of the cooling fan.

'Huh?' grunted Heritage. 'Can't hear you.' He sat forward in his seat.

'The wall,' repeated Conville raising his voice again. 'Around the city. After the Great Wall of China they say it's the longest unbroken wall in the world.' He glanced in the mirror. Heritage was staring at Hamilton in puzzlement. 'Local claim to fame.'

'Fuck the wall,' said Hamilton. 'And turn that bloody fan off,' he added as he sat forward in his seat. Conville obliged.

'Come off it, Alex. He's only trying to break the ice.'

Hamilton slumped back in his seat muttering to himself.

Heritage prodded Conville in the back. 'Alex has been ordered to take a holiday over here.'

'Some holiday,' said Hamilton.

'And if your temper doesn't improve shortly, I'm going back to London for a few days and leaving you all alone in Ankara. And I'll tell your boss what a bad-tempered boy you've been.'

'Don't push me, John,' warned Heritage. Goodison had not forgiven him for the lapse over Duffy's death and had insisted he stay out in Turkey until ASH was completed. 'Anyway, it makes sense to stay out here.'

'Ho, ho. Sense, he says,' replied Heritage. 'That wasn't what you were calling it yesterday.'

Their conversation had completely bypassed Conville, and he concentrated on his driving, speeding past a long convoy of crawling cars and lorries.

'Anyway Francis,' said Heritage. 'What does Kossemlu want?'

'He wants to see you, that's all. Etiquette.'

'But he's going to do it, isn't he?' snapped Hamilton.

'Ninety-nine per cent certain,' said Conville over his shoulder. 'But protocol says he must meet you, haggle over the price, before he actually agrees. And that's got nothing to do with me. I just set up the meeting.'

'Which is where?' said Hamilton.

Conville pointed off to the left. 'Over that way. A village called Dervish Hassan.' Hamilton and Heritage turned their heads to look. A wide expanse of wheat and barley fields stretched out to the rolling foothills in the distance. Men and women working in teams waded through the waving stalks, oblivious to the searing heat, harvesting the crops with sickle and scythe. 'It's his wife's village. He always goes there during harvest time,' he added.

'Hey. What's that up ahead?' asked Heritage.

Conville slowed down and joined the queue of vehicles at the military road block. 'Have your passports ready.'

'Is this usual?' asked Hamilton. There was a note of caution in his voice.

'It's the fighting season,' explained Conville. 'The good weather brings the Kurdish guerrillas out of the mountains and down onto the plains. They shot up a village in the next province the other day. Killed about thirty villagers.'

'I know about it,' said Heritage. 'The PKK, the Kurdish Worker's Party. Bad dudes.'

Conville crept the car forward. A military truck blocked the road ahead and a group of soldiers in green fatigues were inspecting every vehicle. 'This part of Turkey is all Kurds. They spill over into Iraq, Syria, Iran. And of course Russia.'

It took them twenty minutes to pass through the road block. The surly troopers accepted the American and British passports without question and a couple of packets of Marlboro from Heritage. Conville turned off left shortly afterwards on to the Bingol road, and five miles further on, he swung left again on to a narrow dirt track which bounced them down an incline at the bottom of which, nestled in the folds of the hills, lay Dervish Hassan.

They had to pull over to one side to allow an open truck tightly packed with field labourers to pass by. Conville used the opportunity to confront his passengers. 'A few words on protocol, as it were. Kossemlu speaks excellent English. He went to school in Cambridge.' Hamilton nodded. 'Should he choose not to, then don't try to join in or interrupt the conversation. Speak through me.'

'Our Turkish isn't that good,' said Heritage.

'And he doesn't like Americans, either. So take off that class ring,' he told Heritage, who reluctantly did as he was told, much to the amusement of Hamilton. 'Just follow

201

what I do and say. If he gets pissed off, he'll break out into *Zaza*, the local Kurdish dialect, which will be his polite way of telling us to fuck off. Okay?'

'Okay, Franny,' said Hamilton. 'What have you given Kossemlu so far?'

'Just that we have a man being held by the Russians close to the Turko–Russian frontier, and that we want him to take in a specialist to bring out the unfortunate guy. He doesn't like Russians, either.'

'Sounds okay, José,' said Heritage in a deep Texan drawl. 'And that's all he needs to know.'

III

A clump of gnarled and drooping poplar trees commanded the centre of the village and provided the only shade for the motley zoo of animals that gathered there: a pair of panting hounds, a scruffy donkey, and several brindled cats. Further afield, a herd of penned cows bellowed their protests as victims of the harsh sun, while a flock of sheep wandered down to the discoloured water of the village pond to join a band of squawking ducks.

Conville parked the car close to the trees and opened the back door for Hamilton and Heritage. Both men stretched themselves as they got out, looked about, and immediately wrinkled their noses at the overpowering stench of unwashed humanity and itinerant livestock. 'Shit,' said Heritage.

'Exactly,' confirmed Conville. Young children, dirty and unkempt, and leading infants by the hand, began to appear in the mean gaps between the grey clay houses, while their mothers, off to one side, refused to acknowledge the foreigners, kneeling with bowed heads among a huge mound of cattle droppings, moulding the drying pats with their hands into circular briquettes and stacking them in neat rows to dry hard in the sun for use in winter as fuel. The village elders, the lazy, the crippled, sat in small knots at front doors, pretending not to notice the arrival of the red Renault and its occupants, intent upon their conversations of affected importance.

'We'll say hello to the *muhtar*, the head man, first,' said Conville. 'But don't drink the water if he offers you any. You name it, the water will have it.' He made a face, then carefully picked his way across to a large house set apart from the others. Heritage and Hamilton followed exactly in his footsteps.

The *muhtar* sat alone as was his privilege. He rose from his rickety cane chair to greet Conville, shook hands vigorously with Hamilton and Heritage, and without further preamble, he took them over to Kossemlu's dwelling.

Ramazan Loretin Kossemlu was in his late forties, tall and lean, with black, piercing eyes. He met them at the door dressed in his best clothes, a sign of respect for his visitors. He wore a well-cut dark blue blazer with silver buttons over his *yelek*, the traditional black waistcoat, and a collarless white shirt. The *salvar*, Turkish trousers, were grey worsted, loose and baggy on the thighs, pulled snugly in at the knee, and skin-tight down the lower leg to the ankle, to show off a pair of black Gucci slip-ons. On his head he wore a beautifully embroidered *sapka* which he removed with a flourish to usher in his guests, much in the same way that a doorman doffs his hat. '*Evime Hos geldiniz*' he said, and stood to one side.

The house consisted of a single oblong room that was cool and airy. The windows had been boarded up and the subdued lighting came from a gas lantern hanging from the centre of the ceiling. Small, square Hereke silk rugs covered the rough clay walls while a larger one had been thrown down on the earth floor beneath the lamp.

The four men sat in a circle on this rug and a woman ghosted up to them to deliver a large plastic bowl, four smaller ones and several spoons. Kossemlu ladled out a portion of white goo into a bowl and began to spoon it into his mouth after gesturing that the others should follow suit.

Hamilton and Heritage both darted a questioning look at Conville. 'It's *mahallebi*,' he said, as he helped himself. 'Very good. You might find it a bit sweet. It's just rice and milk.' He began to eat. His companions reluctantly followed suit.

As he ate, Kossemlu kept his eyes on Conville. Before Hamilton and Heritage realised it, Kossemlu and Conville were in quiet conversation. In Turkish. Between mouthfuls.

Otuz tufek. Kalashnikovs. Ve cephane,' said Kossemlu. It was the mention of the Kalashnikovs that alerted Hamilton and Heritage to the fact that negotiations had started.

'He says he'll go, but his price is thirty Kalashnikovs and ammunition,' said Conville to the two men.

Heritage nodded. 'Tell Mr Kossemlu that's fine with us.'

Before Conville could reply, Kossemlu spoke. '*Ve elli bin dolar*.'

Conville shrugged. 'He also wants fifty thousand dollars,' he said to Heritage.

'Tell him ten thousand,' said Hamilton.

Conville turned to Kossemlu expecting to be inter-rupted. But he was not. '*On bin dolar,*' he said.

Kossemlu snorted in disgust. '*Haylr. Kirk bin dolar.*'

'He's come down to forty thousand,' said Conville.

'Not a cent more than twenty grand. Tell him that's our final offer. Go on, tell him,' commanded Heritage when he saw the hesitation in Conville.

Conville could not make out Kossemlu's expression. He wondered if Hamilton and Heritage had overplayed their hand: he could see them coming away with nothing. But then, that was not his problem. He took a deep breath. '*Son yirmi bin dolar verirm.*'

'Twenty thousand dollars,' said Kossemlu in perfect English. He pursed his lips and stroked his chin. 'Mr Conville says it is an offer I can't refuse.' He roared with amusement and clapped his hands. Hamilton and Heritage joined in.

'Is it a deal?' asked Hamilton tentatively, as the merri-ment subsided.

Kossemlu put out his hand. 'Twenty thousand dollars, thirty rifles and ammunition. Agreed.' They shook hands.

Conville withdrew from the negotiations, and while he enjoyed another helping of the delicious *mahallebi*, the three conspirators put the final touches to their plans.

IV

The driver of the yellow cab struggled with the slack fan belt, quietly cursing to himself as the sweat ran down his brow and trickled onto his nose. His passenger in the rear seat patiently whiled away the time by occasionally scanning his surroundings through a small pair of high-powered binoculars. He paid particular attention to the village of Dervish Hassan at the bottom of the hill, and when he saw the three men climb in the red car, he ordered the taxi driver to cease his labours and to continue along the Bingol road until they reached the next petrol station. Nihat Sargin had seen all he needed to see.

V

Shenay stacked the bowls to one side and swept the carpet with her hands, flattening the ridges which the visitors had kicked up. When she had finished, she collected the bowls and went to stand next to her husband at the front door.

Kossemlu was watching the red Renault climb the incline in a pall of dust. 'What did they want?' she asked him.

He put a hand on her shoulder. 'They want me to take a specialist into Russia for them.'

The woman considered this for a moment. 'What is a specialist?'

'Someone who kills for them,' replied Kossemlu. 'That's why they pay more than they should!'

ENGLAND

I

White inhaled deeply as he rolled the long cigar between thumb and forefinger and moved it slowly below his flared nostrils. 'Wonderful,' he said. 'Partagas Visible Immenso. Wonderful aroma.' He went over to the small Sheraton table, chopped a thin slice from the Cuban cigar with the gold and ivory cutter, and returned to his seat next to the Davenport which held the prize of Goodison's Mughal collection, the fourteenth century Rashid al-Din manuscripts, *History of the World*, entombed in a glass case.

'Castro has an awful lot to answer for,' drawled Homer Miller from the other side of the room. He drew carefully on his cigar, holding the smoke in his mouth for a full five seconds before allowing it to drift out again. Tiny flecks of grey ash spotted the front of his dinner jacket.

'And Guevara,' said Goodison, ensconced in a large maroon leather wing-chair between his two guests.

'Spoilt one of the best tourist resorts in the world. A lot of good people, friends of mine, lost a pile of money when Batista caved in,' said Miller. 'Now you've got to travel halfway around the world to smoke a decent cigar.'

White warmed the goblet of Cognac Delamain with his hands and smiled. 'A journey, Homer, that I am sure you look forward to every year.'

'You'd better believe it,' replied Miller. 'More so this year when I have the favourite for the Eclipse.'

'He might be favourite, Homer. But he still has to beat my mare,' said Goodison smugly.

'No, no, John. We're not going to run that one again,' said Miller. I'm not going to raise the stakes we set over dinner. I know your crafty ways too well.'

'As you wish, Homer.' Goodison turned to White. 'Perhaps you would like a share of the action, Michael?'

'Too rich for me, sir,' replied White. 'I'm completely neutral. Spectator's role only.' White was still basking in the pleasure of Goodison's invitation to the Esher estate which bordered the Sandown Park racecourse where the Eclipse Stakes, named after the stallion that ensured the survival of the Darley Arabian bloodline, was run on the first Saturday in July. Such invitations to Goodison's Sandown weekend were the most sought after in racing circles. All-male affairs, except at bedtime when Hamilton's specially selected young women made themselves available in the guests' rooms. White was a little disappointed on this, his third invitation in five years: Miller was the only other guest, and he had seen no sign of Hamilton since his arrival.

'A very wise decision, Mike,' said Miller. 'When it comes to horses and bloodlines, John will have you down to your undies before you can say Uncle Sam.'

'Don't worry, Homer, Alex Hamilton has briefed me fully on the subject,' said White. 'That is why I'm only a spectator. And speaking of Alex,' he added, 'is he not down for the weekend?'

'Hmm,' murmured Goodison, seemingly far away, his eyes staring at the wall. 'Alex has been a disappointment to me of late, Michael. A very big disappointment. He seems to have lost his touch, his powers of concentration, as it were.'

White was crestfallen. The prospect of a weekend with some of Hamilton's compliant young ladies had been on his mind since he had first been notified of the invitation, and his body had been geared up, as had his imagination, to the pleasures in which he knew he could indulge at whim. 'I'm sorry to hear that,' he said with obvious disappointment.

'Yes,' continued Goodison. 'Even the simple task of providing suitable companions for the weekend is apparently beyond Alex these days.' He shook his head and looked to White, who in turn shook his head. 'A big disappointment.'

The three men sat in silence for a few moments, contemplating their drinks, until they were interrupted by the presence of Dominic, Goodison's butler. 'Excuse me, sir,' he intoned. 'Your other guests have arrived.'

'Thank you, Dominic,' said Goodison, without turning round. 'Put them in the study will you.'

'Very good, sir,' and he left the room as silently as he'd entered.

Goodison waited a few moments before offering an explanation, paying particular attention to Sir Michael White and his quizzical expression. 'I couldn't let my guests down after all,' he said. 'The weekend would not have been the same. Alex may have let us down. But I wasn't going to let my friends down.' He smiled at White and then at Miller.

'I didn't think for a moment you would, John,' said Miller and guffawed loudly.

'So I arranged for the young ladies myself,' said Goodison. 'Six of them.'

'That was, er . . .' began White.

'Think nothing of it, Michael,' cut in Goodison. 'And for his sins, Alex is to stay out in Turkey and see our little project through to its conclusion. And that reminds me. Thank you again for young Conville's assistance out there.'

'That's perfectly all right, sir,' said White. 'Any time I can be of assistance, you only have to ask.'

'Well,' said Homer Miller. 'I don't know about you two, but . . .'

Goodison waved him back to his seat. 'Allow the young ladies time to remove their coats and freshen up,' said Goodison. 'There's no rush. After all I am expecting you to stay through until Monday morning.' He glanced quickly at his two guests for confirmation. 'That's settled, then. We'll have a nice long weekend together.'

White was all smiles. Miller stood up and wandered off to refill his brandy glass. Goodison beckoned to White to sit a little closer. 'There is a tiny problem, Michael, that you could help me with,' he said in a low voice. 'We'll discuss it tomorrow in greater detail.'

'Anything at all to be of help,' replied White.

'That reporter I mentioned to you some time ago. What was his name now . . .?'

'Garner, I believe.'

'Everything at your fingertips, Michael,' said Goodison, and White's face took on a shrewd and knowing expression. 'He's getting to be very troublesome. And I don't really trust Mackenzie.'

'Understandable,' confided White.

'I knew you'd understand,' said Goodison. 'And Alex has been a disappointment of late. There's no one else I can trust.'

'Leave it to me, sir. I have just the men who can help.'

II

Garner stopped typing as Tariq came into the office. Both men glanced quickly across to Veronica who was busily clacking away on a small Olivetti portable. Tariq nodded slowly at Garner when he saw the questioning frown on his face.

Tariq shrugged and was about to leave again when Veronica spoke. 'Still there, is it?' she asked without looking up from her work. She pulled out the sheet of typescript, placed it with the others, and nimbly inserted a fresh piece of A4 into the machine. 'The blue van I mean.'

'Blue van?' said Garner and stood up.

'Yes, the blue van,' reiterated Veronica. 'A Ford Transit. It's been parked outside most of the evening.

Tariq grinned sheepishly and left the room. Garner worried at a thumbnail with his teeth. 'I didn't think you'd . . .'

'Spotted it?' finished Veronica. 'And stop biting your nails.' She too stood up, pulling her cardigan from the back of her chair and slipping it on over her shoulders. 'Tariq's spent an awful lot of time in the loo over the past four hours.' She reached out and pulled Garner's hand away from his face. 'Stop it,' she chided him, and led him out of the office and along the corridor to the toilet where Tariq was stationed, balancing on the rim of the bowl and peering out of the small window above.

'I wondered why there were footmarks on the bowl,' she said. 'So I climbed up and took a peek. And there was the blue van.'

'It could be just parked there,' said Garner without any enthusiasm for his own suggestion. 'There mightn't be anyone inside.'

'But there are,' said Veronica in her school mistress voice. 'They parked too near the street lamp for a start. And in the floor at the rear of the van is a hole through which the occupants relieve themselves while they are on watch. You can see where the urine has drained away from the van.'

'That's right,' said Tariq. 'Two trails.'

'Which means there's at least two people in the van,' said Veronica. 'And that they've been there for some time.'

'Or one man with a very weak bladder,' said Garner, trying to make light of the situation. He clambered up next to Tariq, leaning against him, and looked out. 'Tariq saw it pull up just as we arrived this evening,' admitted Garner.

'And you didn't want to worry the little lady, did you?' said Veronica sarcastically. 'And all night you've been nodding secretly at one another and frowning. It's a wonder your heads didn't fall off.' She turned and marched off down the corridor.

212

'Veronica,' shouted Garner as he jumped down. He chased her back into the office. Veronica was back in her seat, typing again. 'I didn't want to worry you unnecessarily,' he said, standing over her. 'It could have been a false alarm.'

'After Cormac Duffy's death. After Christian's?' She eyed him angrily. 'Look, we're in this together. Remember? And I'm a big girl, you know. I can look after myself, too.'

'I know you can. But that's not why I didn't tell you,' said Garner with little conviction.

'Then why?' She got to her feet and pushed him back. 'I know these people and how dangerous they can be. I went into this with eyes open wide. And I don't need any overly protective man doing a heroic, protect-the-lady-at-all-costs act which, as far as I can see, always ends up with someone getting hurt. Understand?' She prodded his chest. 'I want and I need to know everything. Understand? We're in this together, we're a team. And I'll not have you holding out on me.' Her face was fixed in anger.

Tariq coughed politely from the door. When he spoke he did so directly to Veronica. 'There could be three in the van. A third urine trail.' Then he smiled broadly, showing his discoloured, disfigured teeth. 'Or one of the two might have a weak bladder.'

'Perhaps,' said Veronica, and her face softened. 'The thing is who are they, and what are they after?'

'Or, who are they after?' said Garner. 'You or me?' he added, pleased to see that Veronica's anger had evaporated, yet worried about the implication of the van outside.

'Both of us,' she said with a shudder.

'Are you alright?' asked Garner, and he put his arms around her and pulled her in close to him. 'Don't worry. They're just snooping. Probably trying to put us on edge.'

'Do you think it's Police?' asked Tariq.

Garner shook his head. 'No. But I've a good idea who they are. Probably D15.' He rubbed Veronica's back as he felt her shiver. 'It is getting a bit chilly up here. I think it's time to go.'

'It's after two,' said Tariq. 'Everything's more or less ready to print. No point in staying.'

'Phone a taxi then,' said Garner.

'Wait a minute,' said Veronica and pushed back from Garner. 'We'll walk.'

'What?' said Garner, 'Are you crazy?'

Veronica slipped her arms into the sleeves of her cardigan. Slowly she buttoned it up, taking time to compose herself. She was frightened but she was not going to show it, either in her manner or in her voice, which had to be confident if she was to succeed. She had made up her mind that she was not going to be mollycoddled by Garner, that she was just as entitled as he was to have a point of view, to put forward suggestions, to demand her own way. She was not going to tolerate any macho, overly protective stances from him and she would ensure that by overruling his suggestion of a taxi. They would walk. 'Look, they've probably followed us here from the flat. They're here to keep an eye on us. So let's see exactly what they're up to, see if they follow us when we walk. We can pick up a taxi later.'

'Are you sure?' asked Garner. 'A few moments ago you seemed frightened. And now you . . .?'

'I'm okay,' said Veronica, as she collected her bag from the desk. 'Not frightened, just concerned that we should be the focus of attention for the mob outside, D15, or whoever. I suppose it was inevitable that they'd sit on our tails sometime.

'And you want to walk?' asked Garner. 'You sure?'

'It'll inconvenience them, having to follow us that way. I don't think they'll do anything. They're just keeping an eye on us.'

Tariq began to turn off lights as Garner, frowning to himself, put on his jacket and switched off his desk lamp. He had a fair idea of what she was up to. She was making him pay for not confiding in her over the blue van. Silently he cursed himself. Had he suggested walking she would have argued in favour of a taxi, just to make her point. He should have remembered from their earlier days how perverse she could be; if he said white, she would say black. It was his own fault. He prayed that his own stupidity in not recognising her mood was not going to lead them into trouble.

'Come on,' said Veronica in the doorway. The only light now came from the bare bulb above the stairwell, and she now moved along the darkened corridor close to the wall with its peeling paper and pot-holed skirting. She paused at the top of the stairs to allow the two men to catch up with her. 'Which way do you go home, Tariq?'

'Out the door, then right and . . .'

'Then we'll go left,' said Veronica bossily and led the way downstairs.

Tariq opened the front door and allowed Garner and Veronica to pass through. He turned off the last light before slamming the door shut behind them. The three of them stood on the pavement. On the opposite side of the road, ten yards away on the right, stood the Ford Transit van. It was half bathed in the yellow lamplight, motionless and menacing like a predatory insect frozen to the landscape waiting for unsuspecting prey.

'Off you go, Tariq,' said Garner and patted him on the arm. 'I'll see you this evening.' Tariq nodded once, then twice, and set off, his long, thin legs taking him past the van in a couple of seconds. Nothing stirred within the vehicle.

'Come on,' he said to Veronica. They turned left and walked away from the van, linking arms, Garner matching his pace to hers, their footsteps echoing on the pavement. As they reached the corner they heard the sputtered cough of an engine coming to life. They felt rather than saw the sudden surge of light as the van's headlights came on. Neither of them looked round. But the hairs on the back of Garner's neck stood on end.

The van crept forward, slowly at first, then quickly began gathering speed as the driver raced through the gears. Garner's heart began to beat rapidly as he realised what was about to happen. He pulled Veronica round the corner. 'Run,' he screamed.

He was ahead of her by a yard, dragging her forward, faster, by the hand. 'Run. For Christ's sake.' Veronica squealed as she staggered under Garner's sudden burst, but she maintained her balance and tried to catch him, pounding her feet into the pavement as she, too, suddenly realised what was going on.

The scream of brakes and the whine of a decelerating engine filled the night and Garner glanced quickly over his shoulder to see the van lurching round the corner, catching them both in the glare of its lights. Gears crashed again as the driver raced towards the running

216

couple. The van mounted the pavement directly behind them, and Garner let out an involuntary whimper.

The post box saved them. Set back from the kerb by a couple of feet, it enabled Garner and Veronica to flee past it, but stopped the van which was too wide to pass through the gap between the box and the gable end of a house.

The van driver swung hard to avoid the obstacle, braked, then continued to accelerate, assuming that Garner and Veronica would continue to run straight ahead. But as they passed the post box, Veronica saw the darkened mouth of an alleyway and she tugged at Garner's arm, ducking into the void. Garner sidestepped nimbly and followed her down the alley.

Their feet struck cobblestones. Behind them the van screeched in protest in a turning loop and came after them again. It paused at the mouth of the alley as if gathering strength for a final effort, savouring the knowledge that the victims were finally trapped.

Garner again looked over his shoulder as he ran and was blinded by the headlights as they moved towards him. He knew then that it had been a mistake to enter the narrow alleyway: there was no room in which to avoid the charging van. He clasped Veronica's hand tightly, urging her on, trying desperately to increase his pace. Ahead he could see the faint outline of the exit from the alley. It was their only hope. He prayed they were going to make it.

'Nearly there,' gasped Veronica, but Garner sensed they would never get out of the alleyway alive.

The silhouette of a man suddenly appeared at the head of the alley. Garner choked back a cry of anguish as Veronica screamed. The figure seemed to raise something to its shoulder. A flash of light and a loud bang emanated from the figure, quickly followed by the screech of the van's brakes. Another shot, then another, and the headlights died quickly. The side of the van struck one wall, then another, as it bounced and tried to veer away out of control in response to the sudden application of the brakes. Garner and Veronica kept running as the silhouette disappeared from view.

They came out of the alley and onto the street. Garner pulled to the right, Veronica to the left. The van was stationary behind them. 'This way,' ordered a voice. It passed through Garner's mind that he knew the voice. He stopped and looked around, bringing Veronica to a halt at the same time. 'Here,' beckoned the voice.

A car moved towards them, it's lights out. 'Come on Garner,' said the voice as Garner began to back away. 'Get in now before those goons start after you again.' The car drew level with them and the rear door opened.

Voices came from the direction of the van. 'Open that fucking back door before I bleed to fucking death,' roared a hysterical voice.

Garner pushed Veronica into the back seat of the car, which accelerated away before his backside hit the seat and before he could pull the door closed.

III

Veronica was slumped sobbing against him in the back of the car. 'So why were you there?' asked Garner, trying to keep his voice calm against the violent pounding in his chest.

218

Arthur Piechler sat in the passenger seat. He was dressed all in black except for a plaid cap which was a green and brown check. 'I was coming over to see you last night, to talk about Duffy's death. To warn you, really, that you and Duffy seemed to have struck a sensitive spot. I saw you leave the flat and the blue van follow you.'

'So you followed them?' said Garner. He took a deep breath.

'That's right. And when I saw you were in for the night I called up reinforcements.'

'Who did the shooting?' asked Garner.

'I did,' said Piechler. 'Take the Epsom Road,' he added to the driver.

Veronica sat upright. 'Where are we going?' Tears glistened on her cheeks and her whole body quivered.

'To a safe house,' said Piechler.

'Hang on. Hang on,' said Garner. 'Safe house?' He sat forward. Piechler nodded. Garner ran his hand through his hair. 'Look, I don't know what's going on here. What . . .?'

'You've upset someone,' said Piechler quietly. 'That someone sent those men to kill you. Just as that someone sent other men to kill Duffy. That's why you need a safe house.'

'But the shooting. Someone might be dead.' Garner looked up suddenly and grabbed Piechler's arm which hung over the back of the seat. 'You told me you were an investigator for that Centre. What was its name?'

'I am an investigator,' replied Piechler.

'And you shoot people?' said Garner. 'Who were they, anyway, those men in the van?' Garner's voice betrayed more than a hint of hysteria. Veronica pulled him back into his seat and wrapped her arms around him.

Piechler leaned over into the rear. 'My work sometimes puts me up against some pretty unsavoury characters. It's not all searching files and archives. Sometimes I meet the men I'm pursuing and I am only alive today because my employers insist that all investigators know how, and are trained, to defend themselves. Okay?

'Okay,' shouted Veronica. 'That's okay by me. I'd sooner have dead men in a van than me dead in an alleyway.'

'As for who the men in the van were,' continued Piechler. 'I suspect they were D15 men, possibly D16.'

'You must be kidding,' protested Veronica.

Piechler shook his head. 'Oh you won't find them on the books as employees. But they work for D15 or D16 just the same. A special bunch of toughs who were called upon from time to time to do dirty work for the service.'

'You can't be sure,' said Garner weakly. But he knew that Piechler was close to the truth.

'Pretty sure,' answered Piechler. 'Four-wheel drive on the van, short-wave radio and bullet-proof windscreen. My first shot only starred it. Vans like that you don't find among the ordinary criminal classes.' He paused and looked at his two assengers. Veronica's eyes were heavy with sleep and her face was lined with worry and fright. Garner sat slumped in the corner, exhaustion and relief written all over him. 'So you can see,' added Piechler, 'why you need a safe house. Someone wants you dead.'

RUSSIA

I

He could hear Chebrikov's voice as if it were there in the distance, like an echo which resounded in his ears. But he paid no attention to it. It was something the KGB chairman had said earlier, something about war, about fighting in the streets, which had flashed through the pages of his memory and had transported him back in time to a summer, thirty-seven years ago, when he had been a chubby, red-faced schoolboy in the village of Privolnoye in the North Caucasus region. On a sweltering Saturday night he had gone to bed as a child and had awoken a man in a different world.

For in the early hours of Sunday morning, along a fifteen hundred kilometres front, from the Baltic to the Black Sea, three million Germans and their allies had marched, ridden and flown into the heart of Mother Russia to exact a terrible toll upon her people. A hurricane of pitiless cruelty and butchery, unsurpassed in the history of mankind, descended across Russia and the vast green fields of Stavropool, images of which were branded forever upon his mind.

War. Countless millions had perished horribly. War. It

was not the politicians and bureaucrats who suffered at times of war. It was the people, the ordinary people. It was they who had to make all the sacrifices. He had seen it all, and he did not want to see it again.

He had bypassed the Party machine in his own country and had appealed directly to the people. He had repeated this approach to the people in the West and he had been overwhelmed by the reactions he had been given. Bypass the power structures, he had told himself. Go directly to the people, to the people who would have to bear the brunt of the mistakes the politicians made.

But now there was talk of war within the boundaries of Mother Russia. Had the pace of his own reforms been too fast? Had he offered too much too soon to a people who had been prisoners within their own country? National and ethnic violence was flaring across the country. Ancient rivalries and envy were being played out on the streets of major cities and the situation was explosive. He understood what lay behind the troubles, the impatience of a nation finally released from the grip of tyranny. But he also knew that certain factions within Russia were content to see, and openly encouraged, the dissent and the nationalistic rivalries. The Pamyat was to the fore right across Russia in many disguises. And he knew also that the cautious reception his reforms had been given by governments in the West were also counterbalanced by certain elements who wished him to fail, and that those same elements were active in encouraging and fermenting unrest throughout Russia. The conservatives in the West could not afford to allow the Russian bear to pull in its claws and to take out its teeth. Without the Russian bear, armed and hostile, the western industrialised nations would be on the verge of bankruptcy.

'. . . more fighting in the streets,' said the KGB chief.

Chebrikov's words broke the premier's dreams. 'I'm sorry, Viktor. What were you saying?'

'You must let me send in my people to arrest the troublemakers. The local militias cannot control the situation and there will be more fighting in the streets. The conservatives, the hawks, the critics, are blaming your programme of glasnost for all the troubles.'

'I know they are, Viktor. But if I am too heavy-handed with the Armenians and Azerbaijanis, glasnost and perestroika will be ridiculed as a sham. No, Viktor. I have informed the leaders that I will personally intervene and listen to the problems of the Armenians and Azerbaijanis later this month after the Special Party Congress. The streets will be quiet from now on.'

'But there are skirmishes every day now,' protested Chebrikov.

'But it is not as serious as you make out, Viktor. You are a victim of your own intelligence reports. I will not have the Army or your special troops complicating matters further. The unrest will subside in the next day or two. And then I will talk with the leaders again. I am scheduled to visit Yerevan to pay homage at the monument in Tsitsernakebard Park. The Armenians will appreciate that. It is a long-standing engagment.'

'And what about the Azerbaijanis?'

'They have been invited too. And they will come. The essence of glasnost is talk. We will settle matters then, Viktor. There is no room for force.'

'As you wish, Mikhail.'

'Thirty years ago, Comrade Krushchev came to power. He was, like me, an agricultural specialist. He attempted

223

a very delicate balancing act between the demands of agriculture, the military, consumer interests and the Stalinists. He failed because the Cold War was at its height and he could not keep his feet on the narrow line he had drawn between all the competing interests. We have exactly the same problems as Comrade Krushchev but without the added burden of the Cold War. So we have been able to cut back on the nuclear arms build-up. We can now concentrate all our efforts on the remainder of the balancing act. We have the people with us. But we will lose them if we meet legitimate protest with force.' The Premier stood and went across to the window. It was a grey, overcast day in Moscow and it matched his subdued mood. 'Tell me, Viktor. What is the latest on Churbanov and his scheming with the conservatives in the West?'

'I cannot tell you any more than I told you last week. He is up to something. And we know the people he is involved with. But so far we do not know exactly what it is they are planning. But we are still monitoring the situation very closely. We are using our illegals so we have to tread very carefully.'

The Premier considered for a moment. 'We have reached a very critical point in the programme of glasnost and perestroika. We need all our wits about us.' He turned to face the KGB chief. He had to give him something before he decided to take matters into his own hands, in secret. 'We cannot afford diversions. Perhaps you had better send someone for Comrade Churbanov.'

II

Yuri Churbanov laughed heartily to himself. He was drunk, and the sight of the Premier's earnest face on television was too much for him. 'Carry on, Mikhail,' he roared loudly. 'Carry on while you can.' He swilled back the last of the *ryabinovka*, ashberry flavoured vodka, and rummaged about his feet for the bottle. He found it but it was empty. 'Nina,' he shouted. 'Another bottle, *ma petite*.'

He slumped in the corner of the settee, looking down the length of his chest and fat stomach, squinting at the images on the screen, and began to giggle. 'Yerevan is a lovely old city,' he said. 'The Armenians take great pride in it. They will love you when you get there.' And his naked flesh wobbled like a jelly on a plate.

Nina came into the room carrying an open bottle of chilled vodka. She too was naked and she knelt next to Churbanov on the settee. Holding his hand steady, she poured him a liberal measure of the fiery drink before depositing the bottle on the floor.

'Look at him. The pig,' he told her, and raised his glass in a toast. Nina put an arm round his neck and began to nibble his ear. 'Ah,' he moaned. She kissed his cheek. 'Soon, Nina, this will all be over.' Her free hand roamed over his abdomen. 'Stop,' he suddenly commanded. 'Stand up.'

Nina pushed herself up and stood in front of him. She was medium height, very thin, and her breasts were tiny, the size of a pair of young apples. Her auburn hair was bunched at the back and her eyes had been made up to accentuate their oval shape. 'Here?' she asked, standing

225

provocatively with her legs apart and her arms on her hips. 'Like this?'

Churbanov stared at her, a dryness in his throat preventing a reply. He examined her body and once again marvelled at his mistress of seven years since he had picked her out from a Bolshoi training class. From time to time she had brought some of her young friends to his home to enjoy the privileges he could dispense, but of late the supply had dried up as his power and influence had waned. But he was sure that in a few weeks' time, once ASH was implemented, he would regain his former glory and ensure that the present director of the Bolshoi did not ever again interfere with Nina's friendships in the ballet company.

His penis stiffened and he opened his legs. 'Kneel,' he ordered.

She smiled at him and slowly inserted a thumb into the corner of her mouth as her other hand moved down to her own pubic region. 'And what will you do for me?' she whispered huskily.

Suddenly there came the sound of running feet from outside on the stairs. Nina apparently did not hear it for she dropped to her knees and grabbed hold of his shaft. Churbanov struggled to sit upright. He felt her hot wetness as her lips caressed him. The door shook and voices were raised above the din of the pounding. Churbanov could not gain his balance and his voice failed him. Nina took him full in the mouth, oblivious to her master's panic, and she gripped him firmly with lips and teeth.

The door burst open and his three shadows fell into the hallway, one of them propelled so forcefully that he tumbled into the room as Churbanov, tears in his eyes, swung at Nina with all his might, knocking her sideways away from him, as he tried desperately to hide his nakedness from the arresting officers.

ENGLAND

I

Veronica awoke in slow motion. She knew that she was going to waken and so her dream obligingly began to subside and her consciousness slowly took command, gently and drowsily prompting and coaxing her to open her eyes.

The heavy curtains on the windows were drawn and there was no clock on the bedside table. But she guessed that it was late morning for she had fallen asleep in the knowledge that she was weary and exhausted and that her mental alarm clock would not respond until at least six hours had elapsed. She turned on her back and her left side came into contact with Garner. His mouth was partially opened and his breathing was subdued. She moved away from him so that their bodies did not touch but then slipped her hand under the bedclothes and rested it on his thigh.

Her mind was doubly troubled and agitated and for the first time for several years she felt in need of help. Garner: she had fallen for him all over again. She knew why she had sought him out to ask for his assistance when there were others in London who would have, and could have, provided her with the same, if not better, back up. That she had had a persistent and nagging feeling all the time she was in America that there were still matters unresolved between them could be used as an explanation of why she had searched him out; but it could not explain why she was in love with him again.

She realised that she would have to admit to herself that a latent spark of love and affection, which she had always denied existed, had, nevertheless, existed within, and that it had burst forth from the moment she had first seen him in the flat, despite her efforts to smother it with rebukes. He was the old Garner again, the funny cynic, the plodder, the man who started and who never stopped until he was finished. The *wilderness* years were gone. And she now surmised that it was a two-way process, her falling for him, for her contribution was that she was so much at ease with herself and had some direction to her life which she had not had before and which Garner had constantly sought for her. In the past she had seen this as interference, and later criticism of herself, when in truth her happiness was of great importance to him. He had simply wanted her to do what she wanted to do, to be involved, to shoulder some responsibility, but she had never been able to make up her mind. And she had adopted feminism not as a belief but as a weapon against him. This had wounded him deeply. He had been asking for her help, but she had been unable to recognise his plea.

While in America she had kept up a reasonable corres- pondence with Gerda de Roos and she was sure that this had helped her come to terms with herself. European women had a much more positive and open approach to female matters, and under Gerda's guidance she had now come to accept that the battle of the sexes was simply a battle between people.

She tried to keep her thoughts on herself and Garner but the reality of their present predicament, the second part of her troubles, would not be denied. They intruded into her mind, demanding her attention. What had she got herself and Garner into? From where was the danger coming? From Hamilton and Heritage and her Contragate investigation? Or from Garner's meeting with Piechler and his pursuit of Goodison? Perhaps they were all connected as Dickson had suggested when they had met up in Carolina. But what had prompted the violent response, hers or Garner's investigation? At what point had they, either as individuals, or as a team, crossed the line beyond which death was the response to their inquiries?

Veronica began to recall the American side of her probings and she placed them in her mind next to all that she had learnt from Garner. If they were connected then she had, according to her understanding, a global conspiracy. But a conspiracy to do what? There was something missing, the end product. And were they so near to finding out what the end product was that the murderous attack was the result?

The more she thought about it the more she became confused. And frightened. Not that she needed any assistance in that particular department. She smiled to herself. 'Under this calm exterior is a blob of jelly, a terrified blob of jelly,' she said to the ceiling.

Then the terrifying events of the previous night impinged upon her consciousness. She couldn't avoid them. 'Stupid bitch,' she told herself. She had almost killed both of them with her stubbornness and her determination to get her own way. Garner had refused to hear her apology.

'Don't worry about it,' he had told her. 'Forget it.' But her mistake in insisting on walking instead of the safety of a taxi was not something she would forget. That was a mistake a man would not have made under the circumstances. She had been trying to make a point, while Garner had been thinking of their safety, of not taking unnecessary risks. It wasn't the time or the place for trying to assert herself; she should have looked at the facts rather than the immediate issue. But it was a valuable lesson, and thank God she was alive to prosper from it.

Garner snorted and began to smack his lips together. She turned on her side and began to caress his thigh. She loved him, she didn't know why, but she was not going to try and find out. Too much soul-searching destroyed the soul.

Garner screwed his eyes together and yawned. As he closed his mouth she kissed him.

II

'What are you doing?' he asked.

'Making brunch. I thought we would have it out on the patio.' She opened the oven, lifted the pan from the gas ring and forked the bacon rashers on to a plate in the oven. 'Eggs, bacon, mushrooms and tomatoes. And I'm only doing it because I'm the better cook. Besides, I'd starve to death if I had to wait for you to get up and cook me something.'

'Great,' he said distractedly. It was the smell of the frying bacon which had eventually dragged him from the bed. Veronica had showered and dressed after their love-making but he had dozed off again. 'Any sign of Piechler?'

She cracked two eggs into the frying pan. 'No. We're all alone here. I've had a scout round. No message, nothing.' As the eggs were frying she took down a couple of plates from the cupboard above her head, placed them in the sink for a moment, splashed hot water over them, and then put them in the oven after dabbing them dry on a towel. 'What do you make of Piechler after last night?'

Garner, hands in the pockets of his dressing gown, shrugged his shoulders. 'I just don't know,' he said. He wandered round the kitchen, opening doors. He inspected the back yard which ran on to the garden, examined the cool pantry and the laundry room. 'What's this?' he asked, as one door, next to the laundry room, failed to open. 'It won't open.'

'Don't know,' replied Veronica. 'I think it must lead down to the cellar. I had to look for a key but couldn't find one.'

Garner shrugged his shoulders again and continued his tour of the kitchen which was large and square, and in the centre of which stood an antique pine kitchen table covered with an oil cloth. He lifted the cloth and ran his fingers over the smooth scrubbed ridges in the wood. 'I've got to phone Nihat sometime today.' He wandered off to the far end of the room. 'That's nice,' he said, pointing at the pitch pine Welsh Dresser.

'For goodness sake, Peter. Why don't you make your phone call. Or set the table on the patio. Do something instead of your prowling act.' She knew from past experience that he was nervous, worried, and that he had to be directed and pushed to overcome it. 'Go on. Set the table.'

'I think I'll have a quick shave,' he said, as he stroked his chin. He kissed her on the cheek as he made his exit.

'Make it very quick. Yours is ready.' As she put the finishing touches to the breakfast, the second, sound-activated tape recorder in the cellar behind the locked door once again picked up activity in the *en suite* bathroom.

TURKEY

I

It was early evening and they sat in the alcove at the far end of the restaurant where they could watch the entrance and the coming and going of their fellow diners – mainly well-to-do Turks with their secretaries and mistresses – and the horde of waiters who far outnumbered the patrons of Chef-le Belge.

'I can't finish this,' complained Hamilton. 'My stomach won't take it.' He dropped his hands below the table and held his stomach, leaving the veal untouched.

'Bread and water and some Norit tablets,' said Heritage as he forked a thin slice of veal into his mouth. 'I warned you about the sis kebab yesterday. Too hot for pork this time of the year.'

Hamilton grunted, farted, and reached for his Perrier water. 'God,' he said.

Heritage sniffed. 'That wasn't very ozone-friendly, Alex.' He sipped his wine. 'You should try this,' he added. 'Villa Doluca. Very good. Try a glass with some Perrier.'

Hamilton shook his head. 'No thanks. Anyway, go on with what you were saying. Do you really believe all that shit Lewis and Bryant were telling us the other day?'

Heritage swallowed a mouthful of zuchini. 'Not really,' he replied. 'But a lot of people do. Blackmore and Becksmith do. They're firm believers in the American way of life of the southern states. It's a growth industry down there and you ignore it at your own peril.'

'And what was all this *Exterminans* nonsense?'

'Nonsense to you, Alex. But not to them. Certainly not to Lewis and Bryant. You see Bryant's father named him Apollyon, which is Greek. The Hebrew equivalent is Abaddon and the Latin translation is *Exterminans*. Our Mr Bryant is the exterminating angel.'

'God almighty,' exclaimed Hamilton. 'Bryant's father really had his son's life mapped out for him, didn't he?'

Heritage raised his eyebrows. 'Sounds like it.' He gave up on his dinner and pushed his plate to the centre of the table. Two waiters raced up and without a word scooped up the plates and serving dishes. 'I don't want anything else,' he said as the Maitre, head cocked to one side, ready for the barrage of complaints, approached cautiously.

'Me neither,' said Hamilton, and waved away the man, much to his relief.

'The first verse of Revelation 9 refers to five angels,' continued Heritage. *Exterminans* is the leader and he has the key to the bottomless pit where the other four live. Now *Exterminans* sends out his minions to slaughter one third of mankind.' He poured himself another glass of wine. 'Sure you won't join me?' Hamilton shook his head. 'Those that are to be slaughtered will be those who have the seal, or mark, of Cain on their foreheads.'

'And they believe this?'

'The Bible is a living, modern book to these people,' said Heritage. 'Lewis and his fellow believers take it quite literally. When the Russian Premier came to power, men like Lewis couldn't believe their eyes. The Premier wore the mark of Cain on his forehead. The Bible had foretold it all.'

'And the Russian people are the followers of Cain and are about to be slaughtered?'

'Precisely. A few years ago when the President referred to Russia as the Evil Empire, that wasn't political rhetoric talking. That was pure religious fundamentalism in full spate, inspired by the likes of Lewis and his co-religionists.'

'Unbelievable,' said Hamilton. He had to smile despite the serious look on his partner's face.

'You may well laugh, Alex. But I was brought up on this kind of stuff at Sunday School and I know how deeply engrained it becomes. Lewis and Bryant are firmly convinced that they are engaged upon a divine crusade, that they are the chosen servants of the Lord.' Heritage's features betrayed a smile. 'I'm not joking, Alex. And when you put Bryant next to Lewis with a middle name of *Exterminans*, then you have all the pieces they need for their crusade.'

'What did Lewis first say when you approached him? He's, er, what would you say, er, Bryant's guardian?'

'Yes, guardian. When I first talked to them about this, Lewis told me he had been expecting me. Even when I told him Bryant would only be a back-up, Lewis said it was ordained that Bryant would do the job.'

'So when you came back and said Stefano was out and Bryant was in he must have done cartwheels.'

'He dropped to his knees and prayed. No kidding. It was just another confirmation that the task was pre-ordained, that it had the Lord's approval. The final showdown between the good and evil empires is about to take place, according to Lewis, and Bryant, the exterminating angel, is going to light the fuse.'

'Well I don't care about motives,' said Hamilton. 'Just so long as Bryant remembers that it's us and not the Almighty giving the orders, then we should be okay. I want him in and out. And he can keep the religious mumbo-jumbo to himself.'

'He'll do the business, Alex. Don't worry about that,' replied Heritage. 'There are a lot of motives driving ASH forward. Some of them coincide and overlap, others are as different as shit from sugar. But the job will get done.' He beckoned the waiter and asked for the bill.

'Let's hope so,' said Hamilton as he got to his feet.

The waiter intercepted them as they crossed the room to the cashier's desk. Hamilton paid but didn't leave a tip. The bright evening sunshine hurt their eyes as they emerged from the gloom of the interior. Their taxi, which they had hired for the week, was parked on the opposite side of Konya Asfalti and they crossed the busy street at a trot. They had to wake the sleeping driver before they could get into the car, climbing into the rear seat and instructing the driver to take them back to the Kent Oteli.

They sat in silence as the taxi roared through the wide, concrete avenues and boulevards of central Ankara, the driver pointing out places of interest in a desultory, automatic manner as if compelled to do so by the mere presence of foreigners in the vehicle. Finally the taxi swept into Mithatpassa Caddesi and squealed to a halt outside the hotel. The driver jumped out and opened the boot, and began to unload the parcels and packages onto the pavement. Hamilton and Heritage watched as their purchases were carried inside by a pair of elderly bellhops. 'Room 203,' said Hamilton. Then he turned to the taxi driver. 'Go home,' he said in a loud voice, measuring each word carefully to ensure he was understood. 'Have something to eat. Come back here at nine o'clock.' He pointed at his watch and then the hotel. 'Okay?'

'Okay, mister,' affirmed the driver. He jumped into the taxi and drove off.

Heritage spoke and he tapped Hamilton's shoulder. 'Conville,' he said and nodded towards the hotel entrance.

Francis Conville had seen the two men arrive from his vantage point beyond the revolving doors and he came down the short flight of steps to greet them. 'I see you have been busy shopping for your trip into the wilds. We'll take a walk up the street if you don't mind,' he said.

'I mind,' said Hamilton. 'I've got some pressing business inside.' And with that he dashed up the stairs and made for the elevator.

'Attaturk's revenge,' said Heritage. Both men followed Hamilton inside.

II

Heritage paid off the bellhops after they had stored the parcels in the closet, and then he and Conville sat on the bed drinking Coca Cola while they waited for Hamilton. He came out of the toilet five minutes later looking pale and shaky.

'Lie down on the bed,' said Conville, getting to his feet. Heritage followed suit, allowing Hamilton to stretch full length.

'I'll be okay in the morning. I took some Norit tablets,' said Hamilton, and he closed his eyes.

Heritage switched on the radio. 'Business or pleasure, Francis?'

'There's no pleasure for Francis in dealing with us, John,' said Hamilton. 'So it has to be business.'

'The KGB arrested Yuri Churbanov two days ago.' When there was no response from either man, Conville continued. 'London seemed to think it was important, that it was a matter for urgent attention.'

'We heard this morning,' said Heritage. A courier from the CIA station at Diyarbakir had brought the news at breakfast time.

'Anything else?' asked Hamilton.

'Your principal confirms that you are to accompany the expedition all the way,' replied Conville.

'I don't need reminding of that,' said Hamilton sourly.

'What about Kossemlu?' asked Heritage.

'His caravan is well on the way to Igdir. His guns have arrived so he's happy.'

'And Bryant's still due in tomorrow?' asked Hamilton.

'As far as I know. And the day after tomorrow you all meet up with Kossemlu at Diyarbakir.'

'Okay,' said Heritage. 'Anything else?'

Conville shook his head. 'Nothing more I don't think.'

'See you, Francis,' said Hamilton, opening his eyes for the first time. 'Be good.'

'Good luck,' answered Conville as he left.

'Stuck up bastard,' said Hamilton.

Heritage sat down on the edge of the bed. 'Can Churbanov hurt us?'

'He only knows the general outline. No details or specifics,' replied Hamilton. 'The KGB will be after details of his black market activities. And he knows we're close to the final stages of ASH. He'll keep his mouth closed.'

ENGLAND

Garner carried two cups of tea into the bedroom. Veronica was still asleep, sprawled across the bed on her stomach, one arm reaching into the space he had recently vacated. He put the cups down and moved her arm. 'Wake up,' he said and climbed in beside her.

'I don't want to,' she said, her speech muffled by the pillow. 'Mick Jagger has just proposed and I said yes.'

He playfully slapped her on the buttocks. 'You'd turn down a cup of my tea for Mick Jagger?' he asked.

'Now you're talking,' she said, and rolled over on her back. He bent over and kissed her on the cheek. 'Tea first,' and she pushed him away and propped herself up on her elbow. 'Egg and bacon to follow?'

He shook his head and passed her a cup. 'Piechler's just been on the phone. He'll be down about noon.'

She sipped her tea deep in thought. 'Are we doing the right thing, Pete?'

'Who knows,' he said with a sigh. 'But we have got to see this thing through to the end. There's nothing else we can do.'

'The police?'

He glanced across at her, saw the frightened look on her face, and put an arm round her shoulder. 'We've been over that before. What kind of protection could we expect from them against DI5 and whatever else Goodison could put against us?'

'Nothing I suppose.'

'Piechler's right. There's something going on, something very important, and while it is going on we're not safe.'

'But Piechler says we should get out of the country and lie low for a while,' protested Veronica.

'And what if this thing that's going on goes on for a year, maybe two. Are we supposed to lie low until then?' She finished her tea and handed him her cup, then curled her body into his. 'We've come this far. We can't give up now. Otherwise we could be running for ever. We have to find out what they are up to.'

'Did you speak to Nihat?'

'Yes, Hamilton and Heritage are still in Ankara but it looks as if they are about to move on. Nihat thinks they are moving out into the country with that Turkish contact of theirs, Kossemlu, I think he's called. Nihat has them covered in Ankara. Their driver is Nihat's man and he spent all day yesterday with them shopping for heavy clothing and boots and sleeping bags. And Nihat said he's placed a man with Kossemlu's caravan.'

Veronica sighed. 'What is going on? What are they up to?'

'Search me,' said Garner. 'But whatever it is they're up to we're going to be right behind them.'

'Are you going to tell Piechler?'

Garner shook his head. 'No. He's arranging for some passports this morning. He said we'll be out of the country tomorrow night and he wants us to make for

Paris and to contact the Documentation Bureau he works for. They'll look after us he said.'

'But we're heading for Turkey?'

'Definitely. Nihat has booked us flights from Bordeaux to Ankara with the names Piechler gave us yesterday.' He pulled her closer to him. 'Nihat's a good man. He'll take care of us. We've been behind Hamilton and Heritage this far and now we're going to find out what they're up to. After all, that's why you came to England, wasn't it?' He stared into her eyes.

'Perhaps,' she said, pulling him closer. 'But I never thought it would turn out like this.'

'Neither did I,' said Garner.

TURKEY

I

The river Tigris winked playfully in the hot morning sun as it wound its tireless, ancient way through the gorges and gullies below the black basalt walls of Diyarbakir, and beyond to the Arab borderlands and Iraq, one arm of the Fertile Crescent which has witnessed the passage of mankind since time immemorial.

Like the river, the ancient, toothless crone who sat at the upstairs window of the ramshackle coffee-house in the Genelev district of the city had seen much of life and it tribulations, but unlike the river, she had been forced by old age to retire. Now all she could do was watch as the participants in the oldest game in town continued without her. Young girls, elderly women, paraded their wares along the narrow, cobbled streets and alleyways of the Genelev, desperation prompting them to converge in droves upon any unattached male, for these were the unlucky ones who had failed to catch a partner the previous night and who would be sorely pressed to find the money for food, for themselves and their relatives, before the heat of the day closed down the district until nightfall.

A niggardly grin creased the hag's face as she looked down from her perch at the antics in the streets. She had been one of the lucky ones who had found a permanent bed after she had given up the game in exchange for some basic cleaning in the coffee-house which her nephew owned. Now she could laugh at those who had taunted her about her age when she had walked the streets, hungry, despised, an empty shell, incapable of attracting even the elderly drunks who managed to stagger her way.

Below her, on the narrow pavement where three tables and a few chairs were crammed together, sat Kossemlu and Conville, the only customers at the coffee-house, who had spent the half hour since their arrival shooing away the whores with their ever-increasing extravagant gestures. They had not spoken, nor had they ordered any coffee, the crone's nephew receiving the same treatment as the whores when he had sidled up to inquire of their preference.

A young Turk broke through a barrage of grasping prostitutes further along the street and marched towards the seated pair, a look of anger on his face, his lips still mouthing the obscenities he had inflicted upon the women. He sat next to Kossemlu and whispered something in his ear. Kossemlu nodded and turned to Conville. 'He has finished. We can go now.'

They got to their feet and walked in the direction the young Turk had arrived from, swatting at the whores as they went until they came to a neat, wooden-fronted house outside of which stood another young Turk. As he saw Kossemlu and his companion approach, he rapped on the door which was immediately opened by Bryant. He glanced outside, turned back for a moment, then stepped into the street. Just as the door closed, Conville glimpsed the form of a young girl, naked to the waist, standing in the darkened room.

The two young Turks walked on ahead and hailed a passing *faton*, a horse-drawn carriage, into which the men climbed, Conville being the last to board. '*Demir Oteli*,' he said to the craggy horseman, who responded with a wave of his whip which set the droopy mare in motion.

II

'They're here,' reported Hamilton from the hotel window. He watched them climb out of the *faton*, Conville first, looking the worst for wear after their bone-jarring trek across the city, followed by Bryant and the three Turks. They entered the lobby. 'Poor old Francis looks fucked.'

'What about Bryant? He's the one who should look fucked,' said Heritage.

'Looks fine to me,' said Hamilton. He let the blind fall back into place, and returned to the bed and put on his boots. 'I can't believe that Lenny Bryant and all that poppycock about saving fallen women.'

'I wish he'd save one for me,' replied Heritage with a grin. 'But seriously, that's what they do. They search out the women of the night and try and teach them the error of their ways. The Reverend Lewis's favourite pastime.'

'I'll bet. And it's rubbed off on his protégé, eh?'

'Seems like it.'

Conville led the way into the hotel room. 'Good morning, gentlemen,' he said.

'Fuck you Francis,' replied Hamilton, tying his laces.

246

'Come off it, Alex,' said Heritage. 'We've got company.'

Kossemlu's black eyes flared in anger for a fraction of a second. He glanced quickly from Conville to Hamilton and then to Heritage as the anger subsided. 'We will go now?'

'Yes, indeed,' said Heritage. He picked up his body-warmer and put it on.

Conville interrupted the general exodus to the door. 'Could I have a word with these three gentlemen, Ramazan? It won't take a minute.'

Kossemlu nodded and went outside with his two bodyguards, closing the door behind him.

'What is it, Francis?' asked Heritage.

'Make it fast,' said Hamilton as he donned a lightweight combat jacket.

'Okay,' said Conville. 'London reports that the journalist, Garner, and the woman, who turns out to be his wife, have managed to elude their pursuers.'

Hamilton shrugged his shoulders. 'So what?'

'The report states, among other things, that they have been dogging your tracks for some time now,' continued Conville. 'And that there is a distinct possibility they may have followed you here.'

'No chance,' protested Hamilton.

'Are you sure, Alex?'

Before Hamilton could reply Conville spoke. 'London believes they followed you to Carolina.'

'When engaged in the Lord's work, always expect the worst,' said Bryant. He stood with his eyes closed and his hands joined as if in prayer, rocking back and forth on his heels. 'The devil makes work for idle hands, and none more idle than those of a journalist.'

247

Hamilton and Heritage exchanged knowing glances. 'Amen,' they said in unison.

'As a precautionary measure, I have been advised to guard your backs,' said Conville. 'And I have a team of twelve men, some of them loaned to me by Ramazan, deployed in the area.'

'Photographs?' asked Heritage.

'They arrived this morning and are being distributed now,' said Conville.

'Airport, bus depots and the like all covered?' said Hamilton.

'Yes,' said Conville. 'And a few other places besides.'

Hamilton took a deep breath. 'Okay, Francis, that's good.' It was the nearest thing to an apology that Hamilton could muster and Conville nodded his appreciation. 'But if those two turn up, Garner and the girl, I don't want any messing about. Understand?'

'I understand,' said Conville reluctantly.

'Make them disappear like they never existed,' added Heritage.

Conville nodded his head several times in confirmation. 'Understood.'

Bryant interrupted the pause that followed. 'An hour to catch the flight, gents,' he announced, checking his watch. 'We shouldn't really keep Mr Kossemlu waiting.'

III

'Half an hour,' said Nihat between mouthfuls of cake which the stewardess had doled out as if she had been

248

dealing playing cards to her charges. He sipped some water. 'Then we hit the road.'

Veronica, sandwiched between Nihat and Garner and clutching a glass of lemonade, merely nodded, and Garner could see sleep waiting to take over in her eyes. He had refused the in-flight cuisine, and for the first time in some months he longed for a cigarette and a stiff drink.

He pushed his seat back further, stretched his legs and closed his eyes, allowing the steady murmuring of the Fokker to lull him into a half-sleep. His toes tingled and his legs ached slightly as the tension within him began to subside and the blood reached parts which seemed to have been restricted over the past few days.

Piechler had obtained, and delivered, the new passports as promised, and had arranged for Veronica to travel to France on the Dover-Calais ferry, while he, Garner, had reached France on the Portsmouth-Cherbourg route. They had met up at the Gare du Nord, avoiding Piechler's contact and travelling straight down to Bordeaux from where, using the tickets Nihat had arranged, they finally reached Ankara via Zurich and Istanbul. Nihat had been waiting for them and had hurried them off to a small flat in the Salam Sokak, Copper Alley to the tourists, where they had been provided with a meal of warm Turkish bread and slices of *kilic*, swordfish, and two restful single beds in which they had slept uninterrupted for ten hours. Their host, a coppersmith, and Nihat's second cousin, had wakened them at seven in the morning as he went down to open his shop to the prowling early-morning tourists.

For breakfast they had been served *asure*, a glutinous mixture of nuts, oats, wheat and juicy raisins by two young girls who had giggled as they stood in the doorway of the bedroom watching them eat. Then

Nihat had arrived and whisked them off to the airport for the flight to Erzurum. On the drive to the airport, Nihat had produced a set of photographs which showed Hamilton and Heritage in conversation with a third man whom Garner and Veronica recognised as the fourth man on the steps of the Administrative Centre in the religious theme park in Carolina. 'Who is he?' Nihat asked, but Garner had been unable to supply the missing name.

'We tried to find out who he was before we left England,' Veronica had explained. 'But no luck. So he's turned up in Turkey, eh?'

Nihat had then gone on to tell them that Kossemlu's caravan had reached Igdir, and that Kossemlu, in company with Hamilton and Heritage, and the unknown man whom Nihat referred to as Uncle Sam, had left the previous day by air for Erzurum. 'From there, it is two hundred kilometres to Kars, where Kossemlu will pick up some additional trucks before moving off down to Igdir to join the caravan.'

'And you think that their final destination is Russia?' Veronica had asked.

'Erzurum to Kars is part of the ancient silk road. From Kars you can travel north along the caravan routes to Batumi and the Black Sea. South from Kars takes you along the Iran transit route, bypassing Igdir.' Nihat had explained. 'Igdir is twenty kilometres from the Russian frontier, and once crossed it is but a further thirty to Yerevan, the capital of Armenia. Caravans assembling at Igdir have only one destination. Russia. And only one purpose. Smuggling.'

Garner's ears began to pop as the aircraft began its descent to Erzurum. His mind wandered back into the past, the recent past and the days with de Roos as they worked together to seek and cement the involvement of the neo-Nazis with the soccer thugs of Europe. He moved on to Cormac Duffy and the tragedy he had unfolded. Both men were now dead, and in his half slumber, Garner felt a lump in his throat and a heavy pressure on his chest. He had moved on since those days. Into what he did not know, but he was sure he was working on a common thread which Hamilton and Heritage were trailing out behind them. The answer, or so it would seem, lay inside Russia. Smuggling? Smuggling what, and to whom?

Veronica nudged him in the ribs. 'Put your seat up. We'll be landing shortly.'

Garner obliged, swallowed hard a couple of times and rubbed his ears to equalise the pressure. 'You okay?' he asked her.

She took his hand and smiled, hiding the traces of weariness in her face. 'Fine,' she said.

The plane banked and swept in low towards the city set on a reddish plateau and surrounded by black hills out of which grew the awesome Paladoken Mountain, casting a dark shadow across Erzurum, as if holding the city to itself in a gesture of protection. The airport was teeming with soldiers and military police in addition to the usual array of security guards and police. Nihat explained that Erzurum was home to the Turkish Third Army, one of NATO's most important frontline units. 'From here to Kars you will see the military everywhere,' he said as he guided them through the crowded passageways. 'But they don't bother you, unless you get too near their convoys or guard posts. Then they are likely to shoot first and not worry about questions after.'

Garner carried their only luggage, a small brown case which Piechler had supplied and which contained a change of underwear, a couple of shirts and toothbrushes. Veronica, like Garner, wore a denim shirt and jeans and a pair of cheap trainers, all courtesy of Arthur Piechler. Outside the terminal building Nihat led the way to a grey Land Rover parked at the end of the taxi rank. The driver, whose name was Kemal, welcomed them politely and ushered them inside before stowing Garner's bag in the rear.

They set off eastwards, bypassing the city, meeting up with the main Kars road which was flowing with traffic. Progress was slow and after half an hour, Nihat instructed Kemal to pull in at the Mobil station which he did. He did not buy any diesel but parked next to a pump, got out of the Land Rover, and made out as if he was filling the tank. The traffic thundered past in both directions; heavy trucks, army convoys carrying tanks and field guns, taxis, private cars and the occasional brave motorcyclist. Nihat did not speak and Garner and Veronica sat there in silence wondering what was going on. Finally a second grey Land Rover pulled into the station and stopped directly behind theirs. Nihat got out and spoke to the four men inside, before returning to his seat. Meanwhile Kemal had given up his pretence and was behind the wheel again.

'We are being followed. A blue Nissan with three men inside,' reported Nihat over his shoulder. Kemal drove out of the station. 'They'll probably be waiting for us up ahead.'

They had not driven more than five kilometres when they saw the blue car parked by the side of the road, the three men standing outside examining the wheels. As they saw the Land Rover pass, they jumped into the car and followed, five or six vehicles behind. 'Who do you think they are?' asked Garner.

'Friends of your friends I suspect,' replied Nihat. 'We will find out soon enough. The other Land Rover will have them in its sight.' And with that Nihat put his head against the window, closed his eyes and fell asleep. Veronica snuggled against Garner and for the next hour and a half Kemal babysat three snoring adults.

IV

Garner woke with a start and startled Veronica from her sleep. He had felt a different motion in the Land Rover and as he looked out of the window he saw that they were turning south off the main highway onto a secondary road which seemed to run into a bank of low hills. Over his shoulder the sun was setting and the reds and oranges cast a strange glow across the countryside. 'Where are we, Nihat?' he asked.

'About thirty kilometres from Kars,' he said.

'But . . .'

'We have to see what our friends are up to,' interrupted Nihat and he told Kemal to speed up. Kemal put his foot down and cruised along the road, which was deserted. Just as well as Kemal drove down the centre, cutting through the curves and making life in the passenger seats very difficult for Garner and Veronica as they were thrown from side to side.

The road descended into a long, curving dip, and as they came out of it and began to climb again, Nihat ordered Kemal to pull over to the side. As soon as he stopped, Kemal jumped out, opened the rear door, pushed aside Garner's bag and lifted the floor of the

Land Rover. Nihat joined him and both men returned to the front of the vehicle carrying Kalashnikov rifles. 'You'll be better outside,' Nihat informed Garner and Veronica. 'Over there by those rocks.' He pointed with the rifle further up the road.

Garner could not find his voice. He took Veronica by the hand, helped her out and walked her to the rocks. They stood side by side, like two children about to witness the strange antics of grown-ups.

'Are you scared?' Veronica asked.

'Terrified,' said Garner. He squeezed her hand and pulled her behind a rock at waist level. 'If there's any shooting, duck.' He tried to smile but he knew he wasn't fooling her.

As he spoke, the Nissan came into view. It slowed down as its driver saw the Land Rover at the side of the road, and then came to a halt at the start of the incline. Nihat and Kemal stood at the front of the Land Rover, one on either side, their weapons hidden by the bonnet.

Garner could see the three men clearly. They were all young and heavily moustachioed. They simply sat there and stared ahead, making no move whatsoever. Then the second Land Rover came round the bend, slowly, crawling along, closing the door on the trap which Nihat had set up.

The men in the Nissan realised what had happened. The Land Rover came to a halt twenty metres behind the Nissan whose occupants became very excited, twisting and turning from back to front, shouting and arguing among themselves until the driver managed to calm his two passengers down. Garner saw no way out for them and he prayed that they would give themselves up. But he prayed in vain.

He heard the Nissan revving up. The driver put both hands on the wheel, sat back in his seat and let the clutch in with a roar and a screech of tyres. The car shot forward. The two passengers rolled down their windows and produced their weapons, Uzi machine pistols, and opened up, the man on the far side leaning out of the window up to his waist in order to get a better shot at Garner and Veronica.

Nihat and Kemal brought up their rifles and returned fire immediately at the charging car. Veronica reacted quicker than Garner and pulled him down and away from the first burst of gunfire. Bullets splattered the sandy earth and ricochetted from the rocks, throwing up shards and splinters which flew above their heads like a swarm of hyperactive wasps. The four men in the second Land Rover jumped out, fully armed, and attacked the Nissan from the rear with controlled, accurate volleys.

Nihat's Land Rover was struck along the side but Nihat and Kemal stood their ground and killed the driver and one of the assassins with their opening shots. The second assassin was struck from behind, almost being cut in two as the bullets tore into his exposed body. The racing Nissan had barely reached half way to the Land Rover when it exploded into a raging ball of fire, continuing along the road for a few more metres before turning on its side as it careered against a cluster of rocks. Garner peered out from his hiding place to see the car ablaze and Kemal jumping into his vehicle to drive it away to safety. 'God almighty,' said Garner.

Veronica, on hands and knees, joined him at his vantage point. 'Oh my God,' she exclaimed. Garner helped her to her feet, steadied her, and then with his arm around her, marched her towards Nihat who was calling up the other Land Rover.

'We will go and leave the others to clear up the mess,' said Nihat, as Garner and Veronica approached.

Garner looked about him. 'The smoke from the fire will be spotted miles away,' he said. 'God almighty. I can't believe this.'

'The police will think it's the army and the army will think it is the police,' said Nihat firmly. 'Don't worry.'

Using shovels, two men from the second Land Rover began to spade the sandy soil onto the burning wreck, while a third attacked it with a small fire extinguisher. The flames and the dense black smoke began to subside.

Nihat led the way back towards Kemal who was busily packing away the two Kalashnikovs.

V

The fertile plain of Igdir, watered by the river Aras, runs across the border into Russia as far as Yerevan. Because of its low altitude relative to the mountains which surround it, the plain is a climatic anomaly: it is permanently warm and the Azeri Turks who inhabit it harvest rice, cotton and citrus fruits. The Azeri Turks are the only Shiite muslim community in Turkey whose muslim population are of the Alevi persuasion.

The Azeris, migrants from Azerbaijan, take their inspiration, religious and political, from Iran, and since the overthrow of the Shah of Persia, the Azeris have become more and more insular in their tightly knit communities. While not openly hostile to strangers, they do not make them welcome, and view all incursions with suspicion.

Kossemulu always used the same village just to the south of Igdir as the assembly point for his caravans crossing the border. He had courted the *muhtar*, the village head man, and his family for many years with presents and gifts and the head man, in return, had allowed Kossemlu to smuggle whatever he wanted back and forth across the frontier, provided there was work for his people and the pay was good. In addition, the head man provided guards and guides who knew every rock of the passageway into Russia and how to avoid the patrols. And it was one of the Azeri guards who uncovered the traitor in their midst.

Hamilton and Heritage stood in the doorway of the brick-built hut that Kossemlu used as his headquarters. His second-in-command, Hasan, a giant of a man with a huge stomach, easily held the young man with the battered face whom the Azeri guard had caught sneaking out of the camp. The Azeri was explaining to Kossemlu what had happened, with sweeping gestures and facial contortions, while Kossemlu stood beneath the gas lamp, his eyes fixed on the young man whose face was white with fear. Bryant pushed his way into the hut past Hamilton and Heritage and went to stand behind Hasan.

Finally, the Azeri finished his speech and fell silent. Kossemlu told him to go and he left with a wide grin on his face. 'I promised him a bonus,' said Kossemlu.

'Who is he?' asked Hamilton, nodding at the young man whom Hasan now allowed to fall to the floor by releasing the strangle-hold he had used to restrain him.

'He wouldn't talk for the Azeri so he won't talk for us,' replied Kossemlu. 'The Azeri had spotted him three nights in succession leaving the camp to meet up with another. Tonight he killed the watcher and captured this man.

'Is he one of your people?' asked Heritage.

A flash of anger burned in Kossemlu's eyes for a fraction of a second. 'No he is not. But he is known to me and has been on one or two caravans before. He is just an extra we hired for this trip.'

'Not very good judgement on your part, Ramazan,' said Hamilton slyly.

'The man was spying on you, not me,' said Kossemlu. 'He already knows what I do.'

An embarrassed silence followed which was broken by Bryant. 'I could maybe find out who he was spying for.

'It is not important now,' said Kossemlu. 'We will be moving out in an hour's time, at ten o'clock. He knows nothing about our final plans and I doubt whether you could break him by then. He is a Kurd.'

'Kill him then,' said Hamilton.

Kossemlu stared at Hamilton. 'You kill him. He was spying on you.'

The young man was on his knees and his head was bowed forward, almost touching the floor. Hasan stood to one side to allow Hamilton through. Hamilton remained where he was, glaring back at Kossemlu. Heritage broke the deadlock. 'Okay, Lenny,' he said.

Bryant stepped forward, made a blade of his right hand, and brought it down across the man's neck. There was a sharp crack and the man crumpled over to one side, his lifeless eyes staring up at the blackened gas lamp.

Bryant cracked his knuckles, nodded at Heritage and went outside. Hamilton finally broke his eye-contact

258

with Kossemlu and marched outside, quickly followed by Heritage.

Hasan dragged the body to the doorway, barked out a command, to which two men responded, and they carried the body off into the night. 'Mr Hamilton and I will have our day of reckoning,' said Kossemlu to himself, but loud enough for Hasan to hear.

'You will have to have a day of reckoning with all of them, Ramazan,' said Hasan. He crossed the square room to the table at the side and took a long swig from a bottle of *raki*.

'What did you find out?' asked Kossemlu. 'About Bryant?'

'Bryant's case contains a rifle. A high-powered rifle with special scope. An assassin's weapon.'

'Did he suspect you had been near it?'

Hasan shook his head. 'No, I don't think so. He had left a hair across the leather strap but I saw it and replaced it exactly.'

'Good. We will have to keep our eyes open, wide open from now on. Perhaps I have involved us all in something we should not be involved in,' said Kossemlu.

'Perhaps,' said Hasan and attacked the *raki* bottle again.

On the other side of the village where Bryant, Hamilton and Heritage slept in a ramshackle hut, Bryant was explaining to his two accomplices how his case had been opened and searched. 'The hair had been replaced on the front but the one on the trigger guard had fallen off as it had been pulled out of the case.'

'You sure you didn't do it yourself as you pulled out the gun?' asked Heritage.

'Positive,' replied Bryant. 'I think it was Hasan. He's been hanging about all day.'

'Just that bastard Kossemlu being nosy,' said Hamilton. 'When this is over . . .'

'Never mind that now, Alex. What interests me more is that Kossemlu has a down on us at the moment. And if he starts getting funny, we could end up with zilch.'

'All he has to do is get me to the hotel,' said Bryant.

'Which means that we have to be nice to him, Alex,' said Heritage. 'Until it is all over, that is. So no more snide remarks, Alex. Let's not get him angry. Okay?'

VI

'They are crossing the border tonight,' said Nihat. He spread the map on the floor and Garner and Veronica joined him on their knees. 'The Aras runs parallel to the border. Kossemlu will cross somewhere here,' said Nihat, and he pointed with his pen. 'There are many fords and crossings.'

'What about patrols?' asked Veronica.

'The Turks do not bother too much. They turn a blind eye to the illegal caravans. Most of the colonels and brigadiers in this area receive a pay-off from the likes of Kossemlu and the other regulars.'

'And the Russians?' asked Garner.

'Kossemlu prefers to avoid them. That is why he uses the Azeris who are expert at deceiving the Russians. But our guides are just as good. We will have no problems crossing.'

'When do we go?' asked Garner.

'Tomorrow night. About ten. It will only take three or four hours. I hope your backsides are prepared for a rough ride,' laughed Nihat.

'It's a long time since I sat on a horse,' said Veronica.

'Me, too,' said Garner.

'Don't worry. You have come this far. You will make it,' said Nihat. He pointed at the map again. 'Once across we will follow the railway into Yerevan.'

'Your man definitely said Yerevan?' asked Veronica.

'Yerevan,' confirmed Nihat.

They talked together for another half an hour, then Nihat said he was ready for bed. They were sharing a long single room in an old farmhouse on the northern outskirts of Igdir. The three sleeping bags had been thrown on the floor beneath the window. The only furniture in the room was a rough wooden table where the remains of their evening meal, Turkish bread and dried beef strips, sat on a big oval platter. Next door, Kemal and the four men from the second Land Rover shared an even smaller room.

They had made the final run from Kars to Igdir without any further incidents and Garner and Veronica were relieved to hear that the police were not pursuing them. They both shuddered at the thought of spending time inside a Turkish prison for their part in the shoot-out and Nihat had reassured them that Turkish prisons were not as bad as they were portrayed. 'It is a state of mind being in prison,' he had told them. 'If you can make the mental adjustment from day one, then there is nothing your captors can do to you, there are no conditions under which you cannot live.'

And as Nihat took off his shirt and climbed into his sleeping bag, Garner could not help but wonder at the

261

man who seemed capable of taking all challenges in his stride without showing any emotion whatsoever. 'Let's go outside for a walk,' he whispered to Veronica.

They went outside the farmhouse, into the warm night. 'It's hot,' said Veronica, tugging at her shirt. 'I'm all sweaty.'

'Me too,' said Garner.

Veronica stopped and looked upwards. 'Look at the stars,' she said. The sky was a deep blue-black and the stars looked as if they were suspended beneath the canopy of sky. The night air was clear. 'Isn't it beautiful?' she said.

He stood in front of her, placed his hands on her hips and looked into her eyes. It was the first time they had been alone for some time and he had sensed that there was something troubling her. 'How are you doing?' he asked.

'I'm fine,' she said, avoiding his stare. There was a tremor in her voice. 'Honestly I am.' She snuggled into his chest and he put his arms around her.

'Frightened?' He could feel her heart pounding.

'I've been frightened since the day I walked into your flat,' she said.

He kissed the top of her head. 'About Russia, I mean.'

'I don't know really. I was scared during the gun fight, terrified by the blue van. But going into Russia? I don't know.'

'I'm a bit like that myself,' he said.

'It's almost a relief,' she interrupted. 'We have to go to Russia. That is where it will all end. At least we know that. Before we were working in the dark and we didn't know where to look for danger. Now we know. It's in Russia.'

'You've been very brave,' he said, and kissed her again.

'And so have you.' She looked up into his face and smiled. 'We've both been brave, haven't we?'

He squeezed her close. 'Yes, that's true. We've both been scared out of our wits but we've managed to cope.'

'We're a good team, aren't we?'

'The best. And we'll come through. Together.'

'We have to, together I mean.'

'Look, don't worry about the crossing into Russia. Nihat won't let us down.'

'I'm not,' she said.

He held her away from him and stared into her eyes. 'Then what?'

'I think I'm pregnant.'

RUSSIA

I

Kossemlu sat on his haunches on the bank of the trickling stream waiting for the sun to rise. The twenty-six pack-horses and seven camels were being watered by his men following the arduous night crossing, and everyone, the animals included, was in need of rest. They had encountered no difficulties with either the Turks or the Russians as they had crossed the frontier, the Azeri guides steering them well clear of even the slightest hint of Russian presence, and as they had taken the first steps into Soviet Armenia, the Azeri guides had left them, promising to return for them in two days' time. The next step of the journey, thought Kossemlu, was the easiest part as they would mingle with the other caravans coming from Leninaken in the west and set up camp on the outskirts of Yerevan.

He watched the dawning sky for the first rays of sun which would be the signal to move off. On his left Bryant lay stretched out on the dewy grass, apparently asleep. Next to him lay Hasan who was now under orders not to let Bryant out of his sight at any time. Bryant's skin had darkened under exposure to the summer sun, and having rid himself of his western clothes and dressed in the loose trousers and shirt of the local Armenian peasantry, Kossemlu thought he looked a lot more like a native than many of the natives did. He would certainly blend in once they were in Yerevan.

As the sun came up, Kossemlu gave the orders to move out, and the caravan took up formation once again and began the short trek across the plain to the city. They joined the main road about ten kilometres inside the border, and tagged on to the end of a much larger caravan which had come from Leninaken. The road was jammed with traffic of every description, from stubby donkeys overburdened with huge sacks, to roaring juggernauts whose drivers apparently had forgotten where the foot brakes where. But progress was steady and uneventful so that by noon they had reached the outskirts of the city and the camping ground which was a wide open field through which ran a small stream. Hasan organised the men into groups, unloading the animals, erecting tents, cooking food, and by two o'clock, Kossemlu's caravan was bedded down for an afternoon siesta, Hasan and Bryant sharing a tent.

Towards evening, Hasan took Bryant over to Kossemlu's tent where he was introduced to Hagop Hagopian, Kossemlu's agent in Yerevan. Bryant sat to one side with Hasan as Kossemlu and Hagopian discussed the goods the caravan had brought and the prices that could be expected. Their discussions were long and involved from what Bryant could hear, frequently interrupted by Hagopian insisting he inspect the fare, and Kossemlu would then lead out the party to examine the quality of the goods. Then, as the sun was setting, Hagopian announced that he was returning to Yerevan. Bryant went with Hasan back to the tent where Bryant collected his gun case which he placed in a holdall and Hagopian stowed it away in the boot of his Fiat.

Hasan sat in the rear of the car while Bryant sat up front with Hagopian. 'You will like the Dvin Hotel. I have a room for you on the sixth floor, facing the Park. A very fine view indeed.'

'Thank you,' said Bryant.

'The room was very difficult to come by as Kossemlu did not give me much notice. The place has been booked for weeks because of the Premier's visit to the martyrs' shrine in the Park.'

II

'I've sent Kemal on ahead to locate Kossemlu's caravan,' said Nihat.

'How far to go?' asked Garner.

'Another hour or so,' replied Nihat.

'My backside is killing me,' said Garner. He patted the long, muscular neck of his mount.

'Mine too,' said Veronica.

Garner ignored her. They had not spoken all night. They had argued ever since Garner had learnt that she could be pregnant. 'Are you sure?' he had asked her.

'I'm usually as regular as clockwork,' she had told him. 'But I'm a week late this month. Chances are I'm pregnant.'

And that was where the argument had begun for Garner had insisted that she stay behind in Turkey and not make the crossing into Russia. 'Not only is it dangerous because

266

of the terrain but what if the Russians spot us and start shooting.' But he knew he was on to a loser as soon as he had opened his mouth.

'I will risk it,' Veronica had said. 'I was in this state the other day when there were people shooting at me, so it should make no difference now. And anyway you've only just been telling me that the Russian crossing would be easy.'

Garner had tried to enlist the help of Nihat, waking him from his sleep. But Nihat had sided with Veronica. 'Turkish women make this crossing all the time,' he had said. 'On foot, too. And heavily pregnant. I don't think Veronica should be excluded because of her pregnancy. She looks strong enough to me.'

But Garner would not give in and had skulked off to his sleeping bag, leaving Nihat and Veronica to carry on the discussion; and he had sulked away the night in his bag, ignoring Veronica when she lay down beside him and tried to make amends. And in the morning he was no better. Throughout the day he had kept to himself, except at lunchtime when once again he had tried to convince Veronica to stay behind. But she was adamant. She was going.

That night they had changed into the clothes that Kemal had brought for them. Veronica put on jeans and a heavy cotton shirt embroidered at the front, and swopped her trainers for a pair of ankle boots. She covered her head with a wide square of red cotton cloth which she tied under her chin. Garner too wore jeans and a cotton shirt, over which he slipped a rough woollen pullover. Nihat and his men were similarly attired.

Their party consisted of the four guards from the Land Rover and Kemal, together with six other men, who would look after the dozen pack horses that made up their caravan and guide them over the frontier.

The riding and pack horses were of the local Kabardin breed; strong, sturdy and agile with a calm, responsive temperament. Nihat selected a grey with a very long flowing mane for Veronica after consulting his wrangler, while Garner was mounted on a tall bay of fifteen hands.

By midnight they had crossed the Aras river into Soviet territory. Garner had slipped from his saddle as he had urged the short-backed horse up the steep river bank. Veronica had allowed herself a short, amused titter and even though it was dark, she could have sworn that she had seen the anger in Garner's face. And his mood did not improve either when Veronica in her turn slid from the saddle and landed with a bump on her backside. 'I told you to stay behind,' he had hissed at her as he helped her back into the saddle. Nihat had warned them to keep quiet. A few minutes later one of the guides had reported to Nihat that there was the possibility of a patrol up ahead. They had dismounted from their sturdy mounts and had waited in trepidation for over an hour until the guide had returned to give the all clear.

'You can't go on like this, ignoring me,' said Veronica. 'I made it across okay, didn't I? We are supposed to be a team, aren't we? Me and you, both in it together.'

'That's not the point,' said Garner. 'We don't know what we are going to be up against here in Russia.' But he knew he was being contradictory and that he would have to give way eventually.

'Will you two stop arguing,' implored Nihat. 'If there's trouble up ahead, then I'd prefer it if we acted as a team and not have any divisions between us which could cause problems.'

'He's right, Pete,' said Veronica.

'Okay, okay,' said Garner. He glanced beyond the railway line at the wide expanse of cotton fields, then turned back to Veronica. 'I'm sorry,' he added. 'But you know . . .'

'I understand,' she said. 'It was my fault for telling you. But I thought you would be glad. I thought we understood one another.'

They rode on in silence until Kemal reappeared to inform them that he had located Kossemlu's camp and spoken to their man. He led the way to the encampment where they set up their tents before having something to eat. As they ate, Nihat brought them up to date. 'Uncle Sam went in to Yerevan last night with Hasan. He's Kossemlu's lieutenant. They haven't returned.'

'Does he know where they've gone in Yerevan?' asked Garner.

'And what about Hamilton and Heritage?' said Veronica.

'Hamilton and Heritage remained behind in Turkey. They didn't cross over.'

'You mean we've lost them?' said Garner.

Nihat shook his head. 'No. I still have a man watching at Igdir. If they move out we will be able to follow them.'

Garner stroked his chin. 'What is going on? Why has Uncle Sam gone off on his own?'

'Uncle Sam went with an Armenian, one of the city fat cats who run the black market and the smuggling. He is well known in these parts. Hagop Hagopian.'

'What's the connection, then?' said Veronica.

'I am not sure. But my man says that Uncle Sam is armed with a very powerful rifle. Hasan told him so. Perhaps Uncle Sam is going to shoot someone.'

269

III

Kossemlu sat alone in his tent, brooding. He had made a mistake. A very big one. He should not have become involved with Hamilton and Heritage. They were evil men. He sensed it. And Bryant? A cold-blooded killer.

He had Conville to thank for it all. He liked the young Englishman and he had wanted to help him when he had first called to make the request to bring the man Bryant into Russia. He suspected that Conville did not know the true purpose of the mission, while he, Kossemlu, had guessed it from the start. He should have pulled out then, after he had met Hamilton and Heritage. But he had gone on. Why? Greed? The rifles, the money? No, he had money and the rifles were not really necessary as his armoury was well stocked as it was. Something new, something different? Had that been the motive for taking up their offer, to smuggle a killer into Russia, something he had never done before, something with an edge of excitement to it that his usual smuggling exploits could not give him. He was getting old, becoming bored. Could that be the answer?

Whatever the answer, he regretted the deal. His friend Conville was treated with contempt, especially by Hamilton, and that offended his sense of propriety and made his own position even more uncomfortable. And then there was Bryant himself. He would kill someone in Yerevan, which was virtually on his own doorstep. He had been under the impression that Bryant was to travel on once inside Russia and he had only learnt that Yerevan was his final destination a week ago. He did not like the idea of such an intrusion upon his territory. He would finish it today, he thought. Hasan would take care of Bryant, and he would see to Hamilton and Heritage when he crossed back into Turkey. They would simply disappear and he would report them missing to Conville, who would not question him too closely. In fact he believed that Conville would be highly delighted by the news.

IV

Lenin Square is the centre of Yerevan. Built as an architectural whole in the Armenian style, it is without doubt the best example of a city centre in the entire Soviet Union. The Square is dominated from the south by Government House which houses the Council of Ministers and the Supreme Soviet of Armenia, while on the north-eastern side stands the Historical Museum whose magnificent fountain reflects the whole panorama of the Square.

Nihat had taken Garner and Veronica into Yerevan in the evening to buy some provisions and they had come upon Lenin Square, not by accident, but as part of a human press of bodies that had carried everything before it. Nihat had told them to swim with the tide and they had done so, finally being deposited in the Square along with thousands of others, all of whom appeared to be waving the Armenian flag. Above the noise of the chanting and singing, Nihat explained what was going on. 'There is an enclave in neighbouring Azerbaijan, Nagorno-Karabakh, which is home to Christian Armenians and Muslim Azeris. They are killing one another, and the people here are protesting, wanting the enclave to be part of Armenia, and demanding action to protect their countrymen.'

The huge crowd was growing all the time as many more of the city dwellers surged into the Square with flags and banners. The singing and shouting became more frenetic and it was directed at Government House where the Council of Ministers was sitting, trying to decide upon a course of action.

'Where are the police?' asked Veronica.

'They've probably joined in with the crowd,' said Garner. 'It's been going on for a few weeks now, one of the side-effects of glasnost, and I think the police are fed up with it and have thrown in their lot with everyone else.'

'A bit like old times in London,' said Veronica with a grin.

'And once you're in you cannot get out,' said Garner. 'There's no way we can push out of here.'

'We can try,' said Nihat. 'Over that way.' He raised an arm, indicating the direction he was taking and set off.

As Nihat made his way towards the fountain, on the other side of the Square, Bryant and Hasan found themselves trapped in front of the Trade Union building. No matter which way they moved they were confronted by row upon row of chanting Armenians. But Bryant's search for a way through the crowd was very different from Hasan's. Bryant had promised Hasan a drink and Hasan was thirsty. His throat felt dry and he wanted out from the crowd. He turned and twisted, as did Bryant, until finally Bryant saw a gap and headed for it with Hasan close on his heels.

Bryant waited for his moment to strike. He half turned as if to urge on Hasan, and then under cover of the many bodies, he slipped a short-bladed knife from his pocket, palmed it and waited for Hasan to close. As the Turk came up to his shoulder, Bryant stuck the knife into the man's chest between the fourth and fifth ribs, and pierced his heart. Without stopping to check up on his handiwork, Bryant continued to push himself free.

Hasan stood still, a look of horror etched upon his face. He was held up by those around him until his legs gave way and he slumped against an old man who tried to push him aside. Then Hasan slowly slid to the ground, the crowd parting to allow him. By then Bryant was away, moving round the edge of the Square, back to the Dvin Hotel.

Nihat led them out of the Square past the Armenian Hotel and into Lenin Prospekt. Sweat was dripping from Garner's nose as the night was very warm. 'I'm glad to get out of that,' he said.

Suddenly, Nihat put out an arm and stopped dead in the street. 'I've just realised what the crowd were chanting back there,' he said. His eyes were wide and he looked shaken. 'They were shouting for the Soviet Premier to put in an appearance.'

'All the way from Moscow?' said Garner.

'No,' said Nihat. 'He's here, in Yerevan. Now. He's at the meeting in Government House.'

'Uncle Sam and the rifle?' exclaimed Veronica. 'No. It can't be. They wouldn't dare.'

'Of course,' exclaimed Garner. 'They are going to shoot him. And I think I know where.'

273

V

'Please sit down,' said Kossemlu. Garner remained standing while Veronica and Nihat sat on the small square of carpet. 'Some tea?'

'No thanks,' said Garner. 'We have precious little time as it is.'

'Is there a hurry?' asked Kossemlu, as he poured the tea into a bowl. 'You are very early risers.' Dawn was just breaking and there was a chill in the air.

'Where is the American?' demanded Garner.

Kossemlu ignored him. 'I'm glad to see that you made it, particularly you, Mrs Garner. But then Hamilton arranged for your welcoming committee so I wouldn't have expected anything else.'

'Thank you,' said Veronica.

'As for the American, he is in the city.'

'We know that,' said Nihat. 'We would like to know precisely where.' It had been Nihat's idea to approach Kossemlu, an outside chance that he might help if they told him the purpose of Uncle Sam's visit to Yerevan. 'You know that the Soviet Premier is also in the city?'

'I learnt of that last night,' said Kossemlu. 'He will come to no harm.'

'Is that why Hasan is with Uncle Sam?' asked Nihat.

'You are well informed,' said Kossemlu. 'And Uncle Sam, as you call him, is known as Len Bryant. He is a professional assassin. But Hasan will see to it that Bryant is off target, as it were.'

Garner glanced across to Nihat and then to Veronica. 'Can you be sure of that?' he asked.

'Certain,' said Kossemlu, and sipped his tea. 'If you would like to check for yourself, you can find Mr Bryant on the sixth floor of the Dvin Hotel, room six-four-five. I am sure he will make you most welcome.'

Veronica got to her feet. 'Thank you,' she said.

Kossemlu stood and shook her hand. 'You are a very brave woman. I wish you luck. If there are any problems, please come back.'

They left the tent and hurried back to their own encampment. 'What should we do now?' asked Garner. 'Do we trust him?'

'Can we afford not to?' said Nihat.

'So we go to the Dvin Hotel and confront Bryant?' said Veronica.

'If he's there,' said Garner. 'He could be just using it as a base. He could be anywhere about that Park.'

'Are you certain about the Park?' asked Nihat.

Garner nodded his head. 'I read it in a newspaper just before we left England. The Premier had arranged the visit some months ago. He is to pay his respects at the Genocide Victims' Memorial in Tsitsernakaberd Park. And then he is going to use the visit to sit down with the Armenians and Azerbaijanis. It was only when you mentioned the fighting in the enclave last night that I remembered what I'd read.'

'What about 'phoning the police and telling them?' said Veronica.

'Out of the question,' said Nihat. 'The Premier gets a hundred death threats a day. Nobody would believe us, even if we managed to overcome the intricacies of the Yerevan telephone system. And besides, I've got no change.'

'Okay, so we go to the Dvin Hotel,' said Garner.

'Yes. Where's Kemal? Kemal!' shouted Nihat.

Kemal ducked into the tent carrying a pair of Smith and Wesson hand guns. He gave one to Nihat and offered one to Garner who shook his head. Both men tucked the guns into their waistbands beneath their shirts. 'The truck is ready,' said Kemal.

They set off in the battered truck which Nihat had hired the night before from a local farmer. But the highway into the city was clogged with traffic which was almost stationary. 'What is happening up ahead, Kemal?' asked Nihat impatiently.

Kemal climbed out of the cab and onto the roof, returning a minute later to report that there was a roadblock ahead. 'They are letting some traffic through but turning most of it back. And they are checking papers.'

'We'll have to walk,' said Garner. 'Come on.'

They walked down the road until they reached the roadblock. The militia waved through the pedestrians, being concerned only with the traffic, allowing only essential vehicles through, trying to lessen the congestion the Premier's visit had brought to the city.

As they entered the city again along Tsereteli Street, they were swallowed up by the crowds moving along the Park. Their progress was slow and Garner began to feel a wave of panic building up inside him as he pushed his way forward. 'Which way now?' he asked Nihat as they reached a junction.

'To the left. The hotel is on the other side of Lenin Square. We passed it last night. Just off Lenin Prospekt.'

Veronica caught up to Garner and gripped his hand. Her forehead was dotted with beads of perspiration. 'Wait for me,' she said.

Garner pulled her along with him as Kemal and Nihat brought up the rear. They crossed into Echiadzini Street which they followed into Lenin Prospekt, from where they could see the top stories of the Dvin Hotel over to the left. 'That's it over there,' said Nihat, gasping for breath. All four were now blowing hard as they alternated between a fast walk and a steady trot, depending upon the density of the ever-growing crowds.

They crossed Marx Street, heading north, and just as they reached the corner of Lenin Square, Garner collided with a man who was walking against the flow of pedestrians. The man was knocked to the ground. Garner stood over him and put out a hand to help him to his feet as the crowds pushed past. He wasn't hurt but he complained loudly and would not release Garner's hand once he was upright again. Nihat intervened, speaking slowly in Armenian, but the man would not be mollified. Garner tried to extricate his hand but all his efforts were resisted. The panic began to rise again within him. 'Let go will you!' he shouted out to the man.

Some of the people on the pavement were stopping to see what was going on. The man looked at Garner, a puzzled frown on his face. Garner realised his mistake and tried to pull away again. Veronica tried to help, but the man wrapped himself about Garner and held him tightly. Kemal faded into the background. Veronica had seen Nihat slip him his gun.

Two men in grey suits approached the scene. Garner could feel his heart beating wildly as there was no doubt in his mind that the men were police. They flashed their identity cards at Garner and spoke to him in Russian. He understood the general drift of their questions, and he shook his head slowly as they repeated them. Veronica clutched his arm while Nihat stood to one side. Then the man began to speak and the two policemen listened before turning their attention back to Garner. Two more policemen arrived, one of them carrying a walkie-talkie. They backed Garner, Veronica and Nihat up against the wall and once more asked them for their papers. When they were not forthcoming the policeman spoke into his radio and within minutes two police cars arrived at the scene.

VI

The Genocide Victims' Memorial in Tsitsernakaberd Park commemorates the death of a million and a half Armenians, murdered by the Turks in a nationwide pogrom just after the outbreak of the Great War. Pilgrims to the shrine enter along the wide, paved Alley of Mourning which leads to an open-air Mausoleum wherein twelve truncated pyramids surround twelve flights of steps which descend into a circular chamber in which burns the eternal flame. The grim, hollow silence within the chamber is broken only by the sombre funeral music, the work of the Armenian composers Yekmalin and Komitass.

As he looked down on the Memorial from his hotel window Bryant could see tiny knots of workmen putting the final touches to their preparations; the half built wall along one side of the Alley which depicted various scenes from the slaughter was being draped in a purple shroud, while bouquets of wild lilies were being placed at the bases of the pyramids.

Bryant watched the activity through his 'scope, and then tiring of it, he opened the window, locked it in place, and returned to the table where he had left his Remington. Gently he stroked its barrel, then picked it up and fitted the telescopic sight, and stood the rifle against the settee. Next he moved the long table closer to the window, positioning it exactly along the angle he would use. He lay on his stomach on the table, supporting himself on his elbows, and smiled in satisfaction at the result. Pushing himself up from the table, he collected the rifle, stretched out and began to adjust the sight. He would get the Premier as he descended the stairs into the chamber, a head shot which would propel him forwards down the marble steps, an added measure that would ensure the success of the job.

VII

Garner had lost his head after the dark-haired policeman had hit him for the third time across the mouth. Like Veronica, his hands were handcuffed behind his back and he sat on the edge of the rear seat trying to explain what was going on. The dark-haired policeman leaning into the back from the passenger seat threw out a backhand every time Garner tried to speak. After the third blow Garner had tried to drive his head into the man's face, but instead had banged his head against the top of the seat. As the policeman again raised his hand to strike, Garner had sat right back in his seat and kicked out with both feet. 'Bastard,' he had shouted above the screams from Veronica.

And so when they were delivered into the cobbled courtyard of the nearest police station, both Garner and Veronica were assaulted as they were dragged inside and deposited, smeared with their own blood, in a bare room.

'Bastards,' screamed Veronica as the heavy iron door was slammed and locked.

'Idiots,' said Garner. 'Why don't you listen to me! They are going to kill your Premier!' He ran at the door and kicked it with the sole of his foot. 'Idiots. Come and take these handcuffs off.'

'I can't believe it,' cried Veronica. She sat down on the floor and began of weep. 'To have come this far and now this.'

'Fucking idiots,' said Garner and went and sat next to Veronica. 'Let me see your face. If they've harmed the baby . . .'

She turned her face towards him. 'They just caught my mouth.' A thin trickle of blood, already drying, marked the corner of her mouth. 'And a couple in the kidneys.' She tried to smile. 'You're going to have a lovely shiner tomorrow.'

'There may be no tomorrow for us,' he said. 'Bastards. Hey, did you see what they did with Nihat? And what happened to Kemal?'

'I think Nihat is here. The car he was in was behind us all the way.'

'I hope he gives them what for,' said Garner. Then a thought struck him, the memory from a few nights ago about prison being a state of mind. 'Yes, he'll be giving them some problems. They won't know how to handle him.'

'Meaning we're easy to deal with? Just beat us up, then lock us away?'

'Yes, something . . .' Before he could finish, they heard the key turning in the lock.

The door began to open. Garner started to get to his feet and then he froze. 'My God,' said Veronica.

Before them stood the man they knew as Arthur Piechler, dressed in the uniform of a KGB colonel. He ushered in two guards who set about releasing Garner and Veronica from their handcuffs.

'I'm going crazy,' said Garner, rubbing his wrists to restore circulation. 'This just doesn't make any sense at all.'

'Same here,' said Veronica, getting to her feet. 'What the hell are you doing here, Piechler?'

'Where are Hamilton and Heritage?' asked Colonel Volsky.

'Are you really KGB?' asked Garner skeptically.

'Yes, I am. Now where are the two men?'

'They are still inside Turkey. I thought the KGB knew everything,' said Garner.

'I had a man in the camp who kept me up to date on things. They broke his neck two nights ago. Now where are they?'

'I told you. They're still inside Turkey. But it's not them you should be worrying about. Bryant's your problem.'

Volsky took a step forward. 'Bryant. Leonard Bryant?'

'Yes, he's . . .'

'Where is he?' shouted Volsky, almost dancing on his toes.

'That's what he's trying to tell you,' shouted back Veronica. 'He's in the Dvin Hotel getting ready to kill the Premier.'

Volsky closed his eyes momentarily as if fully registering the news, then he acted. He rattled out orders to the two guards who left the room as if they were going into orbit. 'Come with me,' he ordered as he turned on his heels and ran out, Veronica and Garner hot on his heels.

281

As they left the station Volsky gave orders to make contact with the Premier's security guard either by radio or by messenger. 'And alert all units in the vicinity.' They rushed out onto the pavement. 'Where's the damn car,' he shouted, searching the road for his two men. But the answer lay under his nose: the pedestrians were spilling over into the streets and all traffic was at a standstill.

'You won't get a car through that crush,' said Garner. 'Is it far away?' But Volsky was already off and running. 'Come on you two, follow me.'

VIII

The Soviet Premier was on walkabout, attended by the Council of Ministers.

The barriers, both human and metal, could not contain the enthusiasm of the Armenian people. Gone were the harsh, strident chants of the previous evening. In their stead, smiling grinning faces roaring their approval, giving vent to their emotions as the Premier moved amongst them, ignoring his own security guard, as eager to get to the people as they were eager to greet him. He moved along the narrow passageway between two banks of the seething masses grasping hands, patting heads, slapping shoulders, occasionally disappearing from view, much to the consternation of his bodyguard, beneath a welter of small flags and clapping hands.

Bryant followed the Premier's every movement through his 'scope as he lay flat on the table, ready for action. The Premier climbed the short flight of steps to the entrance of the Alley of Mourning. He turned at the top, removed his

282

hat and gave a huge wave above his head. The ministers
and the bodyguard gathered on the lower steps and then,
as a party, they walked along the Alley, pausing from time
to time to examine one of the massacre scenes. Four of the
security guards went ahead and took up position around
the top of the twelve flights of stairs. Bryant tensed and
pressed the butt of the rifle firmly against his shoulder.

The Premier walked around the pyramids and at one
he picked up a wild lily. One of the ministers came
to his assistance as he fixed the flower to his lapel.
Bryant could feel sweat on the palms of his hands.
Too late now, he told himself. The Premier stepped
towards the descending stairs. Bryant took a deep
breath.

Behind the Premier Bryant noticed one of the security
men clutching his ear. He looked up and above. To Bryant
he seemed to be looking at him from the other side of
the 'scope. Bryant hesitated as the Premier put his foot
on the first step. Suddenly the guard ran forward and
stood between Bryant and his target while the three other
guards converged on their leader. The Premier was lost
from view. 'Shit,' swore Bryant. And the room began to
tremble.

IX

They reached the Dvin Hotel and sprinted up the steps
into the lobby and through reception to the elevators.
Volsky banged all six buttons watched by a startled
manager whose glasses were perched on the end of
his nose 'They do not work,' he said, frowning in

dismay that anyone should be foolish enough to expect the elevators to work. 'Use the stairs.' The sight of Volsky's uniform did not deter him as he barked out the order.

'This way,' said Garner, pushing open the fire doors. They charged up the stairs, Veronica falling behind, the two men cursing under their breaths. When they reached the sixth floor they stopped and gathered themselves before entering the corridor. Volsky drew his pistol, a standard Makarov, and checked the magazine. 'Six-four-five?' he asked, breathing deeply.

Garner could only nod his head in confirmation. He sucked in air through his mouth. 'Let's go,' he whispered, and pushed open the doors, stepping into the corridor ahead of Volsky.

'This is my show,' said Volsky, and nudged Garner to one side. As he did so the corridor began to shake and shudder, the floor began to sway. Chunks of ceiling plaster thudded down onto the thin carpeting. Garner staggered and almost fell, grabbing hold of Volsky to maintain his balance. 'Earthquake,' cried Volsky. Cracks appeared in the walls, and more of the ceiling fell, accompanied by a fine choking dust.

Veronica screamed. 'Veronica,' said Garner in anguish. He lurched towards the doors, coughing hoarsely, as a tremor passed beneath his feet. Veronica had almost reached the top of the stairs. Part of the bannister had broken away and she was gingerly trying to climb the last few steps, her back to the wall, which seemed to be rising and falling in waves. Garner reached out a hand and pulled her to his side. 'Keep tight hold of me,' he said. The entire hotel was swaying.

Up ahead they could see Volsky picking his way through the debris, making for Bryant's room at the top end of the corridor, one arm above his head as a shield. Garner and Veronica followed in his wake, taking care to watch for the falling ceiling. When Volsky reached the room he turned to Garner and Veronica and indicated they should stay where they were. But Garner wanted to be in on the kill, and he led Veronica along the twisting corridor. Then, just as suddenly as it had begun, the tremor passed, and the hotel stopped moving. 'It's stopped,' said Veronica in a hushed tone. 'The earthquake's over.'

'He's going in,' said Garner and he jumped a pile of debris and raced to Volsky's side.

Volsky raised his leg and kicked open the door, dropping to his knees as he entered. Garner was right behind him, crouching low.

Slowly Volsky stood up. The scene which greeted them turned Garner's stomach. Bryant was stretched out on the table, his rifle on the floor beneath the window. A piece of the concrete ceiling beam had been dislodged by the tremor and had crashed down upon Bryant's head, crushing it to pulp. Garner staggered back to the door just in time to stop Veronica entering. 'Come on,' he said weakly. 'It's all over. There's nothing for us in there.'

They walked slowly down the corridor which was now eerily quiet and still. A door on their left opened and a wide-eyed man, white with fear and plaster dust, poked out his head demanding an explanation. 'Earthquake,' said Garner.

X

'We will get you back in a day or so,' said Volsky. 'But first you need some rest. And then there will be some questions to answer.'

'What about the earthquake?' asked Veronica.

'It was centred on Leninaken. There's been great devastation up there. Yerevan only caught the tail end, a large tremor.'

'A lucky tremor, too,' said Garner. 'Probably saved the Premier's life.' They were in an office in the same station which Volsky had commandeered from the Police Chief. It had hardly been touched by the quake though a fine film of plaster dust covered the furniture. 'I think the Dvin Hotel will have to come down,' he added. 'It looks like the leaning tower of Pisa.'

'I think we can say that Veronica and yourself were mainly responsible for saving the Premier,' suggested Volsky.

'And Nihat,' said Garner. 'By the way, where is he?'

'He'll be along shortly.'

'I hope no harm has come to him,' said Garner. 'He's a good friend. Without him we wouldn't have made it.'

'I have a great deal of respect for Nihat Sargin,' said Volsky. 'After all, he did spirit you away from me, didn't he?'

'I'll tell you about it one day,' said Garner.

'Indeed, indeed,' said Volsky. 'And what about your story?'

'How do you mean?' asked Garner.

'You will have a good story to tell now, won't you? Goodison will be exposed. Heritage and Hamilton will be unmasked. And then there's Bryant and the whole American connection.'

'To tell the truth I haven't given it much thought of late,' admitted Garner. 'How about you?' He turned to Veronica.

'Neither have I,' she said.

'Understandable,' said Volsky. 'But you will write it up. We will help you, not only with the American side but also with the Russian side of the conspiracy.'

Garner eyed him suspiciously. 'We will only write the truth.'

'That is all we ask of you. That is all de Roos and Duffy would have asked of you. The truth.'

TURKEY

Hamilton and Heritage strolled to the outskirts of the village beneath a starry sky. 'He should be back later tonight,' said Hamilton. 'And then we can go home.'

'Is that all you are thinking about, Alex? Home?'

'A hot bath, a decent meal and a good bottle of wine. I've had enough.'

'And the success or failure of ASH?'

'That's all over, John. By now the Premier is dead. I can feel it in my bones.'

'There was nothing on the afternoon or evening news broadcasts.'

'The earthquake saw to that. The Premier is dead and they will keep back the news for a couple of days while the Politburo juggles with the contenders for the succession.'

'I hope you're right,' said Heritage.

'Trust me, John.'

They walked on slowly. 'I was out here a few years ago,' said Heritage. 'South, on the other side of Mount Ararat. I came with Stan Oliver.'

'Really? Whatever for?' Neither man heard the stealthily approaching footsteps.

'It was when the Delta Force boys were trying to rescue the hostages from the embassy in Tehran. Stan and I were involved in the logistics of the operation. So Stan and I came out here. We were right on the Iranian border, as close as we could get to the mission without actually being inside Iran. A night just like this. Wonderful.'

'It's a pity the mission was a failure. Good idea, but badly executed.'

'Bad luck, really,' said Heritage, staring up at the sky. 'It should have . . .'

He never finished the sentence. Kossemlu shot him in the back of the head before turning the gun on Hamilton and shooting him in the temple.

ENGLAND

Glorious Goodwood; Goodison grinning.

He had drunk too much celebratory champagne: his face was flushed and his features were set in a permanent smile while his eyes glistened with proud fulfilment. His horse had stormed away with the Goodwood Cup, its second long-distance victory after Royal Ascot, and he was looking forward with great anticipation to York the following month and the Yorkshire Cup, the third leg of the stayers classics which his horse was certain to win. And then there was ASH. He was expecting news of that result sometime in the early hours of the following day, and his stomach felt like that of a nervous bridegroom on his wedding night. Undoubtedly it was the champagne which was responsible for his out-of-character behaviour throughout the evening, but he did have reason to celebrate and feel good.

He slouched rather than stood in the library alcove, close to the door which led through into the study into which his guests had spilled. He had broken a golden rule of his own household and allowed the young ladies to join the men straight after dinner. And both sides had responded with an animal zest. He had even permitted one of the young ladies to approach him and nuzzle his ear, but he had declined her further blandishments in favour of more champagne.

Now he cast a paternalistic eye over his friends and companions. Sir Michael White had returned to the library without the redhead he had left with some twenty minutes ago and was now ensconced in an armchair close to the fireplace, a young blonde at his feet, a leggy brunette at his side, both girls apparently intent on what he was saying. Sir James Ffitch-Heyes and Sir Alfred Brond, giants of industry and commerce, were at the shelves handing down books to their four companions, playing games of I-know-everything with the girls. Homer Miller was content with one young lady, and as Goodison watched, Miller took her by the elbow and marched her out into the hallway.

Goodison finished his champagne. It was time, he decided, to go to bed and he followed Miller into the hallway. Dominic was on duty outside the door. 'Wake me if there are calls,' he said.

'Yes sir,' replied Dominic. And he bowed goodnight to his master.

He walked slowly up the winding staircase and along the corridor to his suite of rooms, passing straight through the day room and into the bedroom where he was greeted by the sound of running water from the bathroom to his right. He quietly pushed open the door and gazed down into the bath. His heart leapt at the sight, and he stood silent and still, watching the young blonde fondle himself in the bath which was filling with water. Hamilton had accomplished one thing successfully, he told himself, in finding this young man for him in New York. Since then, he had accompanied him wherever he went. The boy was almost perfection, from the clear blue eyes and blond hair, to the broad, sloping shoulders and flat stomach. Goodison could not get enough of him.

'Stop,' said Goodison gently as the young man's self-directed pleasure neared its climax.

The young man glanced up slowly and smiled sweetly, innocently almost, at Goodison. 'Are you going to join me?' he asked.

Goodison approached the bath and sat on the edge near the taps, oblivious to the running water from the taps. 'No.' He turned and shut off both taps before returning his attention to the Adonis before him. 'Did you have enough to eat?'

'Yes. It was fine.' He sat up in the bath and put a hand out to Goodison. 'Won't you join me please?' he asked again. He took hold of Goodison's arm and pulled him along the edge of the bath towards him. 'Please,' he pleaded while his other hand returned once more to his erection.

Goodison's throat was dry and his voice was husky when he spoke. 'Just for a minute.' His left hand dropped to the youth's thigh, then climbed higher to the groin.

The young man arched his back and pushed his face closer to Goodison's, their lips meeting in a brief, crisp kiss. Goodison closed his eyes as he felt the soft, gasping breath of the boy on his neck. He never opened them again.

Using his left elbow for leverage on the side of the bath, Ivan Pozemsky lifted Goodison over the edge of the bath and into the water, rolling on top of him and pinning him flat with the weight of his muscular body to the bottom of the bath. Despite the struggling panic beneath him, Ivan held his victim firmly in place and lay on top of him until all activity had ceased. Even then he remained in position for a further couple of minutes to ensure that the man was dead.

Then he climbed out of the bath without a second glance at Goodison, quickly towelled himself dry and dressed again in the expensive clothing his former patron had bought for him in Paris.

Goodison had his own private alarm, independent of the main house alarm, and Ivan checked to see if it was active. It was not, so he opened the window and climbed down the front of the house as he had practised earlier that week, and dashed across the lawn towards the wall on the other side of which waited his Spesnatz colleague in the car.

II

'If it's a boy we'll call him Peter. A girl, and it's Veronica.'

'That's hardly original,' said Veronica, as they walked through the arrivals hall at Heathrow. 'I like Laura. I have an Auntie Laura'.

'And so do I,' said Garner. 'Well she's not really an aunt. She was a good friend of mum's and I always called her Auntie.'

'Well that's settled, then. Laura for a girl. But Peter for a boy? I'm not so sure. What about Nihat?'

'Don't you think that's carrying friendship a bit too far?'

Veronica smiled. 'I'll settle for Peter.'

They approached the queue at Passport Control. Garner gave Veronica her passport. 'I hope they don't check out our passports too thoroughly,' he whispered.

'They'll just glance at them,' said Veronica. 'Don't worry, they won't know they are forged.'

As they joined the queue, Garner felt someone at his elbow. 'Mr Garner?' said a voice. 'I wonder if you and your wife would accompany me to the office. I have some inquiries which I believe you could help me with.'

All Sphere Books are available at your bookshop or newsagent, or can be ordered from the following address: Sphere Books, Cash Sales Department, P.O. Box 11, Falmouth, Cornwall TR10 9EN

Please send cheque or postal order (no currency), and allow 60p for postage and packing for the first book plus 25p for the second book and 15p for each additional book ordered up to a maximum charge of £1.90 in U.K.

B.F.P.O. customers allow 60p for the first book, 25p for the second book plus 15p per copy for the next 7 books thereafter 9p per book.

Overseas customers, including Eire, please allow £1.25 for postage and packing for the first book, 75p for the second book and 28p for each subsequent title ordered.